THINGS THAT BREAK US

ALSO BY MICHELLE HEARD

In Reading Order:

MAFIA ROMANCE

Mafia / Organized Crime / Suspense Romance
All books can be read in this order or as stand-alones.
Mafia Empire

The Hermit

The High Priestess

Death

The Empress

The Devil

The Kings Of Mafia Series
This series is not connected to any other series I've written, and there will be no spin-offs.

Tempted By The Devil

Craving Danger

Hunted By A Shadow

Drawn To Darkness

God Of Vengeance

ST. MONARCH'S WORLD

The Saints Series

Merciless Saints

Cruel Saints

Ruthless Saints

Tears Of Betrayal

Tears Of Salvation

The Sinners Series

Taken By A Sinner

Owned By A Sinner

Stolen By A Sinner

Chosen By A Sinner

Captured By A Sinner

Corrupted Royals

Destroy Me

Control Me

Brutalize Me

Restrain Me

Possess Me

CONTEMPORARY ROMANCE

Beautifully Broken Series

Beautifully Broken

Beautifully Hurt

Beautifully Destroyed

Enemies To Lovers

Heartless

Reckless

Careless

Ruthless

Shameless

Trinity Academy

Falcon

Mason

Lake

Julian

The Epilogue

The Heirs

Coldhearted Heir

Arrogant Heir

Defiant Heir

Loyal Heir

Callous Heir

Sinful Heir

Tempted Heir

Forbidden Heir

Stand-Alone Spin-Off

Not My Hero (young adult / high school romance)

The Southern Heroes Series

The Ocean Between Us

The Girl In The Closet

The Lies We Tell Ourselves

All The Wasted Time

We Were Lost

STAND-ALONE

Lifeline (FBI suspense romance)

THINGS THAT BREAK US

MICHELLE HEARD

This is a work of fiction. Names, characters, organizations, places, events, and incidents are either products of the author's imagination or are used fictitiously. Otherwise, any resemblance to actual persons, living or dead, is purely coincidental.

Published by Montlake, Seattle

www.apub.com

EU product safety contact:
Amazon Media EU S. à r.l.
38, avenue John F. Kennedy, L-1855 Luxembourg
amazonpublishing-gpsr@amazon.com

ISBN-13: 9781662536809 (paperback)
ISBN-13: 9781662536816 (digital)

Cover design by Caroline Johnson
Cover image: © Michelle Lancaster PTY LTD; © Valery Kraynov / Shutterstock; © ShutterWorx, © Wirestock, © Jackyenjoyphotography / Getty

Interior image: © sense / Adobe Stock

Printed in the United States of America

Dad,
it's an honor to be your daughter.

SONG LIST

Another Kind of Love—Madilyn Paige

Falling Star—Raphael Lake, Royal Baggs

Please Don't Go—Stephanie Rainey

My Life with You—Ryan Star

This Side of Heaven—Riley Clemmons

As It Seems—Lily Kershaw

Forever & Always—Written by Wolves, Becks

Born to Love—Ashes & Arrows

I Choose You—Forest Blakk

Always & Forever—Lily Kershaw

AUTHOR'S NOTE

This book contains subject matter that may be sensitive for some readers.

Loss of a family member to cancer
Grief
Domestic abuse and PTSD

There is triggering content between these pages.
Please read responsibly.

Chapter 1

Nova

Easton Rowe, 35. Nova Allen, 28.

I stare at the peeling wallpaper in the cheap motel room until my sight begins to blur. When I blink, my eyes sting, so I keep them closed while a deep breath shudders from my chest.

Like a thief in the early morning hours, I ran from the place I've called home for the past three years. Except for a single bag of luggage, I left everything behind. I've heard the words "I'm sorry, it will never happen again" one too many times.

God, why did I stay so long?

In my defense, Trent wasn't always abusive. Our first year together was good, but then he lost his job. With him being unemployed and my meager income from my part-time jobs, we struggled financially, and it brought out a mean streak in him.

With the despondent thoughts milling in my head, I open my eyes and glance around the room. There's only a bed, a TV, and a small closet. Even though everything is old, it's clean, at least.

When I suck in another deep breath, my ribs ache from where Trent kicked me the night before, but I know from bitter experience nothing is broken.

Glancing down, I stare at the angry handprint on my bicep. Unable to stomach looking at it any longer, I get up, and grabbing a sweater out of my luggage, I quickly put it on.

As I let out another heavy sigh, I sit down on the edge of the bed again, the hopeless feeling in my chest growing.

God, what am I going to do?

My life hasn't been easy. Living in the small town of Verona in the Sugar River Valley area, it's hard to find a decent job that pays well. At least, that's what it's been like for me. I also seem to attract the worst kind of men. Trent wasn't the first one to abuse me, but I've had enough, and I'm swearing off all men from now on.

Why do I end up with men who beat women?

It's time to make peace with the fact that a healthy romantic relationship isn't in the cards for me.

It doesn't look like anything good is in the cards for me.

My mind keeps jumping from one thought to the other, and I'm unable to focus on anything long enough to come up with a plan for what I should do next.

My phone rings, scaring the ever-loving crap out of me. I turn my head, and for a few seconds too long, I stare at my handbag that's lying beside me on the bed.

I don't want to talk to Trent. He's probably calling to tell me to get my butt home.

I consider letting the call go to voicemail before I tentatively dig the device out of my bag.

I suck in a quivering breath while my hands tremble, and I brace to see Trent's name, but when Rachel's shows on the screen, I answer as quickly as possible.

"Rach?" My voice is hoarse from all the chaotic emotions warring in my chest.

She sobs, and it takes a moment before she gasps, "Nova."

Instantly, my own problems vanish, and with urgency and worry lacing my tone, I ask, "What's wrong?"

"I need you."

"Are you okay?" I rush to grab my handbag and the luggage I haven't unpacked yet. "Did something happen to Lainey?"

"No, Lainey's fine," she replies, her voice strained.

I suck in a deep breath before I dare to ask, "Easton?"

It would've been all over the news if something had happened to him.

"Easton is fine. I'll tell you once you're here. I don't want to talk about it over the phone."

"I'm on my way." I take one final glance around the room before hurrying to yank the door open.

"Thank you."

"Is there anything I can do right now?" I ask, heading to the beaten-up truck I bought four years ago after saving my butt off. It's so old it's a miracle it hasn't given up the ghost yet.

"No. Just hurry." Rachel sobs. "I'm sorry to ask you on such short notice. I'll pay for the flight and send you the address."

"Don't worry about anything. I'll drive." My breaths rush over my lips. "I'll be there soon."

"Okay," she whispers. "Drive safely."

I stop walking and shut my eyes. "I love you."

"Love you too, Nova," she squeezes the words out before she sobs again. "Please hurry."

"I'm already on my way, Rach," I tell her as I open the passenger door and haul the luggage onto the seat. Shutting the door, I rush to the driver's side. "I'm coming."

"Let me know when you're close so I can notify security."

"Okay."

Rachel ends the call, and I drop the cell phone on my lap. Starting the engine, I glance around the area for other vehicles before I reverse out of the parking bay.

Thank God I paid up front for the motel room, so I don't have to waste time settling the bill right now.

Worry for Rachel tightens its grip on my heart as I drive away from the motel. She's been my best friend since our first day of elementary school. Besides my grandfather, whom I hardly get to see because he's a grumpy recluse who doesn't care about me at all, Rachel's the only constant in my life.

Since moving to LA with her older brother, Easton, I've only seen her on the few occasions she's come to visit me in Verona. Apart from seeing Easton on TV or in a movie, I haven't laid eyes on him since they left.

God, it's the first time I'm leaving Verona.

The realization suddenly hits, and it makes nerves spin in my stomach as I steer the truck onto the interstate. I glance in the rearview mirror at the only home I've ever known. My heart beats faster because I'm not just driving toward Rachel but away from a life that's never been kind to me.

Reaching for my phone again, I quickly program Rachel's address into Maps so I can keep an eye on where I need to go.

Looking at the directions, I notice the distance between Wisconsin and California is a twenty-eight-hour drive. That's not including the time it will take to stop for gas.

My teeth tug at my bottom lip while I quickly do a calculation in my head. I should reach Rachel around lunchtime tomorrow if I don't sleep and stop as little as possible.

Please, let me get to Beverly Hills in one piece without the truck breaking down.

After sending up the quick prayer, I settle in for the long drive. As I put one mile after another between Verona and me, I remember when I got a call from Rachel similar to the one I received today. I rushed over to the apartment she shared with Easton as if hellhounds were chasing me.

Barreling into Rachel's bedroom, the words burst from me. "What's wrong?"

Her face is blotchy with tears, and for a moment, I worry something's happened to Easton. The last time I saw Rachel in such a state was the night we learned their parents died in a car accident.

Sobs make her body jerk as she cries, "I'm pregnant."

Shock shuddering through me, I drop down beside her on the foot of the bed. "Oh God." I wrap my arms tightly around her, and at a total loss for words, I comfort my friend.

After a few minutes, her voice is filled with fear as she admits, "I don't know what to do."

"We'll figure out something." I pull back a little, and using my thumbs, I wipe the tears from her cheeks. "Have you done more than one test? Are you sure?"

She nods and points at her dressing table. "I peed on three sticks." Another sob bursts from her, then she whimpers, "They're all positive."

My mind races for the right thing to say. Not coming up with anything better, I mutter, "At least graduation is only two months away."

"Easton is going to kill me," she groans.

I shake my head. "He won't."

I've been in love with Easton since I discovered I had hormones, but he's seven years older than us and hasn't noticed me. It also doesn't help that I'm painfully shy.

It's been a constant battle to bury my feelings for him deep down so Rachel won't notice.

"He won't what?" Easton asks, suddenly appearing in the doorway and startling the ever-loving crap out of us.

My eyes widen, and for several seconds, Rachel and I just stare at him.

Every time I see him, it feels like an intense punch to my heart. The stubborn organ only beats for my best friend's older brother and refuses to acknowledge any other man. With his dark-brown hair, stormy-gray eyes, and features that were clearly chiseled by angels who were in one heck of a good mood when they made him, Easton is the epitome of handsome.

His eyes flick between us as he steps into the bedroom and asks, "Why are you crying, Rach?"

She grips my hand as she shakes her head, a pleading expression tightening her features. "You tell him," she whispers as she partially hides behind me.

Easton's worried gaze locks with mine, and there's a fluttering in my stomach while my heart beats faster and faster.

My tongue darts out to wet my lips, and I clear my throat. "Don't get angry . . ."

He tilts his head, and when his eyebrows draw together in a frown, my insides spin with nerves.

"Rachel is pregnant," I blurt out the news.

Shock flashes over his way-too-attractive face, and I quickly wrap an arm around Rachel.

His gaze flicks to his sister. "You're what?"

"I'm sorry," she sobs. "I don't know how it happened. We used protection."

"Who?" Easton growls.

"Who what?"

"Who got you fucking pregnant?" he snaps, anger tightening the lines around his mouth.

Rachel shakes her head and presses her lips together, which has Easton turning his angry gaze to me.

Oh crap.

I quickly shake my head as well. "I don't know."

He glares at his sister again. "Tell me, Rachel!"

She looks downright miserable as she admits, "It was a one-night stand at the end of January. He doesn't go to our school. We hooked up after one of the games."

I remember the guy. Rachel was so upset when he didn't call her the week after the basketball game. But that was months ago, and she's gotten over him since then.

"Christ," Easton grumbles while pulling his fingers through his hair.

He stares at his sister until she begins to ugly cry, sobs shuddering through her body.

Shaking his head, he lets out a heavy breath before he moves closer to us. He crouches in front of Rachel and places his palm against her cheek.

She throws her arms around his neck and whimpers, "I'm so sorry."

I scoot to the side, so they'll have some space, and watch as they hold each other.

"We'll find a way through this," Easton says. "I'll get a better job that pays more."

Rachel cries harder, and I reach over to pat her back, my heart breaking for my friend.

Not even a month after Rachel learned she was pregnant, they moved to LA, where Easton got a better job while trying to pursue a career in acting.

It's been ten years since they left Verona.

Besides the four times Rachel and Lainey have come to visit me, we talk regularly on the phone and sometimes have video calls. I never ask about Easton, and Rachel doesn't tell me anything about him. It's been an unspoken rule since Easton became a famous actor.

I haven't talked to Easton in over a decade, and now I'm heading to his house. He was my first and only love, and watching him turn into a devastatingly handsome movie star, my feelings for him have never died. If anything, they've intensified.

My mouth grows dry, and goose bumps spread over my body when I realize I'll be at Easton's place this time tomorrow.

When my heart starts to pound in my chest, I shake my head and focus on the reason why I'm driving to LA.

You're going for Rachel.

I wonder what happened. It has to be serious because Rachel wouldn't ask me to travel so far for no reason.

But crap, what do I do when I see Easton? Do I greet him like he's nothing more than my best friend's older brother?

Well, whatever you do, just don't fangirl and faint.

After I stop for a quick toilet break, I buy a bottle of water and sip on the cool liquid while putting in gas.

The impromptu trip to California is going to take a big bite out of my meager savings.

Crap, I forgot about work.

Letting out a sigh, I lean into the cab and grab my phone. Opening the Messenger app, I type out a text to Sadie, my boss, so she'll know I won't be returning. I've been helping her part-time, but the pet grooming business isn't doing too great to begin with, so I'm sure she'll be relieved to be rid of me.

After I press send on the text, I drop the device back on the passenger seat and finish putting in gas. When I make the payment, I do a mental calculation of what should be left in my bank account.

I'll have to get another job soon. The money in my savings won't even last another two weeks.

Climbing back into my truck, I start the engine while thinking maybe I can find a good job in LA. That way, I can stay close to Rachel and Lainey.

It would be a dream come true.

Chapter 2

Nova

When I pull up to the impressive iron gates in Beverly Hills, my stomach is knotted with nerves. Rolling down the window, it sticks a couple of times, and I have to stretch out my arm to press the button on the intercom.

"Yes?" a man answers.

My stomach spins even more, and I swallow hard. "Hi. It's Nova Allen. I'm here to see Rachel Rowe."

"Follow the driveway all the way to the house and park by the garages, Miss Allen."

"Okay," I say, then quickly add, "Thanks."

As the gates begin to open, my heart pounds a mile a minute.

I'm worried about Rachel, but I can't help feeling anxious as hell about being at Easton's house as I steer the truck up the driveway.

I suck in deep breaths as I drive around a bend and the mansion comes into view.

Holy crap!

I lose my ability to breathe for a moment. The sleek dark concrete and cedarwood with expansive windows make the huge mansion look both serene and super expensive.

Gosh, it's so beautiful.

As I bring my beaten-up truck to a standstill, I feel horribly out of place. I check my reflection in the rearview mirror and cringe because I look disheveled from the long drive.

At the last gas station, I changed into a cute summer dress and tied my hair in a ponytail, but that was it. I'm not wearing a stitch of makeup, and I regret not putting on some mascara at the very least.

"It's too late now to worry about your appearance," I mutter while pushing the door open. I glance over the intimidatingly gorgeous mansion and manicured lawn, and I whisper, "You're not in Verona anymore."

Leaving my luggage in the truck, I grab my handbag and hoist the strap over my shoulder. Tension fills my body as I walk up the steps toward the larger-than-average front door, which is made of frosted glass.

I stop to tap my knuckles against the glass. "Hello? Rach?"

"Nova!" I hear her shriek.

She comes hurrying into the foyer, which is decorated with plants, and in the center there's a glass table that has a massive vase with pretty flowers on it.

I open my arms in time to catch Rachel, and as I engulf her in a tight hug, she bursts out crying.

"I'm here," I say as tears of my own begin to spiral over my cheeks from finally getting to hold my best friend.

God, I missed her and needed this hug so badly. It's been too long since we last saw each other in person.

Even though I'm exhausted from the long drive, worry for my best friend makes me feel wide awake.

I rub my hand up and down her back and press a kiss to the side of her head. "Tell me what happened."

She pulls away, and seeing the fear in her eyes, I try to brace for the worst.

"Come in," she murmurs, visibly trying to regain control over her emotions. "You must be so exhausted from the long drive. Did it go okay? No problems?"

"The drive felt much quicker than it was," I say to set Rachel at ease.

"Oh, that's a relief. I was so worried about you alone on the road with that old truck. You should've let me pay for a flight."

"The truck didn't give me any problems. Please don't worry," I reply while I follow her through the foyer, my eyes darting around.

I'm completely overwhelmed by all the luxury. We walk into a living room with a vaulted ceiling and open sliding doors that overlook a veranda, pool, and picturesque garden.

The living room is a modern open space that blends into a state-of-the-art kitchen that would have any chef drooling.

Geez, the place is next-level amazing.

I've never been in such a lavish house, and it's super intimidating.

"Your home is gorgeous," I murmur in absolute wonder.

Rachel tries to smile but isn't very successful.

"Is anyone else home?" I ask so I know what to expect.

"No. It's just the staff and me," she replies as she sits down on a cream leather sofa. "Lainey's at school, and Easton is in New Zealand, busy shooting a movie."

There's a mixture of disappointment and relief in my chest at knowing Easton isn't here.

I take the seat beside Rachel before giving her a questioning look. "Are you pregnant?"

She shakes her head, then her features crumble, and her words are filled with hopelessness as she sobs and says, "I'm sick." My lips part, but she cuts me off with a shake of her head before dropping a bomb between us. "I have cancer. Glioblastoma." She sucks in a trembling breath, then explains, "It's a tumor in my brain."

Intense shock vibrates through every cell in my body, and for the longest time, I can only stare at my best friend, the words not really sinking in.

Looking closely at Rachel, I notice she's even more beautiful than the last time I saw her. Her hair is longer, and the highlights she mentioned getting a few days ago look good on her. I can't find any visible signs of her being ill.

"I haven't told anyone else," she murmurs, her tone filled with a world of fear and hopelessness. "I got the final confirmation yesterday, and you're the first person I thought of calling. I don't know how I'm going to tell Lainey and Easton."

Again, my gaze darts over her face, which looks so healthy.

Cancer?

Shaken to my core, it takes a moment before I'm finally able to speak. "I'm so sorry, Rach."

My words feel all wrong, and I suck in a shaky breath.

No. Not Rachel.

She hardly ever gets sick. I'm the one who gets the flu from standing in the rain for ten seconds.

She's the strong one.

Rachel scoots closer and wraps her arms around me. I grip her with all my strength, my fingers digging into her silk blouse as I try to process what she's telling me.

"I'm scared, Nova," she whimpers, her tone hoarse from the devastation the diagnosis is causing in her life.

Hopeful that the doctors can treat it, I ask, "Are they giving you medicine? Will you get chemotherapy?"

She shakes her head, and her voice is filled with anguish as she says, "It's too far advanced. There's nothing they can do for me. They're only giving me meds that will help make me as comfortable as possible."

Oh God.

Nonononono!

Unable to be strong as the shock of the horrible news digs its claws into my heart, a sob explodes from me. Our hold on each other tightens, and it makes my ribs hurt, but I don't care.

Sitting on the couch, we cry as empty hopelessness spins a web of fear around us. The harrowing news that my best friend is dying floods my soul with panic.

Not Rachel. She can't die. She's the only good thing in my life.

I brush my hand over her hair, and pulling back, I lock eyes with the person I love most in this world. When I see the fear in her gray irises, it makes me realize I'll have to be strong for her.

Rachel needs me.

Another wave of intense shock hits the air from my lungs. "You're all I have." I sob as my panic and fear rapidly increase. "I can't lose you."

"I'm so sorry," she cries.

Her face crumbles again, and I hold my best friend as she breaks down. Tears roll silently down my cheeks while I try to offer her all the comfort she needs.

God, Rachel's dying?

Everything in me revolts against the fact that I'm going to lose her. I've been through a lot in my life, but I'm not sure I can survive losing Rachel.

Still shocked to my very core, I pull back a little, and my gaze darts over her face. Somehow, I think to ask, "Did you get a second opinion?"

She nods and lets out a heavy sigh. "I've gone for every test there is. They all say the same thing."

My chin trembles as I take hold of Rachel's hand, linking our fingers together. I do my best to fight back the tears and clear my throat before I ask, "What's next?"

She clenches her jaw and glances at the stunning view of the veranda and backyard before looking at me again. "I guess I have to wrap things up and somehow prepare for the end."

My body goes numb, and my voice is barely audible as I ask, "How long do we have?"

Her face crumbles again, and her tone is thick with tears. "A few weeks. Two months if I'm lucky."

"No!" I cry, shaking my head wildly. "There has to be something they can do. I thought, at the very least, we'd have a few years!"

The same dread I see etched into her beautiful features engulfs my heart.

Oh God, this is really happening, and there's nothing we can do to stop it.

No. No. No. No. No.

Rachel is so young.

She's all I have.

For a moment, my emotions spiral into chaos until I see the despair in her gray irises.

This isn't about me. I have to be strong for Rachel, Lainey, and Easton.

I suck in a quivering breath, and as I stare at my friend, I do my best to shove all my feelings deep down so I can focus on her.

"What do you need me to do?" My voice sounds much stronger than I feel.

She shrugs while rubbing a hand over her face. "I don't know how to tell Easton and Lainey."

"When will Easton be back?"

"Not for another three months."

I shake my head. "You have to call him, Rach. We don't have time to wait for him to come home."

"I know," she whispers. "But . . . what do I say to him?"

"Just tell him to come home. Say it's important, but you can't talk about it over the phone. Just like you did with me."

She lets out an empty-sounding chuckle. "You're so much easier to talk to."

I rub her shoulder. "Where's your phone?"

"In the kitchen." When she climbs to her feet, I get up as well. As we walk toward the kitchen, she mentions, "If you want something to drink or eat, just help yourself. I want you to feel at home while you're here." Her eyes dart to mine, and her teeth tug at her bottom lip before she asks, "How long can you stay?"

"As long as you need me."

Some relief eases the worried lines on her face. "The pooch parlor won't miss you?"

I shake my head. "Not at all. Business has been quiet, so I quit."

"And Trent?"

Every muscle in my body tenses at hearing his name. The anxiety and fear I always feel when just thinking of him blends with the horror of learning Rachel is terminally ill.

A tremble shudders through me, but somehow, I manage to shake my head and say, "It's over between us."

"Oh, I'm so sorry, Nova." She leans in to give me a hug, then asks, "Why didn't you tell me?"

"We ended things two days ago." I leave out the part about Trent hurting me. *Again.*

Rachel will lose her shit if she finds out, and she has enough to deal with.

Shoving my own trauma away, I gesture at the device on the counter. "Call Easton and tell him to come home. That's all you have to focus on for the next ten minutes."

That's all I have to focus on for the next ten minutes.

She sucks in a deep breath as she picks up the phone, and I watch as she dials Easton's number.

She clears her throat and wipes invisible dust from the marble countertop of the island, then she clears her throat again and says, "It's me. Give me a call as soon as you get this message. It's urgent."

When she sets the device back down on the counter, I lift my arm, and placing my hand on her shoulder, I give her an encouraging squeeze.

"Lainey will be home in thirty minutes," she mentions.

Before I can say anything, Rachel's phone starts to ring, and I see Easton's name showing on the screen.

Just seeing his name is enough to make my stomach flutter as if a kaleidoscope of butterflies is taking flight inside me.

She picks up the device and closes her eyes as she answers, "Hey." I can't hear what Easton says, but Rachel replies, "I need you to come home as soon as possible. Something's happened, but I can't tell you over the phone . . . Lainey is fine . . . I can't tell you now, Easton." She opens her eyes, and they settle on me. "Nova's here with me . . . No, nothing happened to her." She loses the battle against her tears, and her voice grows strained as she snaps, "Stop asking questions and just come home! Please." She sucks in a desperate breath while doing her best not to break down. "I need you here, Easton. I wouldn't ask if it wasn't serious . . . Okay . . . Okay . . . Thank you . . . Love you too."

Ending the call, her shoulders shudder as tears overwhelm her, and I do the only thing I can. Wrapping my best friend up in a hug, I try to comfort her by rubbing my hand up and down her back.

Shock keeps rippling through me, and every time the realization strikes that Rachel is going to die, it hits harder than before. My soul shrivels away from the devastating news, and my heart feels like it's being pulverized to dust.

I can't lose Rachel. She's all I have. She's the only person who understands and loves me. How do I live a life without her?

Shit. Lainey will have to grow up without her mom.

Oh God.

My body jerks from all the strain, and it has Rachel holding me tighter, making my bruised ribs ache.

"I can't lose you," I whimper, clinging to her as if my life depends on it, because it does. "You're the only person who loves me."

What is life without my best friend?

"I don't want to die," she whispers hoarsely. "I'm terrified."

I have no idea how long we stand in the kitchen, and I don't care. I do my best to focus on Rachel's sweet cookies-and-cream scent and how good it feels to hold her.

She's still here.

Chapter 3

Nova

After I take a moment to regain control of my chaotic emotions, I let go of Rachel. Forcing a quivering smile to my lips, I say, "What can I do?"

She shakes her head. "You just being here is all I want." Her fear-drenched gaze locks with mine. "Until the end, Nova. Please."

My chin trembles badly as I nod.

"And after . . ." she sucks in a few shaky breaths as she fights to control her tears, ". . . I'm gone, I need you to be there for Lainey."

Jesus. My heart.

I nod quickly while blinking like crazy to try and stop my tears.

Half of me wants to hide from the unfathomable thought of losing Rachel, and the other half is preoccupied with thoughts of what I can do to make things easier for her.

A smile trembles around her lips, then she says, "We should get you settled. Lainey will be home soon."

"I just need to grab my luggage from the truck."

I walk with Rachel to the front door while sucking in deep breaths of air. My heart feels like it's hemorrhaging from the shock I've been dealt.

When we approach my truck, Rachel shakes her head. "God, Nova. I still can't believe you drove all the way from Verona in this beaten-up old thing."

Completely steamrollered by the news that Rachel has cancer, I can't think of anything to respond with, so I just shrug.

As I haul my luggage from the passenger seat, she asks, "Only the one bag?"

"I left Trent in a hurry," I admit. Just thinking about the man who's made my life a living hell sends a shiver down my spine and has me wanting to curl into myself.

I have never kept any secrets from Rachel except for two. She has no idea about the abuse I suffered at Trent's hands or the feelings I have for Easton.

She'll be so disappointed to hear that after I got away from John, my first abusive boyfriend, I ended up with another bastard.

God, I sure know how to pick them.

After my past relationships that were so violent, I'm now jumpy around men. I don't think I'll ever date again. Just the thought of being alone with a man is enough to make panic grip my heart.

All the thoughts make me tremble, and I hope Rachel doesn't notice while we walk back into the mansion. Again I feel intimidated by all the luxury and wealth. It's like I've stepped into a different world where nothing makes sense.

As I follow Rachel up a staircase that has a cast-iron railing on the left side, I notice framed photos on the wall to my right. I glance over them, and seeing Easton in the photos reminds me who he is and that he's coming home.

"So . . ." I clear my throat as we reach the landing and begin to walk down the hallway. "Um . . . Easton."

Stopping by the first room on the right, Rachel looks at me with an arched brow. When she pushes the door open, she asks, "What about him?"

We step into a bedroom that robs me of my train of thought.

"Holy crap," I whisper, gaping at the king-size bed with cream silk covers and pillows.

There's a modern dressing table that has light bulbs all around the frame of the mirror, and to my left stands a five-tier shelf decorated with expensive-looking ornaments and two plants.

Moving forward, I avoid the fluffy cream carpet, not wanting to track dirt on it.

To my right is a walk-in closet that's as big as the bedroom I shared with Trent.

The instant I think of the bastard, the panic and fear I've grown too accustomed to feeling tighten my insides.

Don't think of him.

My own problems will have to take a back seat to what's happening with Rachel.

"You have your own bathroom, and I've made sure it's stocked with everything you might need," Rachel says as she opens a door to my left.

I peek into the massive bathroom that looks like the ones I've seen in travel magazines when they showcase five-star hotels and resorts.

Not knowing what else to say, I murmur, "Thank you."

She glances at my single piece of luggage. "We'll go shopping soon for more clothes. My treat. It's the least I can do for dragging you all the way to LA on such short notice."

My hand flies up, and I wave it in a don't-worry-about-it manner. "It's fine. I don't need anything."

She lets out a sad-sounding chuckle. "You'll have to get used to shopping because it's one of Lainey's favorite things to do."

I set my luggage down near the foot of the bed and glance around the lavish room again.

"I'll keep you company while you unpack," she says, sitting down in an armchair near the window. "What did you want to say about Easton?"

"Oh . . ." Not wanting to put my luggage on the pristine white covers, I lay the bag on the floor and open it. "Will he be okay with me being here?"

"Of course." A slight frown forms on her forehead.

I place my handbag beside my luggage before removing two dresses. Walking to the closet, I admit, "I'm just going to be straight with you. He's a famous actor, and I don't know what to do when I see him again."

A burst of laughter escapes Rachel, and getting up, she walks to my open bag and grabs a sweater before coming toward me. "He's still the Easton you knew back when we were in school."

"I doubt that," I mutter. I hang the two dresses, then glance at her as she places the threadbare sweater down on a shelf.

She gives me a reassuring smile. "Don't worry about Easton."

Easier said than done.

Not knowing how to explain that I'm super nervous about seeing him, I let the subject go.

While we continue to unpack, I hear my cell phone beep like crazy with incoming messages. The sound instantly sends a wave of apprehension crashing through me, tensing every muscle in my body.

It's probably Trent who's noticed I'm gone. Crap, he must be so angry.

I stare at where my bag is on the floor, thinking how badly he'll beat me for running away like this.

"Aren't you going to check your phone?"

Ripped out of my thoughts, I quickly shake my head. "It can wait until later."

Trent isn't here, and he doesn't know where I am.

I'm safe with Rachel.

Deep breaths.

"So, things are over between you and Trent?" Rachel asks. Staring at me, her eyebrows narrow. "What happened?"

With trembling hands, I place a small stack of leggings on one of the shelves.

All I want to do is run into my best friend's arms and cry my heart out, but instead, I give her a generic answer. "Things just didn't work out between us."

Rachel has enough on her plate.

As I walk back to my almost-empty bag, we hear Lainey calling, "Mom, I'm home."

"We're in the guest room, sweetheart," Rachel replies.

The moment Lainey barrels into the bedroom, a wide smile splits over my face. I only have enough time to open my arms when she slams into me.

"You're here!" she exclaims happily.

I flinch hard from the ache in my ribs caused by the impact of her body hitting mine, and sucking in a harsh breath, I say, "Hey, sweet girl."

We hug, and when we pull apart, she jumps up and down with excitement. "Mom and I made so many plans last night. We're going to take you shopping and show you around LA. It will be so much fun!"

"But first, you're going to do your homework," Rachel reminds her daughter.

"Ugh," Lainey grumbles with a disgruntled expression. "I don't want to."

God, she's grown so much since I last saw her. I can't believe she's ten years old already.

I reach out to Lainey and comb my fingers through her long, straight hair that's the same dark brown as Easton's. "Go do your homework so we can have fun this weekend without having to worry about it," I encourage her.

"Okay." Her gray eyes shine up at me. "I'll be quick."

I nod and watch her jog into the hallway. As soon as she's out of hearing distance, Rachel asks, "Why did you flinch when Lainey hugged you?"

Shoot.

I suck in a deep breath before I meet her gaze. "It's nothing."

She steps closer to me, her eyes narrowing on my face. "What's nothing?"

I hesitate for a moment longer, but when she gives me a concerned look, I can't stay silent any longer.

Darting forward, I throw my arms around her and bury my face against her hair, the wall crumbling down and unleashing a flood of tears.

"Nova?" she whispers, her tone tense with concern as she holds me tightly. "Talk to me."

"Trent hurt me," I squeeze the words out.

Rachel pushes me back a little, and her eyes dart over my face. "What do you mean he hurt you?"

Feeling ashamed, I slowly shrug off my sweater, and the moment her gaze lands on the angry marks on my bicep, shock tightens her features.

"Jesus, Nova!" Her gaze snaps back to mine. "Where else are you hurt?"

I walk to the door and shut it before I lower my head. With trembling hands, I grip the fabric of my dress and pull it up until my ribs are visible.

"Nova!" she cries, her expression horrified as she hurries closer to me. "Did you go to the emergency room? Did they take X-rays?"

"No. Nothing's broken." My voice sounds as fragile as I feel, but not wanting her to worry too much, I lie, "I'm fine. I promise."

Her eyes flick to mine, anger filling them as she snaps, "It doesn't look that way. We need to get you checked by a doctor."

I take hold of her arm, and shaking my head, I give her a pleading look. "I'm fine. Really. I know what broken ribs feel like."

She freezes, and a weird expression ripples over her face. "Why didn't you tell me?"

I lower my head and wrap my arms around my middle. "I was ashamed, and our weekly calls were the highlight of my life. I didn't want to ruin them with my problems." I feel rotten as I add, "And after the crap with John, the last thing I wanted to tell you was that Trent was beating me too."

"Oh, honey." She wraps me in a tender hug, and being held as if I'm precious to her makes me feel safer than I have in a really long time.

"I'm okay," I lie again. Between being abused by my ex-boyfriends and Rachel being terminally ill, I don't think I'll ever be okay again. "I left him, so it's over and done with. Please don't worry."

She pulls back to meet my eyes. "I wish you told me sooner." Letting go of me, she asks, "Are you sure you don't want to see a doctor?"

"Yeah," I chuckle awkwardly. "The bruises will be gone in no time."

I put on the light sweater again and walk to my luggage to grab the last item. Once I've placed it on a shelf, I can't help but notice how lost my clothes look in the massive walk-in closet.

Glancing at Rachel, I try to lighten the mood by joking, "I sure know how to pick them."

She steps closer and tucks a few strands of my ginger hair behind my ear. "It's not your fault, Nova."

I shrug again and say, "You'll be happy to hear I've sworn off dating. I'm done with the male species."

"Honestly, remaining single was the best thing I could've done after I had Lainey." Concern still fills her eyes. "Have you seen a therapist?"

I shake my head. "I don't want to talk to some stranger."

Rachel rests her palm against the side of my neck. "I think you should consider seeing one. It would do you good to talk with a trained professional about the shit you've been through."

Wanting Rachel to drop the subject, I mumble, "I'll think about it."

"Good. Let me know once you've made your decision. I'll help you find the best therapist in LA." She hooks her arm through mine, and we move toward the door. "Let's get something to drink."

When we step into the hallway, I think to ask, "Where's your bedroom?"

She gestures to our right. "My room is next to yours, and Lainey's is opposite mine. Easton's bedroom is at the end of the hallway."

As we take the stairs down and head to the kitchen, I struggle to control all the destructive emotions whirling in my heart.

My gaze drifts over Rachel, and once again, the bitter reality of her illness shudders through me.

With a quivering chin, I take a seat on one of the stools by the island and watch as she grabs two glasses from a cupboard and pours soda for both of us.

God, I need more strength to get through everything. Help me to be strong for Rachel.

I clear my throat and hate that there's nothing else I can do but ask, "How are you holding up?"

Exhaustion and despair tighten her features. "I'm not. A million thoughts are constantly racing through my mind." She glances in the direction of the stairs, then whispers, "There's so much I have to get in order. Just thinking about dying is terrifying the living hell out of me."

When she sits down beside me, I gently rub my palm over her forearm, hoping my touch will give her some comfort. "I'm here. Every step of the way."

I have no idea how to make things easier for her, but I'll somehow figure it out. I just have to.

All that matters now is Rachel, Lainey, and Easton.

Chapter 4

NOVA

(The Past . . .)

I let out an exhausted sigh as I pack the clean clothes into the closet. After a super long day at work where I had to wrestle the biggest dog I've ever seen so we could groom him, every muscle in my body aches.

The Great Dane even managed to drag me halfway down a hallway, and I think I sprained my wrist when I clung to his leash.

God, I wish I could crawl into bed and sleep for a week.

That's not a possibility, though. I still need to vacuum the living room, make dinner, and clean the kitchen.

Letting out a sigh, I head to the living room, and after making sure the worn carpet is spotless, I rush to the kitchen.

My eyes fly to the clock on the wall, and realizing it's already past seven, apprehension twists my stomach into an anxious ball.

Please let Trent stay out late tonight.

He hasn't worked for over two years and spends most of his time hanging out with his friends. For the better part of our relationship, I've felt like nothing more than his glorified slave, but leaving him is easier said than done.

After putting some mac and cheese on the stove, I pour myself a glass of water. I've only taken a few sips when I hear the front door open.

Instantly, fear tightens my muscles, and the glass slips from my hand, landing with a crash in the sink.

Crap!

I quickly gather all the shards, but as I turn toward the trash can, Trent grabs hold of my arm. "That fucking glass cost money we don't have."

I swallow hard. "I'm sorry. It was an accident."

He leans down until his menacing face is inches from mine, and smelling the beer on his breath, my heart sinks, and dread freezes me to the spot.

"I can have any woman in town, but I'm fucking stuck with your pathetic ass," he complains. "You can't even have dinner ready in time."

I lower my submissive gaze to the shards of glass in my palm, trying to brace for whatever pain Trent chooses to unleash on me tonight.

Even though it's happened so many times before, I'm still startled when the flat of his hand connects with the side of my head. "Show some fucking life, bitch!"

I draw my bottom lip between my teeth to keep from crying.

I want to fight back, but I know it will only anger Trent more, and because I'm much smaller, I'm no match for him.

He grabs hold of my sprained wrist, and when he yanks me toward him, a painful cry escapes me while the broken pieces of glass fall to the floor.

"Finally, some kind of reaction," he sneers before twisting my wrist. The intense pain forces me down to my knees, another cry ripping from me.

Suddenly, he lets go of my hand, but before I can think to move, he plants his boot on my shoulder and shoves me backward.

The pain from the first kick blends with the second and third, and I'm barely able to curl into a small ball as a world of hurt is unleashed on me.

(The Present . . .)

Sitting on the side of the bed, one of many memories shudders through me while I grip my cell phone tightly.

After an awful night filled with nightmares and restless sleep, I feel drained and broken.

Letting out a heavy sigh, I unlock my phone's screen. For a moment, I stare at all of the notifications before I open the messages.

Trent: Where are you?

Trent: You better get your ass home!

Fear seizes my heart in a merciless grip, and I can't help but start to panic about what Trent will do if we ever come face-to-face again.

Trent: What the fuck!

Trent: Okay, fine. I'm sorry. It won't happen again.

It always happens again.

Trent: In all fairness, it's not my fault. You know not to push my buttons and that I always go out for beers with the guys on Wednesday nights. How fucking hard is it to make sure I have a clean shirt laid out on the bed when I get home?

How many times have I heard something like that from him? *Too many to count.*

Trent: Come on. Don't be like this.

Trent: Fine, be like that. But send money so I can pay the rent. Mr. Hicks is breathing down my neck, and you know how I hate it.

I spent half the rent money on gas to get to LA. I don't have enough to send him.

Wait. I left Trent. I don't have to pay for anything. The rent is his problem now.

Trent: I swear to God, if you don't get your ass home, you'll regret it.

My heartbeat speeds up, and my panic and fear spike rapidly again.

I can't help it. Trent has beaten me so many times my immediate reaction to his anger and threats is to be terrified.

You're safe in LA. Trent can't get to you here.

Deep breaths.

Trent: I'm sorry. I'm just so worried about you. Where are you, darling? I'll come get you.

Trent: I'm done being the nice guy.

Trent: I will find you.

I stare at the messages for a little while longer as I try to build up the courage, then, sucking in a deep breath that makes my ribs ache, I type out a reply with trembling fingers.

Nova: I'm done with you hurting me. We're over, and I'm never coming back.

Letting out a shaky sigh, I press send and set the phone down on the bedside table.

It's done. Trent doesn't know where I am, so he can't find me.

I'm safe here with Rachel.

I have to calm down and get ready for the day ahead. I have to be strong for Rachel.

After putting on a dress and ballet flats, I grab the same light sweater from yesterday and shrug it on so my bruises won't be visible.

I walk to the door, and sneaking out of the bedroom, I do my best not to make a sound so I won't wake Rachel and Lainey. As I make my way down the stairs, I take my time to look at each of the photos on the wall.

Easton, Rachel, and Lainey look so happy, and I can feel how much they love each other.

I learned what love was from watching Rachel and her family, and she's the only person who's ever truly loved me.

She's the only one who's never hurt me.

I don't know who my dad is, and I was very young when my mother left me with my grandfather. I can barely remember her, but I know she had ginger hair like me, and I think she was loud and bubbly.

My grandfather is a mean recluse who never cared about me.

And now I'm going to lose Rachel.

I lift my hand to cover my quivering mouth while I fight not to burst out in tears.

When I reach the first floor, I glance around the open space, taking in the luxurious living room with the massive TV before turning my attention to the kitchen.

Feeling completely out of place, I walk into the kitchen and take a mug from the cupboard. Thankfully, Rachel showed me last night how the coffee machine works. I pick a flavor from the dozens, and putting the pod into the machine, I watch as the coffee pours into the mug.

Rachel's dying.

Instead of knocking the wind from me like it did yesterday, the thought only makes the pit of fear and hopelessness grow in my chest.

Last night, she went to bed early. I had a good cry in my bedroom before deciding not to take a single second for granted and to cherish the time I still have with her. I'll keep my breakdowns for late at night when I'm alone so she doesn't see them.

When the machine is done, I remove the pod and throw it into the trash before grabbing coffee creamer from the fully stocked fridge.

God, I've never seen so much food.

Slowly, I shut the door and head back to the counter. I add the creamer before returning it to the fridge, and after stirring the beverage, I pick up the cup, taking a much-needed sip.

Soooo good.

While I drink my coffee, I take a seat at the island and glance around the big open space again. I'm used to small homes, and I don't think I'll ever grow accustomed to all this luxury and the sheer size of Easton's house.

My thoughts return to Rachel, and I think back to when we were kids. She's always been my ride or die. Together, we learned how to shave our legs and put on makeup.

God, we experienced everything together. She's in every happy memory.

My throat strains, and I swallow hard on the lump before taking a deep breath.

How am I going to make things easier for her? Can I even help?

My heart squeezes painfully, and my eyes burn with unshed tears.

How will I survive without her?

I can't picture a world without Rachel.

Suddenly, I hear the front door open, then a woman says, "Take care of whatever the problem is so we can get back to New Zealand. Tim is already breathing down my neck. They're losing money every day you're not on set."

The next moment, Easton stalks into the space between the living room and kitchen, and my heart all but stops.

He glances over his shoulder at the woman who's following after him and mutters, "I know. Go home, Sylvia. I'll be in touch as soon as I've dealt with the problem."

Sylvia seems to be in her late forties, and there are tired lines around her eyes and mouth.

"Okay," she replies.

My gaze flicks back to Easton while my heart starts to thunder in my chest. For a moment, I'm too stunned to comprehend that Easton Rowe is actually standing in the same room as me.

God, he's even more attractive than when I saw him in his last movie, *The Elimination Project*.

With the coffee forgotten in my hand, I sit frozen at the island, too nervous to move a muscle. I take in the sight of his unruly dark-brown hair, chiseled jaw, and tall, muscular body. He's even taller than I remember, probably close to six foot five.

The jeans, T-shirt, and boots Easton's wearing look so freaking hot on him. Even though the clothes are ripped in places, I can tell they must've cost an arm and a leg.

Sylvia turns away from Easton and heads to the front door while saying, "We need to be back on the plane by tonight."

Easton only shakes his head before he walks toward the stairs.

Once I'm alone in the kitchen again, I gasp for air and slap a hand over my racing heart. I set the mug down and focus on bringing my rapid breaths under control.

Holy crap, I just saw Easton.

I remain sitting at the island while I process seeing my first and only love turned famous actor, and once I'm able to think straight, I realize I need to get my shit together.

Easton might be famous, but to me, he should be nothing more than Rachel's older brother.

I'm not going to fangirl over him. That would make things weird as hell.

You're going to treat him the same as any other person. You've managed to hide your feelings for him before, and you'll do it again.

I hear footsteps again, and my gaze darts to the stairs. Staying silent, I watch as Easton comes down to the first floor, then he lifts his head, and his eyes lock on me.

He stops dead in his tracks, and there's an intense punch to my gut as he stares at me.

I gasp from the overwhelming sensation in my chest.

Holy shit, he looks good.

Say hi.

Crap.

At least smile!

My lips tremble as I force what I hope looks like a smile to my face.

Easton recovers from the shock of seeing me, and the corner of his mouth lifts. It makes him look devastatingly attractive, which in turn amps up the nerves spinning in my stomach.

"Hey, Nova," he says, his tone not as harsh as when he spoke to Sylvia.

When he takes the last few stairs and walks toward me, I somehow manage to get up from the stool while practically squeaking, "Hi."

My legs feel numb as I move around the island, unsure of what I should do. At least my voice sounds semi-normal as I say, "It's been so long. How are you?"

"It has," he agrees as he stops a few steps from me, his eyes drifting over my face and body. "I'm good. How are you?"

With a thundering heart and sweaty palms, I feel very awkward as I stand in front of Easton, the star of every fantasy I've ever had.

"I'm okay." Fidgeting, I clear my throat. "Thanks for letting me visit." Unable to stop myself, my gaze drifts over him. "You look good."

Jesus. The man knows he looks good. You couldn't think of something else to say?

"You look good too," he replies, his eyes glued to my face with an intense stare that makes me wish I took time to put on some makeup. The corner of his mouth lifts again. "Wow, you're all grown up." He lets out an incredulous-sounding chuckle. "For some reason, I kept picturing the teenage version of you whenever Rachel mentioned your name."

I smile awkwardly before glancing around the kitchen because it's too unnerving to keep eye contact with him. "Ah . . . was the flight okay?" I think to ask. "Can I make you some coffee?" Spinning around, I hurry away from him, and not waiting for his reply, I prepare a cup of coffee while rambling, "Rachel and Lainey are still asleep. It's pretty early, and I don't know what time they usually get up on a Saturday."

For the love of all that's holy, please calm down!

"Lainey won't wake up until ten," he murmurs. "Rachel should be up soon, though."

"Okay." I take hold of the mug, and turning around, I see Easton has moved closer. He's leaning back against the island with his arms crossed over his chest and his eyes locked on me. The muscles in his biceps strain against the short sleeves of his T-shirt, and even though I've sworn off all men, I can't help but admire how amazing he looks.

When I hand him the coffee, I clear my throat before saying, "I added two sugars. I don't know if you take it differently now."

"Still two sugars. Thanks," he replies before taking a sip. "Is it your truck parked out front?"

I nod, feeling super self-conscious and completely inadequate.

I might be imagining things, but I can swear there's a flash of concern on his face as he asks, "Was the drive from Verona okay?"

"Yeah," I reply. "It wasn't too bad."

Easton glances toward the stairs before looking at me again. "Do you know what the problem is?"

I nod while my teeth tug at my bottom lip.

"And?" He gives me a questioning look.

"It's not my place to say." My voice is hoarse, so I clear my throat again before I add, "It will be better if Rachel tells you."

His eyes sharpen on me, making me feel even more nervous while familiar apprehensiveness tightens my stomach.

"Is it serious?" he asks.

I nod and lower my gaze to my scuffed shoes while my heart clenches in my chest.

We hear a door open upstairs, and the sound has Easton saying, "Sounds like Rachel is up."

God. The news is going to devastate Easton and Lainey.

When Rachel comes down the stairs, Easton stares at her. "Hey, Rach."

"Hey," she whispers, her face unnaturally pale.

As I watch Easton move closer to her, it feels as if my heart is shattering to smithereens all over again. I know it's going to kill him to hear Rachel is dying.

Dying.

I lift my palm to my neck, my throat straining as tears burn my eyes.

He presses a quick kiss to her temple, then asks, "What's the problem?"

Suddenly, she bursts out in tears and slams into Easton's chest while sobs shudder through her body.

Oh, God.

My hand moves up to cover my mouth, sadness ripping through me like a destructive storm. Unable to stop my tears, they begin to roll down my cheeks, and I quickly wipe them away.

"Christ, are you pregnant again?" he asks as he pulls back from his sister so he can look at her face.

When she doesn't answer fast enough, his eyes flick to me, and I shake my head while sucking in a shuddering breath.

Noticing I'm crying, Easton's features grow tenser with worry, and his eyes snap back to Rachel. "What the fuck happened?"

Rachel gasps through her sobs, then she reaches for my arm and yanks me to her side while whimpering, "You tell him."

Crap.

I glance between them, my tongue darting out to wet my lips. "I think it would be better if he heard it from you." Hoping to give her strength, I rub my hand over her lower back. "I'm here, Rach. You can do it."

"Fuck, will someone just tell me what's going on?" Easton growls as he begins to lose his temper, making fear grip my insides.

Rachel shakes her head but manages to squeeze the words out with a strained voice, "I have cancer."

A frown forms on Easton's forehead as he stares at his sister, and a long, tense moment passes before he asks, "Did you see a doctor?"

She nods. "I also got a second opinion. I didn't want to tell you until I knew for sure."

Easton seems weirdly calm as he asks, "What did the doctors say?"

Rachel looks up at him, her face torn with fear. "It's glioblastoma. There's nothing they can do. They've given me meds to help with the headaches."

As the blow hits Easton, he takes a step backward, and shock ripples over his features. This time, his voice is filled with alarm as he snaps, "What do you mean there's nothing they can do?"

Her face crumbles as she replies, "I have a few weeks at most. It's too far along to treat, and it's growing at a rapid pace."

"Weeks," he whispers, intense devastation carving hard lines on his forehead and around his mouth.

A few seconds pass before he shakes his head in disbelief. "But you look healthy." Shaking his head again, he takes another step backward. "When I left two months ago, you were fine."

"Remember the headaches? They started getting really bad after you left, and I thought it was something stupid like a hormone imbalance. The doctor says the symptoms can get worse at any time."

Once again, my heart cracks right down the middle as I watch the shock hit Easton. I try to smother a soft sob as tears continue to roll over my cheeks.

Jesus, this is too much for any of us to handle.

Easton turns around and walks a few steps away from us while lifting a hand and gripping the back of his neck.

God. I wish I could take the heartache from him.

Silence falls heavy in the air until Rachel lets out a sob. Her voice is hoarse as she whimpers, "Easton?"

He sucks in a harsh breath before spinning around and stalking back to her. Lifting his hands, he frames her face and says, "We'll get a third and fourth opinion. There has to be some kind of treatment that can help. I'll find the best fucking doctor in the world." He pulls her into a tight hug against his chest and presses a kiss to the top of her head. "I'll find someone."

Maybe there's something Easton can do? He's rich, and he must have connections.

Hope trickles into my heart, and in desperate need of doing something besides just standing around, I walk to the cupboard and take out three mugs so I can make fresh coffee for everyone.

Lord knows I need more caffeine right now.

Rachel cries in Easton's arms while I prepare the beverages, and only when I set the three mugs down on the island do they let go of each other.

I quickly take the two cold coffees to the sink and pour the liquid out before rinsing the cups.

I join Rachel and Easton at the island, and as we all sip on the coffee, a crushing silence hangs around us.

My gaze darts over Easton's face, his features tense with worry and sorrow. The urge to hug him almost overwhelms me, but instead, I place my hand on Rachel's shoulder.

She wipes a stray tear from her cheek as she says, "I don't know how to tell Lainey."

Easton shakes his head, and his eyes settle on his sister. "Hold off on telling her until after you've seen the other doctors. I want to be certain before we break the news to her."

Letting out a heavy sigh, Rachel nods, then she glances between Easton and me. "Nova said she'll stay as long as we need her."

His attention turns to me. "Will you be okay staying indefinitely? What about your job and life back in Verona?"

I shake my head. "Nothing is more important than Rachel." I clear my throat and add, "And you and Lainey. I'll stay as long as I'm needed."

He stares at me for a moment, his gray irises darker than usual from the horrible shock he's been dealt. "Thanks, Nova."

I nod before taking another sip of my coffee. "If either of you need anything, just let me know."

They both give me weak smiles.

My teeth tug at my bottom lip. "I don't want to step on anyone's toes, so if I get in the way, just tell me."

Rachel reaches for me and gives my forearm a light squeeze. "You can never get in the way. You're family."

Family.

Her words act as a soothing balm to my broken heart. Even though we may have to face the impossible, I'm still thankful to be here with them.

Chapter 5

Easton

A weird sense of panic and powerlessness settles heavily in my chest while I sit at the island with Rachel and Nova.

Everything I've ever done has been for my baby sister. Fuck, I hardly dated because I didn't want anything to disrupt our home life. Rachel and Lainey are my entire world. Without my sister, I won't be able to cope with all the pressure. She's kept me grounded over the years.

I look at Rachel, who's only twenty-eight. When our eyes lock and I notice the fear trembling in her irises, my heart breaks a little more.

Getting up from the stool, I move closer and wrap my arms around her. Pressing her head against my stomach, I vow, "I'm going to find someone who can help you. We'll get through this."

Rachel doesn't nod but only grips me tighter.

Fuck. I'm not losing her. I can't.

Letting go of her, I dig my cell phone out of my pocket and dial Sylvia's number. She's been my manager from the beginning and has gotten me out of some serious, shitty situations.

There was one incident where I placed my hand on a teenage girl's back for a photo. The press blew it totally out of proportion, practically making me out to be some fucking pedophile. Since then, I refuse to touch a female fan. Sylvia made sure the media stopped printing the false information.

Another time, a costar, Kate Phillips, spread lies that she had a sex tape of us. Sylvia went to town on Kate's ass and got the rumors squashed.

Thankfully, my manager answers on the second ring. "What's the problem?"

I suck in a desperate breath of air, and for a moment, I'm unable to speak.

"Easton?" Her tone is much more serious as she says, "Talk to me."

When I finally get the words out, they're strained. "Rachel is sick. She has cancer."

It takes a few seconds before Sylvia whispers, "Oh God." I hear her moving around as she continues, "I'm so sorry, Easton. What do you need me to do?"

"Postpone the filming and find the best doctors who deal with glioblastoma."

"Glio . . ." Her voice trails away, and it takes a moment before she exclaims, "Jesus! I'm coming over."

The call ends, and I struggle not to crush the device in my fist as I look at Rachel's pale face.

"I'm so sorry that you have to postpone filming," Rachel apologizes, looking absolutely devastated by the hell that's been unleashed on us.

"Don't worry about work," I say to reassure her. "You come first."

We stare at each other for a moment, then her face crumbles, and folding her arms around her middle, she admits, "I'm scared."

Christ.

My eyes begin to burn as I pull her to her feet so I can gently wrap her in a hug. Dropping a kiss to her hair, I say, "It's going to be okay."

Since Rachel was fifteen, I've been her guardian. I've done everything in my power to give her a perfect life, and I refuse to consider that I might lose her.

It's not an option. I'll spend every last dime I have to save her.

"You're going to be okay," I repeat.

Her hold on me tightens before sobs burst from her again.

I press more kisses to the top of her head, then mention, "Sylvia's coming over. She'll find the best doctors for us." I push Rachel backward, and leaning down, I lock eyes with her red-rimmed ones. "I want the details of the doctors you've seen and all your test results."

She nods while turning away from me and walking toward the stairs. "I'll get everything from my bedroom."

When it's just Nova and me in the kitchen, I glance at her while sitting down at the island again. Even though her face is blotchy from crying and her green irises carry a world of sadness, she still gives me a compassionate look.

"I'm so sorry, Easton." She begins to reach out to me but changes her mind and pulls back her hand. "I'm here if you need anything."

I have no idea how I'm this calm as I ask, "Can you focus on Lainey? Keep her busy so she doesn't catch on that something's wrong until we're ready to tell her."

Nova doesn't hesitate to nod. "Of course. I'll take her out today so you and Rachel can have time to process everything."

"I'll arrange a driver and guards for you," I mention.

"You don't have to."

My eyes lock with hers. "Everyone knows Lainey is my niece. It's for her safety."

Nova's gaze widens slightly, then she whispers, "Oh, right. Of course."

Even though I've just been knocked off my feet, I once again notice how beautiful Nova's become since I last saw her. When I came down the stairs and saw her sitting at the island, I was stunned speechless for a few seconds, which is a rare thing for me to experience.

Every time Rachel told me about her calls with her best friend, I still pictured the sweet seventeen-year-old girl who was always shy and awkward with me. Now she's breathtaking with her ginger hair and dark-green eyes.

Over the years, I've become cautious around people because of my status, but looking at Nova, there's a sense of familiarity that sets me at ease.

"Thank you for being here," I mention.

"Of course," she whispers, looking a little uncomfortable.

Yeah, she might be all grown up, but she still seems to be shy, which I find endearing.

Hearing Rachel coming down the stairs, I glance over my shoulder and watch her walk toward us.

She sets a folder down on the island, then says, "Everything's in there."

Pulling the folder closer, I open it and begin to read through all the documents. When I look at the scans and reports, a fist grips my heart in an unforgiving hold.

Seeing the actual growth in Rachel's brain makes it all terrifyingly real. In one of my movies, *Unhinged Minds*, I played a CSI agent who was dying of glioblastoma, so I know enough about the illness to understand what the reports are telling me.

Fuck, it's bad.

Again, my mind rebels against the thought of losing Rachel, and I search through all the documents for any sign of hope.

Rachel places her hand on my shoulder, and her tone is soft as she says, "I don't think seeing more doctors will make any difference."

I shake my head hard while my eyes snap to her face. "I'm not giving up, Rach."

There's a knock at the door, and Sylvia calls out, "Easton?"

"In the kitchen," I reply.

My manager comes rushing in and makes a beeline for my sister. I watch as they hug each other, which makes Rachel cry again.

"I'm so sorry, Rach," Sylvia says before pulling back. "I found a specialist in tissue pathology and diagnostic oncology at the Royal Prince Alfred Hospital in Australia who's had success with some glioblastoma cases. I've reached out to his office, and as soon as I hear back from them, I'll let you know."

As Sylvia pats my shoulder, I ask, "Who's the doctor?"

"Professor Anthony Fox," she answers. "One of his patients has been cancer-free for two years."

Hope soars in my chest. "I don't care how much it costs. I want him to look at Rachel's case as soon as possible."

Sylvia glances at her wristwatch. "I'll give them a call once their offices open. It's only four a.m. in Sydney." Her attention turns to Nova, and moving closer, she holds out her hand. "Sylvia Sloane. I'm Easton's manager."

"Hi," Nova replies, looking awkward while she shakes Sylvia's hand. "I'm Nova Allen, Rachel's best friend."

"Nice to meet you," Sylvia says. "Are you from Verona?"

Nova nods and starts to fidget with her empty coffee mug. "Yes. I've known Rachel and Easton my whole life."

Sylvia smiles at Rachel. "You have a whole team of people who love you and will stand by you."

Rachel only nods, her face way too fucking pale.

I can kick myself for not asking sooner. "How do you feel, Rach?"

She lifts a trembling hand and presses her fingertips to her temple. "I have a headache that's making me feel nauseated. I need to eat a slice of toast before taking my meds."

"I'll prepare it for you." Nova jumps up from her stool. "Anyone else hungry?"

I can't think about food right now, so I shake my head. "I'm good."

"I ate on the flight home," Sylvia replies.

We all watch Nova as she toasts a few slices of bread, and the air grows heavy again.

Sylvia is the first to break the silence by saying, "I've spoken to Tim. He's not happy. We'll have to sit down for a meeting to discuss how to proceed."

"There's nothing to discuss," I mutter. "Rachel is my priority now."

"I know." Sylvia gives me a sympathetic look but still says, "The meeting has to happen. I'll ask for a postponement of a month or two. I also left a message for Bobby, so you can expect a call from him. As your agent, he needed to know not to look at any other scripts."

Christ, I can't think about work at all.

My temper flares, and I level her with a look of warning as I snap, "We can talk about work later. Now is not the time!"

Nova drops the butter knife, and the sound draws my attention to her. She gives me an apologetic look, and her voice quivers as she whispers, "I'm sorry."

I notice how tense she is and the trembling in her hand and assume it's because she's upset about Rachel.

Sylvia pulls my attention back to her as she agrees, "Okay. I'll take care of everything at work. You take a few days to process the news."

The only thing that matters is Rachel. Once she's receiving treatment, I'll think about work again.

"Uncle Easton!" Lainey suddenly shouts, and as I glance over my shoulder, I see her running toward me.

I quickly get up and give her a hug before pressing a kiss to her cheek. "How's my princess?"

"This is the best day ever. I didn't know you were coming home, and Nova is here."

"I'm going to head out and do some damage control," Sylvia interrupts us.

I nod, staring after her as she walks away from us. "Thank you for taking care of everything."

"Of course. I'll call once I have news."

I turn my attention back to Lainey. "I missed you, so I came home early."

Her face is filled with excitement. "We're taking Nova shopping and sightseeing today. Are you coming with?"

Before I can reply, Nova hurries closer and wraps an arm around Lainey's shoulders. "I haven't seen you in such a long time and was hoping it could be just the two of us today. Would you mind?"

She glances at Rachel, who quickly says, "I think that's a good idea. You can show Nova all your favorite places."

"Okay," Lainey agrees. "I'll go get dressed."

We all watch my niece head back up the stairs before Nova brings the toast and a glass of juice to the island.

"Eat so you can take your medication," I tell Rachel. I glance at Nova. "Thanks for stepping in with Lainey."

"Of course. I'm just going to go grab my handbag."

I pull my phone out and dial the number for my driver, who's on standby during the day. When Izak answers the call, I say, "I need you to drive Lainey and a close family friend around today. Be ready in ten minutes and tell Tyler."

"Yes, sir."

With that taken care of, I let out a sigh while I pick up my half-empty mug. I'm not a big coffee drinker, but seeing as I can't have alcohol so early in the morning, caffeine will have to do.

While I'm sipping on the lukewarm beverage, Nova comes back into the kitchen and asks Rachel, "Where do you keep your medicine?"

"In my bathroom cabinet," she answers. "I'll go up and take it as soon as I'm done with my toast and juice."

Nova seems to think about something before she asks, "Does Lainey have money? In case she wants to go shopping."

When Rachel starts to get up from her stool, I say, "Don't worry. I've got this."

I pull my wallet out of my pocket and take one of the credit cards from it. I place the card down in front of Nova and say, "There's no limit. Lainey can get whatever she wants."

"Okay," Nova murmurs as she carefully picks up the card, as if she's scared she'll break it.

"Get something for yourself as well," Rachel adds, and it has me agreeing, "Yes. Have fun today."

Nova quickly shakes her head, an awkward expression flitting over her features. "Oh no, I couldn't."

"Lainey is going to shop until you're dead on your feet, so you might as well get something out of it," Rachel chuckles.

"No, really, I'm fine," Nova declines again. "I'm just going to enjoy spending time with her."

Any other woman in LA would jump at the chance of a free shopping day with my credit card, but the offer makes Nova look very uncomfortable.

Before I can look too deeply at Nova's response, Lainey comes barreling down the stairs again. "I'm ready!"

I glance at my niece and tell her, "Nova has one of my credit cards. Get anything you want and buy a few things for your aunt."

"Yay!" she shrieks. "There's a new fashion line out that all the girls at school are talking about."

Rachel pulls her daughter in for a hug and plants a kiss on her cheek. "Enjoy the day with Nova."

"I will."

Seeing Lainey's excitement has a smile forming around Nova's lips, and it makes my eyes lock on her breathtakingly beautiful face.

She's definitely going to draw attention while she's visiting.

Getting up from the stool, I walk out of the house with Nova and Lainey.

Tyler, the head of my security team, is having a cigarette while he's talking to Izak.

"Tyler, keep a close eye on Lainey and Nova," I order.

He nods before asking, "Are you planning to go anywhere else today?"

I shake my head. "I'm staying in with Rachel."

They all climb into the black SUV, and after I watch them drive away, I suck in a fortifying breath before heading back into the house.

Chapter 6

Nova

"Oh my gosh!" Lainey exclaims, bouncing on the seat from all her excitement. "What should we do first? A tour? Breakfast at All That Jazz? It's Mom's favorite place because they make the fluffiest pancakes. Oooh, or shopping, then lunch, then more shopping? And there's this place, The Sweet Spot, that makes the best milkshakes. We have to stop there so you can try one. Or we can take it to go and drink it at the beach?"

I let out a burst of laughter. "We can do anything you want to do."

Just being in the car with my goddaughter for five minutes makes me feel better. She's like a dose of sunshine.

I take in her sparkling, gray eyes, wide with innocence and happiness.

Dang, she's pretty. She got all the good genes from Rachel's side of the family.

"I missed you so much," she says while cuddling up against my side. She wraps her arms tightly around me, and when she squeezes, I have to suppress a groan from the ache in my bruised ribs. But because it feels incredibly good to be loved, I try to ignore the pain.

I hug her back and press a kiss on her soft hair. "I missed you, too, my sweet girl."

Today is about Lainey. I'm going to do my best to make this day fun for her because once she learns about Rachel, it's going to break her little heart.

"Okay." I straighten up and give her a serious look. "How about a light breakfast so we can get some energy, and then we shop until we drop. We can have a late lunch and afterward do something fun like bowling or going to an arcade?"

"Yessss!" she practically screeches. "That will be so much fun."

Behaving like a little grown-up, she leans forward and instructs the driver, "Izak, can you take us to All That Jazz for breakfast, please?"

"Of course," he replies. I see a smile tug at the man's mouth. He seems to be in his late thirties, with salt-and-pepper hair and a friendly face, unlike Tyler, the bodyguard, who has a strict air about him. His features are expressionless, and his blond hair is trimmed in a super neat style.

The men make me feel uneasy, but I do my best not to let it show.

I'm going to have to work hard on hiding my past trauma. I don't want anyone to pick up on it.

My thoughts turn to earlier when Easton snapped at Sylvia. I had such a fright I dropped the knife. His heated words had fear engulfing me. Even though his angry response had nothing to do with me, I automatically apologized like I would've done with Trent.

Only no apology was ever good enough for Trent. He always had to teach me a lesson.

"If you turn left up here, it goes to my school," Lainey says, pulling me out of my dark thoughts.

"How is school?" I ask, forcing myself to focus on her while I glance at the wealthy neighborhood we're driving through.

Back in Verona, there are mansions, but they pale in comparison to the luxurious properties here in Beverly Hills.

Lainey shrugs. "Some days, it sucks. I'm still best friends with Porsha, but there's this girl named Shay who's trying to worm her way between us."

Lainey and Porsha have been friends since their first day of school. Just like Rachel and me.

Rach.

My heart clenches in my chest, but I try not to think of the worst-case scenario because Easton might be able to get help for Rachel.

She's not gone yet. You still have time with her.

"Maybe Shay wants to be friends with both you and Porsha?"

Lainey shakes her head. "She never speaks to Porsha and keeps trying to invite me over to her house. It's very annoying. I know Shay's only doing it because her mom probably told her to do it." She rolls her eyes. "It's happened lots of times before where kids try to hang out with me so their parents can meet Uncle Easton."

"Oh no," I murmur while my eyebrows furrow. "I'm sorry that happened to you."

Dang, it must be so hard for Lainey with people using her to get to Easton.

"How long are you visiting for?" Lainey asks.

"For as long as I'm allowed to." A smile spreads over my face. "So you're going to get tired of me real quick."

She lets out a bubbly chuckle. "Never. Mom was so happy when she told me you're coming to visit she cried."

Again, my heart clenches.

Needing to say the words, I tell her, "I love you and your mom very much."

Her smile widens until a dimple appears on her left cheek. "We love you too. You should move to LA so we can hang out all the time."

"You know what?" I say, giving her an excited look. "I might just do that."

"Really?" she gasps. "That would be awesome, Nova."

"It would, wouldn't it?" I murmur while combing my fingers through her hair.

Izak brings the SUV to a stop, and when Lainey pushes her door open to climb out of the vehicle, I do the same. I glance up and down the bustling street, and noticing a long line at the entrance of All That Jazz, my stomach sinks.

Holy crap.

There's never a line at Reggie's Diner, and it's the most popular spot in Verona.

Actually, it's the only place to eat in that one-horse town.

"Come on," Lainey says as she takes me by the hand.

I'm tugged toward the entrance, where a woman is standing behind a podium of some sort. She's dressed in a black pantsuit, and her makeup is done to perfection.

I wish I could do my mine like that.

The moment the hostess notices Lainey, a wide smile splits over her face. "Lainey! What a nice surprise."

"Hi, Bianca," my goddaughter replies.

Bianca gives me a curious look, then asks, "Will your uncle be joining you?"

Lainey lets out a sigh, then mutters, "No. It's just my aunt and me. The usual table, please."

It's only then I realize Easton's fame extends to Lainey as well.

"Of course. Follow me," Bianca says, and with her chin held high, she walks into the busy restaurant, her hips swinging as if she's modeling the latest fashion.

I glance at the other patrons, and seeing all the expensive clothes, jewelry, and handbags, I feel like something that crawled out of a trash can.

I'm really going to have to put in more effort with my appearance while I'm here. I don't want to embarrass Easton, Rachel, or Lainey.

"Bianca has a massive crush on Uncle Easton," Lainey whispers as we follow the hostess. "That's why there's always a table available for us even though he's never eaten here."

"Is that so?" I whisper back while I keep glancing around the fancy establishment.

Some girls and women wave at Lainey, and she returns their greetings with a polite smile.

Gosh, Lainey's so grown up. Rachel and I were making mud cakes when we were her age.

We're shown to a table that overlooks the sidewalk, and as we take our seats, I notice a man hiding partially behind a car with a camera in his hand.

"Ah, Lainey. Shouldn't we get another table inside? There's someone with a camera behind the sports car."

She doesn't even look up from her menu and only shakes her head. "The paparazzi are everywhere. Just ignore them."

God, I'm not wearing any makeup.

I turn my face away from the man, and picking up the menu, I use it to hide behind.

Lainey lets out a chuckle. "You're being silly."

"I am, right?" I say, chuckling. Focusing on the menu, I ask, "So you suggest the pancakes?"

"Yes," she replies. "That's what I'm getting. We can add bacon and share if you want to."

Relieved that I don't have to think about what to get, I nod. "That sounds great."

Lainey gestures for a waitress to come to our table, then orders, "Hi, Stacey, we'll have a plate of pancakes to share, and please add bacon."

Stacey jots down the order on a small notepad, then asks, "What would you like to drink?"

"I'll have orange juice," Lainey replies while looking at me.

Not wanting to keep the waitress waiting, I quickly answer, "I'll have the same, please."

"Great. I'll be back with your order shortly," the waitress says before hurrying away from our table.

When we're alone again, I smile at Lainey. "Tell me everything that's new with you."

She leans forward to rest her forearms on the table. "My grades are good, so Mom's happy."

I let out a chuckle. "No, tell me all the fun stuff."

"Our grade is having a bake sale in two weeks, and Mom said Porsha can come over the day before the sale so we can bake chocolate chip cookies."

"That sounds fun." My smile grows wider. "When your mom and I were sixteen, we tried to bake a cake and almost burned down the apartment."

"Really?" Lainey chuckles. "Did you get in trouble?"

I shake my head. "We just had to clean up the mess and paint the kitchen."

"Did Mom get in trouble a lot?" she asks.

I shake my head again. "No." My gaze drifts over Lainey's pretty face. "You look so much like your mom."

"And Uncle Easton," she mentions, pride shining in her eyes.

Lainey glances to her right, then lets out a groan before mumbling, "Ugh. Don't come over. Don't come over. Don't come over . . ."

I glance at a woman and girl heading our way with wide smiles on their faces. The woman is dressed in a pair of dark-blue pants that fit her like a second skin, a white silk blouse, and white high heels. An expensive-looking handbag hangs over the crook of her arm, and gold bangles jingle on her wrist. Her blond hair is up in a neat bun, and her bangs are perfectly layered around her face.

The little girl looks like a carbon copy of her mother, except that her hair is down in curls.

When they stop beside our table, Lainey gives them a polite smile. "Oh, hey, Mrs. Riley, Shay."

"It's so good to run into you here," Mrs. Riley says while patting Lainey's arm. She glances around, only sparing me a second of her attention. "Is your mom here with you?"

Seeing the uncomfortable expression on Lainey's face, I climb to my feet and hold out my hand to Mrs. Riley. "I'm Nova Allen, Lainey's godmother."

"Ohhhh!" The woman's eyebrows almost rise into her hairline with surprise, but her surprise quickly passes before she looks me up and down with disdain. "I thought you were the nanny." She barely touches me, her fingers only brushing over mine before she pulls back and wipes her hand on her pants.

I'm never quick to judge people, but holy crap, this woman is something else.

Mrs. Riley turns all her attention back to Lainey. "Where's your mother?"

There's a slight frown on Lainey's forehead as she mutters, "Not here. You'll have to excuse us. I'm having breakfast with my *favorite* aunt, whom I haven't seen in a very long time."

"Oh." Mrs. Riley looks visibly taken aback, then she nods. "I'll see you and your mom at the fundraiser in two weeks, but tell her I say hello and I'd like to have coffee with her when she's free."

Lainey only nods.

The rude woman gives me a look that makes me feel self-conscious, then she mutters, "Enjoy the meal."

Lainey waits for Mrs. Riley and her daughter to leave, then she gives me an apologetic look. "Sorry about that. I don't like them at all."

"Mrs. Riley doesn't seem very nice," I reply.

"She's the worst. She only talks to Mom and me because of Uncle Easton." Lainey glances at the other patrons. "Actually, everyone is fake with me because they're hoping to impress Uncle Easton. It sucks sometimes."

I reach across the table and place my hand on hers. Giving my goddaughter a warm smile, I say, "You're important to me, my sweet girl. Don't worry about other people."

A hopeful expression replaces the upset one on her face. "Are you really going to stay here in Beverly Hills with us?"

I let out a chuckle. "Well, maybe not Beverly Hills, but I'll find a place somewhere in LA."

A happy smile returns to her beautiful features. "I'm really glad you're here, Nova."

My heart fills with warmth as I reply, "Me too."

Chapter 7

Nova

Oh my God. My feet are aching something fierce.

Lainey shopped until I was ready to drop. After stopping to get milkshakes at The Sweet Spot, Izak drove us to Santa Monica Beach.

My gaze is glued to the waves rolling in as I push open the door to get out of the SUV.

Oh God. The smells. The sounds. The sights. It's the most amazing thing I've ever seen.

I stand and stare at the ocean for a few seconds before Lainey says, "Take off your shoes so we can leave them in the SUV."

The moment I slip off my flats, I can't help but groan as I wiggle my toes.

That feels sooooo good.

"My shoes were killing me," I chuckle while we walk toward the stretch of sand. When we step onto the beach and I feel the soft sand beneath my feet, a wide smile spreads over my face. "Gosh, it's so beautiful."

"I like coming here," Lainey says.

"I've never seen the ocean before," I admit. "Well, apart from in magazines and on TV."

She points at a spot. "Let's sit over there."

I can't tear my eyes away from the waves as I plop down beside Lainey. For a minute or two, we drink our creamy milkshakes while enjoying the view, then Lainey asks, "Can I tell you a secret?"

I turn my full attention to her. "Of course."

A shy smile ghosts around her lips. "There's this boy. Tyrel. He gave me a chocolate. I was happy until I heard that he gave one to both Casey and Abigail as well."

"That sucks," I mutter.

She gives me a questioning look. "I know I should ignore Tyrel because he's a player. But . . ." I patiently wait for her to finish. "But I really like him. I feel stupid."

Lifting my right hand, I brush my palm over her hair. "Oh, sweetie. You're not stupid. It's okay to like him, but don't let him walk all over you. You deserve the moon and the stars and everything in between."

If only I'd taken my own advice in the past.

Her eyebrows draw together. "Why are boys like that?"

"Not all boys," I reply. I glance at the ocean before admitting, "There are men like your uncle who are amazing. One day, you'll meet a nice boy who only wants to give you chocolates and no one else."

She lets out a sigh. "I hope so." She thinks for a moment, then says, "He has a twin brother, Shiloh, who's always polite. But he's always awkward around me."

My smile widens. "Maybe he's awkward because he likes you."

Her eyes widen. "You think so?"

"I'm awkward around men I like," I admit. "The more I like a guy, the more I turn into a bumbling idiot."

Lainey lets out a bark of laughter. "You're not a bumbling idiot." She looks me up and down. "You're pretty."

I pull her close for a sideways hug. "Aww, thanks, my sweet girl."

When I suck on the straw of my milkshake, she asks, "So what do you think? Best milkshake ever, right?"

I nod. "I love it."

We stare at the ocean again, and my thoughts turn to when I fell in love with Easton. I think I was fourteen. Rachel and I were having a sleepover at her house, and Easton came out of the bathroom only wearing a pair of shorts. His hair was damp, and there were a couple of stray drops on his chest and abs.

I felt hot all over and didn't know where to look. I ended up walking into the doorjamb when I tried to dart into Rachel's bedroom.

Yeah, that day, I was a bumbling idiot.

"Nova?" Lainey asks, her tone soft. "Why did Mom cry this morning?"

Crap.

Trying to avoid answering, I ask, "What makes you think she cried?"

"Her face was all blotchy."

I suck in a deep breath of air, and feeling rotten for lying, I answer, "She was just happy to see Easton."

Lainey thinks for a moment, then says, "She's never cried before when he's come home from filming."

My mind races to think of a better lie, then I say, "Maybe she's happy because I'm here as well. It's the first time we're all together."

Thankfully, my excuse seems to put Lainey at ease. "That's true." She grins at me. "Let's go home, so we can show them what we bought."

"That sounds like a good idea." I climb to my feet and brush the sand from my dress while we walk toward the SUV.

We stop to toss the empty cups into the trash, and I glance over my shoulder at the ocean, hoping I'll get to see it again soon.

After we get back into the vehicle, she says, "We can go home, Izak."

During the short drive, Lainey grins. "Mom's going to love the dress I got for the bake sale."

"You looked good in it," I say. "I wish I had your sense of style. When I was your age, I only wore shorts and T-shirts."

She looks me up and down. "I like the dress you're wearing today. It's pretty."

Her compliment boosts my fragile self-esteem, making me smile. "Aww, thank you."

When the SUV pulls up to the front of the mansion, I'm once again struck by how big and luxurious the place is.

"Let's get all your bags," I murmur.

"Don't worry about it. Tyler and Izak will bring everything inside," Lainey says while shoving her door open.

Earlier, when we were shopping, I was surprised when the driver and bodyguard doubled as pack mules for Lainey. They didn't complain once though.

Gosh, life is very different here.

Again, I'm hit with the fact that I'm at Easton's place, and I get to see him after so many years. Even though a dark shadow hangs over me because of the crap I've been through and Rachel's illness, my heart beats faster for the man I've loved most of my life.

We climb out of the vehicle, and I join Lainey as we walk into the mansion. "Mom, we're home!" she shouts.

"Out here," Rachel replies from the direction of the veranda.

When we step through the open sliding doors, I see Rachel sitting on a lounge chair. Easton's standing in front of a grill, busy flipping a juicy steak. There are worried lines on his face, but he still looks unbelievably good looking.

My attraction to the man knows no end, and I pray to all that's holy I'll be able to hide it from everyone.

"Did you have fun?" Rachel asks, glancing between Lainey and me.

"So much fun!" Lainey replies while I nod.

I sit down beside Rachel, and unable to stop myself, I take her hand and hold it tightly. As her fingers curl around mine, my gaze darts over her features, and I notice how tired and pale she looks.

My heart clenches painfully in my chest, and the urge to grab onto her and not let go almost overpowers me.

Once again, I'm overcome with an intense sense of hopelessness and fear, and I try to breathe through the heavy emotions while Lainey says, "I got new dresses! They're pretty like Nova's. And I got sneakers and shoes, and the cutest handbag, and an adorable hat."

"Why a hat?" Rachel asks with a soft chuckle.

Lainey shrugs. "I'm thinking of making it my new style."

Rachel lets out a bark of laughter. "God help us. I'm still trying to recover from your scarf obsession. You haven't worn most of them."

"But they look pretty as decorations," Lainey argues as she moves to stand beside Easton. "Nova and I already ate, but the food smells yummy."

Easton brushes his hand over her hair in a fatherly manner. "You can have yours later."

I wonder if he'll ever get married and have children of his own. I think he'd make an amazing father.

I once read that he was dating a model, but it didn't last long, and there's been no other news of him being in a relationship.

The aroma of the steaks pulls me out of my thoughts, and even though I'm stuffed from everything Lainey and I ate today, I ask, "Can I make a salad? Or maybe a potato bake?"

"Don't worry," Rachel replies. "Frances already prepared green beans and mashed potatoes."

I give her a questioning look. "Frances?"

"Oh, she's our housekeeper. You'll love her," she informs me. "You'll also see Josh and Randy around the property. They're the groundskeepers. And you'll probably meet the other guards, Noah, Ryan, and Eddie, at some point."

Holy crap, that's a lot of names to remember.

Rachel must read my mind because she says, "I'll keep reminding you of their names until you remember them."

I let out a relieved chuckle. "Thanks."

"All the bags are in the living room," Izak suddenly says from where he's standing by the open sliding doors.

"Thank you," Easton replies. "You can take the rest of the weekend off."

"Just call if your plans change and you need me." Izak offers us a polite smile before heading back inside the house.

Lainey comes to grab Rachel's other hand and tugs at her. "Come, Mommy. I want to show you everything."

Rachel climbs to her feet before asking, "Are you going to give me a fashion show?"

"Yes!" Lainey darts into the house, her excitement easing the constant tension hanging in the air.

From where I'm sitting, I'm able to glance into the living room while staying out on the veranda with Easton so he's not alone.

Lainey babbles about everything we did while emptying one bag after another.

"Thank you for today, Nova," Easton says.

My gaze darts to him, and noticing he's staring at me, my heart skips a beat. My voice is a little hoarse when I reply, "It's my pleasure. I had a great time with Lainey." I look into the house again, and seeing Lainey is preoccupied with showing Rachel all her purchases, I quickly take the chance to ask, "Did you hear anything back from that doctor in Australia?"

Easton flips a steak while nodding, then his eyes meet mine again. "We've sent him all the information about Rachel's illness and put him in contact with the doctor here in LA. He's looking at everything and will get back to us."

My teeth tug at my bottom lip. "Do you think he'll be able to help her?"

Easton lets out a heavy sigh. "I hope so."

I glance at Rachel again and watch as she laughs with Lainey, who's modeling the purple hat while making silly faces.

An intense wave of sorrow and worry knocks the air from my lungs and makes my throat strain as tears sting my eyes. I lift my hand to cover my mouth while I fight with all my might not to break down.

I take in every inch of Rachel's beautiful face and see the fear etched into her features. She looks so pale and tired.

I can't lose you, Rach.

As if she can hear my thoughts, her gaze flicks to me, and for a few seconds, we stare at each other before Lainey catches her attention again.

When a tear threatens to fall, I get up and walk past the swimming pool before heading in a random direction away from the veranda.

"Nova?" I hear Easton call, but I pretend not to hear him.

Not taking in any of the pretty flower beds around me, I suck in deep breaths of air, but I'm unable to calm down. It feels as if heartache and desperation threaten to rip my chest wide open.

I rush to the side of the mansion, and once I'm sure no one can see me, a sob bursts from me. I wrap an arm around my middle, my body bending forward from the devastation ripping through me.

You need to calm down.

Gasping through the pain, I desperately try to regain control over my emotions while wiping the tears from my face.

You have to be stronger.

Suddenly, a hand touches my back, and as my head snaps up, Easton moves to stand in front of me.

Crap, I didn't want anyone to see me cry.

His gray eyes are filled with the same sadness that's suffocating me.

"I'm sorry," I say, my voice strained. "I'll do better."

A frown forms on his face while he tilts his head. "Come here," he murmurs, his tone soft and filled with understanding as he pulls me into a hug, surprising the hell out of me.

Instead of feeling frazzled and overwhelmed that Easton is actually holding me, it has a totally different effect on me.

The instant his arms wrap around me, I'm unable to stop myself from breaking down. It's as if the comfort he's offering me makes the tears come faster.

I curl my arms against my chest and keep a hand over my mouth while my tears soak into his expensive T-shirt. Every time I take a choppy breath, I get a lungful of his woodsy cologne.

If I weren't so broken and Rachel weren't ill, this could've been one of the best moments of my life. But it's not. Because I might lose my best friend, and I don't think I'll ever be whole again.

After a minute or so, my emotions turn from an inconsolable mess to an empty feeling that weighs a ton. My tears stop, and the sobs fade away.

Easton pulls back while tilting his head to catch my eyes. "Better?"

I only manage to look at him for a couple of seconds before I have to avert my gaze because it's just too intense. "Yes." I quickly clear my throat. "Thank you." Then I see the wet spot on his T-shirt and add, "I'm sorry for ruining your shirt."

"Don't worry about it." He takes a step backward while shoving his hands into the pockets of his jeans. "Nothing about this is going to be easy."

I look up at him as I nod. Noticing he's staring at the grass, I don't look away immediately, and I see the worry and heartache etched into his features.

"What can I do to make things better?" The words leave me automatically.

He turns his head toward me, and when we lock eyes, my heartbeat speeds up.

"You're already doing plenty, Nova. Just be there for Rachel and Lainey."

My voice is a soft whisper as I dare to ask, "And you?"

The corner of his mouth lifts slightly. "Don't worry about me."

I'll always worry about you.

He gestures with a nod of his head toward the veranda. "Let's head back."

Not wanting Rachel to notice that I cried, I ask, "How does my face look? Can you tell I've been crying?"

Easton stares at me for a moment too long before he replies, "A little red here and there. Hang back for a few minutes."

I nod while I watch him walk away and disappear around the corner. *As much as I needed that cry, I really have to do better.*

Chapter 8

Easton

It's almost eleven at night when I shut the laptop with a heavy heart after speaking with Professor Anthony Fox, who was able to give us fifteen minutes of his time.

Rachel slumps back in her chair where we're sitting at the dining room table, and for a moment, I'm unable to think straight.

Sylvia reaches across the space between us and gives my shoulder a squeeze.

Fuck, this is really happening.

Nova gets up from her seat and walks to Rachel, then crouches beside her chair. She places her hand on Rachel's arm but doesn't say anything.

There's nothing she can say.

After Professor Fox looked at everything we sent and spoke with Rachel's oncologist, he agreed with the prognosis. The tumor is too big and impossible to remove surgically. He suggests we use the time Rachel has left by enjoying it as a family instead of spending it in hospitals and going for treatments that will make little difference to the outcome, if any.

The four of us sit in silence for a few minutes before Sylvia asks, "Is there anything I can do?"

I begin to shake my head but then say, "Cancel the filming. Cancel everything."

Even though I'm asking for the impossible, she nods. "Don't worry about work. I'll see which commitments I can postpone."

Rachel sucks in a sharp breath, and it has my gaze snapping to her. Staring at the table, her eyebrows draw together. "Oh God. I'm dying."

Christ.

I shoot up from my chair, and grabbing hold of my sister's shoulders, I practically yank her to her feet before engulfing her in my arms.

A second later, the realization slams the air from my lungs.

Rachel is dying, and there's nothing I can do to stop it from happening.

I grip her tighter and bury my face in her hair as a hard tremble shudders through my body.

After everything I've done to protect Rachel, I'm going to lose her anyway.

She doesn't start to cry but just stands numbly in my arms. When I pull back to meet her gaze, it looks like she's in a daze.

"Rach?" I ask.

Her eyes focus on my face, then she asks, "How am I going to tell Lainey?"

Suddenly, emotion after emotion, everything from horror to panic to devastation, flashes over her features.

This moment right here is easily the most difficult I've ever had to endure. But I've always been the strong older brother who handled shit, and now is no different.

Lifting my hands, I frame her face and force her to focus on me. "We'll tell Lainey together. I'll explain it to her. We'll get through this as a family." I lean a little closer, and my tone is filled with determination and urgency. "You are not alone in this, Rach." She nods while puffs of air burst over her lips. "I'll carry you through it." She nods again, her features morphing into a pleading look. "I'm here."

Her voice is barely a whisper as she admits, "I'm so scared."

"I know." No, I don't. I have no fucking idea, because I'm not the one dying. "I'm here with you, Rach. Every step of the way." Nova moves, catching my attention, and I quickly add, "And Nova's here as well." I brush my palms over the sides of her face and hair. "We are going to love you so fucking much to make up for . . ."

Sylvia lets out a sob. "I'm sorry," she murmurs before rushing out of the dining room.

Rachel crumbles under the weight of her death sentence, and as her body goes limp, I move fast to catch her. I've seen my sister cry many times before, but as she breaks in my arms, it obliterates my heart.

I carry her out of the dining room and head for the nearest couch in the living room. Sitting down, I cradle my sister like a baby and try to will every ounce of strength I have to her.

I would swap places with her in a heartbeat.

Nova sits down beside us and begins to rub her hand up and down Rachel's back.

It takes a good ten minutes before Rachel is able to regain control of her emotions. Looking feverish and trembling badly, she moves off my lap to sit beside me. Nova hurries to the kitchen to grab a chilled bottle of water from the fridge and brings it to Rachel.

We watch as she takes a few sips, then she asks, "Nova, can you bring me my painkillers? My headache is worse from all the crying."

Nova darts away as if hellhounds are chasing her.

I wrap my arm around Rachel's shoulders and try to think of something to say, but everything I think of feels horribly lacking for the gravity of the situation we're facing.

"I love you, Rach."

She closes her eyes and leans against my side, which has me holding her tighter.

Sylvia comes out of the guest restroom and takes a seat on the other couch across from us. Her face is blotchy from crying, and she gives me a compassionate look.

"I'm so sorry, Rachel," she says, her voice scratchy.

Not opening her eyes, my sister can only nod.

As Nova comes rushing down the stairs, Sylvia climbs to her feet. "I'm going to head out so I can get to work on clearing your schedule."

I give her a grateful expression. "Thanks for everything, Sylvia."

"Just give me a call or shoot me a text if you need anything."

Once Sylvia leaves, Nova crouches in front of Rachel and shakes two pills out into her palm.

I stare at Nova as she folds her legs beneath her so she can sit at Rachel's feet.

Except for when she broke down earlier, she's been a source of strength and comfort.

Rachel looks at her best friend before she once again asks, "How do I tell Lainey? How do I tell my baby girl I'm dying?"

"We'll sit her down and explain everything to her as a family," I answer.

Nova tilts her head. "Maybe take a few days for yourself so you can try to process the shock, Rach. You don't have to tell her today or tomorrow. Right?"

Rachel sits up a bit straighter. "Maybe I can hold off on telling her until the symptoms get worse, and I can't hide it any longer."

I nod. "That sounds good."

"Lainey noticed you cried this morning," Nova informs us. "I told her you're happy because Easton and I are here."

"Shit," Rachel murmurs. "I'll have to hide things better around her." She thinks for a moment, then continues, "I need to get everything in order." Her gaze flicks between Nova and me. "You're both Lainey's godparents. You'll have to do for her what I can't once I'm gone."

Nova nods while I struggle through a wave of heartache that's making my eyes burn with unshed tears.

I suck in a deep breath, and when I let it out slowly, I know I'll have to put up the best performance of my life where Rachel is concerned. I have to be stronger than ever so I can one hundred percent be there for her until the end.

Rachel gives me a pleading look. "I don't want Lainey's life to change. You're the only father figure she knows."

I don't hesitate to vow, "I'll continue to raise Lainey as my own, Rach."

"Even when you one day have kids of your own," she pleads.

I brush my palm over the area where the tumor is growing. "I promise to give Lainey the best life possible and to love her for both of us."

She nods before she turns her attention to Nova, who says, "I'll be there for Lainey the same way you've always been there for me. I promise."

Rachel lets out a sigh that sounds like it was dragged from the depths of her soul. "Thanks, guys."

A strained smile forms on Nova's face. "And you can write letters and make videos, which we can give to Lainey so you're always a part of her life."

Rachel nods again. "I'll definitely do that. I'll start tomorrow and get the letters and videos done as soon as possible." She lets out an empty-sounding chuckle. "While I still look good."

"You'll always be beautiful," Nova says.

Silence falls around us for a little while, then Rachel climbs to her feet. "The pain meds are making me tired. I'm going to bed."

Nova also gets up and hugs Rachel. "Good night, Rach. Is it okay if I check in on you during the night? Just to make sure you're okay."

"That's a good idea," I agree. When it looks like Rachel's going to argue, I add, "You could start having seizures or experience other symptoms at any time, so Nova and I are going to keep a close eye on you."

Her shoulders sag, but at least she nods before she heads toward the stairs.

Nova wraps her arms around her middle, staring after Rachel until she's out of sight before she glances at me and asks, "Can we talk about how we're going to handle things going forward?" When I nod, she takes a seat on the other couch across from me. "We need to bring

Rachel's medication down to the kitchen so it's in a spot where we can easily get to it."

"Okay," I reply. "I'll take care of it in the morning."

Even though I'm tired as fuck, I'm pretty sure I won't be able to sleep, so I think about everything that needs to be done.

"Rachel has a will, but I'll have my lawyer check it again," I mention. "I'll ask Sylvia to find the best nurse out there who can assist Rachel during her final . . ." My voice cracks, and I clear my throat.

"We should do as many fun things as possible while Rachel is still able to be active," Nova mentions.

Shaking my head, I let out a humorless chuckle. "My mind went straight to the end. You're right, we should make the time we still have with her special."

"If you want to spend time alone with Rachel, just let me know, and I'll take Lainey out." An uncomfortable expression flits over her face. "And if you don't mind, I'd like to have some time with Rachel as well."

"Of course," I agree.

"Thank you. I really don't want to intrude on your time with her, and I know you're more important, but it would mean the world to me."

I may be Rachel's brother, but I know how close she and Nova are. "Rachel loves you very much, Nova. You're important to her too."

Her chin quivers, and I watch as she fights her emotions. Her beautiful features strain, but she loses the battle, and a tear spirals down her cheek as she admits with a strained voice, "She's the only person who loves me."

Seeing Nova's pain takes a swing at my already pulverized heart, and my eyes burn again as I struggle to hold back the tears.

She covers her mouth as she sucks in a shuddering breath. "Rachel is my other half, and I'll do anything for her."

"She's the glue that keeps us all together," I add my thoughts.

Nova wipes the tear from her cheek and glances at the kitchen. After a moment of silence, she says, "I can cook, so I can help prepare meals."

"You don't have to. Frances takes care of the household."

"Oh, right." She looks awkward for a moment, then gives me a shy smile. "Coffee?"

I slowly nod while trying to force a smile to my face. "Coffee would be really nice right now."

I watch Nova walk to the kitchen and keep staring at her as she prepares the beverages. Something about the way she moves and the energy she gives off is soothing, and it makes me feel grateful that she's here.

The fact that Nova is completely different from most of the women in my world really makes me take notice of her. She's beautiful in an innocent kind of way and seems to be as kind and caring as I remember.

It's refreshing as fuck, to say the least.

The longer I stare at her, the more I become aware of the attraction I started feeling the instant I laid eyes on her after all these years.

When we lived in Verona, she was just Rachel's best friend, but now that we're older things feel different.

Christ, it's been a long while since I've felt attracted to a woman. I've been too busy working my ass off to think about dating.

And now is not the time either.

"Thank you, Nova," I say, my tone a little hoarse from the unexpected emotion she's stirring in me.

"Oh, it's nothing. I was going to make myself some anyway," she replies as she brings the mugs to the living room.

"I mean, thank you for being here."

She takes her seat again before meeting my eyes. "There's nowhere else I'd rather be."

Chapter 9

Nova

I had another nightmare of Trent coming here and causing a scene, but I'm trying not to think of him. It isn't easy, though.

After showering, I put on a pair of leggings and a shirt that reaches past my butt. When I glance down, I notice the bruises on my bicep are starting to fade a little.

Ugh, I wish they would disappear quicker.

Letting out a sigh, I look through my clothes before pulling a crocheted cardigan out and putting it on over the shirt. I push the sleeves up my forearms while I walk to the door, and as I exit my bedroom, I see Easton coming down the hallway.

"Morning," he whispers, gesturing with his hand for me to walk ahead of him.

"Morning," I reply, hurrying down the hallway and stairs so I don't hold him up. When we reach the first floor, I ask, "Would you like some coffee?"

He shakes his head. "I had too much the past weekend. I'll prepare a smoothie for myself. Thanks, though."

I let out a chuckle. "Without coffee, I'd become a serial killer."

The corner of his mouth lifts in a hot smirk while his eyes flick to me, and it has my stomach doing cartwheels. Today, he's wearing a pair of black jeans and a matching T-shirt that spans tightly over his chest and muscled biceps.

He looks so handsome I can't help but stare at him like a lovesick fool.

"You can't even hurt a spider, never mind kill someone," he mutters with a tone of amusement in his deep voice. I watch as he gathers all the ingredients for the smoothie while he continues to say, "Remember that one time you and Rachel screamed your heads off because there was a tiny spider in the kitchen?"

I do. Even though Easton laughed at us, he got rid of the eight-legged demon.

"But you begged me not to kill it," he reminds me.

"Yeah, I remember. It wasn't tiny. That spider was the size of a small dog." I chuckle as I take a mug from the cupboard.

The sound of the blender fills the kitchen for a few seconds, and when Easton pours the smoothie into a glass, he asks, "Are you still scared of bugs?"

"Yeah." I stir my coffee. "Especially if they have wings."

He takes a seat at the island, all his attention focused on me. "Tell me about the past ten years. What have you been up to?"

Taking a sip of much-needed caffeine, I shrug. "Nothing worth mentioning."

He raises an eyebrow. "What work do you do?"

My life is totally insignificant compared to his, and it makes me feel super self-conscious.

I sit down across from him and place my mug on the marble surface. "The last job I had was at a pooch parlor."

It feels as if Easton's gaze burns into me, and I shift on the stool before I mutter, "I liked it. It was nice to work with animals."

They're not mean like most of the humans I've met in my life.

"The last job?" he asks. "You don't work there anymore?"

I shake my head. "The business was struggling, and with me coming here, I figured it would be better to hand in my notice." Feeling uncomfortable from having to talk about myself, I quickly add, "I'm going to start looking for a job here in LA soon." I nervously glance in the direction of the stairs. "I just want to be here for Rachel while she needs me. But until I find a job and a place to stay, I can help Frances with the cooking and cleaning."

Easton's eyes narrow on me, and my anxiety skyrockets, fear tightening my muscles. My voice quivers as I try to explain, "Money's a bit tight right now, so it will be difficult to pay rent while I'm here. But if it's a problem, I can find a job this week."

His features grow serious, and a frown forms on his forehead.

Whenever Trent had that look, it was usually followed by a burst of anger, which always led to a world of pain.

My heart thunders in my chest, and my shoulders hunch forward. I wrap my arms around my middle to protect myself from whatever pain is about to be unleashed on me. Breaths burst over my lips, and panic threatens to overwhelm me as I plead, "I'm sorry. I didn't mean to upset you."

"Morning," Rachel suddenly says.

My head snaps in her direction, and seeing her walking toward me makes an instant wave of dizzying relief wash over me. She places her arm around my shoulders and pulls me into a sideways hug while asking, "What's wrong?"

I quickly wrap my arms around her, taking desperate breaths of her soothing scent.

Rachel's here. She won't let anyone hurt me. I'm safe.

"I'm not sure." Easton gives me a worried look. "We were talking about Nova's previous job, and it somehow derailed. She thinks I expect her to pay rent."

God, I'm so glad she walked in on the conversation when she did. Why the hell did I say all of that and have a panic attack? Easton must think I'm crazy.

Rachel gives me a comforting smile. "You're doing me a huge favor by being here. You're practically family. I don't want to hear anything about you paying rent."

She brushes her hand over my hair, her eyes sharpening on my face.

She's definitely going to insist that I go for therapy now.

Maybe I should.

I pull back from her, and feeling downright awful for the way I spiraled, I mutter, "I'm sorry."

She gives me another sideways hug, which feels very comforting, and after letting go, she helps herself to a sip of my coffee.

"Can I make you a cup?" I offer.

She shakes her head. "I'm feeling a little nauseated today. I'll just have a slice of toast and orange juice so I can take my medicine."

"Nova and I were talking last night, and we feel you should leave your medication in the kitchen where we can all get to it," Easton mentions.

"Okay. I'll bring the medication down after breakfast." Rachel glances around the kitchen, then says, "We can keep them in the same cupboard as the vitamins but on the top shelf."

Still feeling mortified, I avoid looking at Easton while I get up to make some toast.

When I take hold of the bread, Rachel's hand covers mine, and she shakes her head. "Let me do it. I want to carry on as normal for as long as possible. I don't want to think about dying every second of the day. I want to enjoy every moment I have left to the fullest."

My heart clenches painfully in my chest. Nodding, I step to the side and watch as she pops four slices into the toaster. There's a determined sparkle in her eyes that wasn't there before. Certainly not last night after we got the awful news.

An affectionate smile curves around her lips as she says with a teasing tone, "Make yourself another cup of coffee. I know you need at least three before you're able to function."

"You know me best." I try to chuckle but fail miserably.

As I walk back to the island to grab my mug, Easton gets up from his chair, and my body instantly tenses.

Stop! Easton won't hurt you.

"While you're at it, Rach, will you make bacon, eggs, and pancakes as well?" Easton asks, his tone mischievous.

She gives him a playful scowl. "Now you're pushing your luck." A chuckle bubbles over her lips. "Get the bacon defrosted while I make the pancake batter."

It feels like everyone is putting up a lighthearted act, but the sorrow hanging over our heads is devastating and dark.

I clear my throat before asking, "What can I do?"

Easton points at the stool by the island. "Sit."

Rachel adds, "Make yourself coffee and relax while the Rowes prepare breakfast for you."

Easton lifts an eyebrow at his sister. "The Rowes?"

"Yep." When he sets a carton of eggs down on the counter near Rachel, she pats his shoulder. "You're helping, brother."

I place a pod in the machine, and while the coffee pours into the mug, I watch Rachel and Easton. The moment is bittersweet, feeling like the old days when I used to sleep over at their place.

If this is what Rachel wants, I'll do my best to keep the atmosphere light.

Easton

Rachel playfully nudges her shoulder against my arm while I'm frying bacon, then says, "Don't burn the food."

I look at the bubbles forming in the batter in her pan. "You just pay attention to the pancakes."

I glance at Nova, who's enjoying her third cup of coffee, and I'm relieved to see she looks calmer.

I'm not sure what made her react so strongly earlier, but it has my alarm bells going off. Sure, it's normal for her to be awkward, but I've never seen her have a panic attack.

She looked scared of me, and it doesn't sit well with me at all.

A sound comes from upstairs, and Nova jumps up from the stool. "Shoot! I thought my phone was on silent."

When she rushes out of the kitchen, I stare at her until she's out of my sight. Turning my attention to Rachel, I ask, "Did something happen to Nova?"

My sister glances at me. "Why?"

"She had a panic attack just because I asked her about her job."

Rachel glances over her shoulder in the direction of the stairs before saying, "Yes, something happened. A lot of somethings."

"What?" My tone is unexpectedly gruff, and the bacon is forgotten in the pan.

She shakes her head. "It's not my place to say."

"Was it bad?" I ask, trying to get more out of her as worry for Nova trickles into my chest.

Rachel hesitates, then nods.

Christ.

A hundred scenarios rush through my mind, and it makes my body tense and my jaw clench.

When we first moved to LA, I felt bad for leaving Nova behind, but she was a minor and in her grandfather's care. Afterward, life got busy, and it's been one rollercoaster event after another.

Rachel glances over her shoulder again before locking eyes with me. "Once I'm gone, will you look out for Nova? Please." Her features draw tight with sadness. "I don't want her to be alone."

Nova's been a part of our lives since she and Rachel met on their first day of elementary school. I know how much my sister loves her best friend, and honestly, some part of me has always cared about Nova too.

I nod, and just as I'm about to pull Rachel in for a quick hug to comfort her, the smell of something burning hits us.

"The bacon!" Rachel bursts out laughing while I move the pan off the stove.

When I walk to the sink, I hear her mutter, "Shoot, the pancake burned as well."

"That's what you get for laughing at me."

We throw the burned food in the trash and drop the pans in the sink before getting clean ones from the cupboard.

"Let's try again," Rachel says, putting a dollop of butter in her pan. When I join her at the stove to fry more bacon, she asks, "So, you'll look out for Nova, right?"

"Yes." Seeing the pleading look in Rachel's eyes, I add, "I promise."

I hear movement, and a moment later, Nova joins us in the kitchen again. She looks a little pale, and when she smiles, it's strained and doesn't reach her eyes.

Knowing something bad happened to her and seeing her pale complexion makes the worry I already feel double in my chest as I ask, "Are you okay?"

Nova nods as she picks up her empty mug, taking it to the sink. Suddenly, there's a burst of laughter from her. "You burned the food."

The corner of my mouth lifts. "Rachel distracted me."

"Don't blame me," Rachel playfully grumbles.

When Nova walks back toward us, she teases, "Maybe I should take over making breakfast."

Wanting to include her, I say, "Come take over from me before I burn everything."

I only move enough to make space for Nova between Rachel and me, and leaning my hip against the counter, I can't help but admire her beautiful face.

What happened to you?

I take in the nervous way her teeth tug at her bottom lip and the anxious expression that keeps her from looking relaxed. My eyes get stuck on a faint scar above her eyebrow, and it makes me wonder how it got there.

Wanting to know everything I've missed in her life, I ask, "How's your grandfather?"

She shrugs. "Still a recluse and grumpy as hell. I haven't seen him in a long while."

I shake my head. "And Verona? What's changed?"

Her gaze darts nervously to my face before she flips the bacon. "Everything's still the same." She looks at me again, and this time, a shy smile tugs at her mouth. "When your first movie came out, they put up a huge screen on the football field. The whole town came to watch."

I've gotten used to the fame, but hearing that my hometown celebrated my first movie makes warmth trickle into my chest.

When Nova places the bacon that's ready on a paper towel so she can fry another batch, I steal one and nibble on it. It's crispy, just the way I like it.

Usually, I couldn't care less, but with Nova, I'm interested to know her opinion of the movie, so I ask, "What did you think of *Infinite Assassin*?"

Her gaze darts between the pan and me for a few seconds, and a blush creeps up her neck. It makes her look even more shy and awkward.

Making my own assumptions about her reaction, I ask, "Did you hate it?"

"Oh God, no!" she exclaims, her eyes going wide. "It was good, and you were great, and it was . . . really good." Looking more flustered by the second, she rambles, "It was all every woman in town talked about for months. You know . . . because you did that shower scene . . . and . . . there were abs, and your chest was all wet . . . and—"

Rachel lets out a bark of laughter and pats Nova on the back. "Please stop. I don't want to hear about my brother's bare chest."

"Sorry," Nova mutters, looking downright miserable as her face flames up with embarrassment. "This is why I never talked about Easton during our calls."

"Mmmh. Do you have a thing for Easton?" Rachel teases her best friend.

Nova freezes for a moment, and her eyes widen again. She actually looks guilty. I give her a questioning look that has her cheeks turning bright red, and she starts to shake her head.

"Nononono! Of course not." She quickly places the rest of the cooked bacon on the paper towels, then hightails it in the direction of the sink. She sounds panicked again as she hurries to say, "He's your brother. I would never cross that line."

Her strong reaction hits me square in the chest, and it's quickly followed by a wave of disappointment.

"I'm just teasing you," Rachel says with a chuckle.

I force a smile to my mouth and grab another piece of bacon to eat.

Why am I disappointed that Nova will never cross the line?

Do I want her to cross the line?

I glance at her again, and noticing her flushed cheeks and parted lips has my cock hardening at the worst possible time.

Fuck.

I turn away from the women and keep myself busy by grabbing four plates from the cupboard.

"We can eat at the island," Rachel mentions. "Nova, will you go get Lainey?"

"Sure."

My eyes follow Nova as she heads toward the stairs, and I take in her slender body that's a little too skinny. I find the way she moves really attractive, and it's only then that I take notice of the cardigan.

"Is it cold in the house?" I ask.

"No. Why?"

"Nova's wearing a cardigan," I mention.

"Oh." Rachel carries the pancakes to the island before looking at me. She lets out a sigh, then whispers, "I'm only telling you this so you won't think she's being weird."

I take a step closer to my sister, giving her my undivided attention.

"Nova's been in abusive relationships, and the cardigan is to cover bruises on her arm."

The fuck? Is that how she got the scar above her eyebrow?

"Relationships?" I ask for clarity. "More than one?"

Rachel nods. "Those bastards did a number on her."

A frown darkens my forehead, and I glance in the direction of the stairs again. Knowing men hurt Nova makes anger bubble in my chest.

"She's too kindhearted for her own good, and that made her an easy target for the bastards in Verona." Rachel crosses her arms over her chest and lets out another sigh. "Anyway, she's probably terrified of the male species right now, so be careful around her."

I nod, and as I continue to move the food, plates, and cutlery to the island, my thoughts revolve around Nova and what she's been through.

Fuck, I should've brought her to LA after she turned eighteen.

The thought has me feeling a deep sense of guilt and regret for leaving her behind, especially knowing we were all she had.

I hear a commotion, and Lainey comes rushing down the stairs, shouting, "Yay! Pancakes."

When my eyes land on Nova, who's right behind Lainey, a protective feeling toward her pours hot and fast into my chest.

Her gaze meets mine, and a shy smile tugs at her lips. Again, I notice the anxious expression on her face.

I'll prove to her not all men are assholes.

Chapter 10

Nova

When Lainey heads out to go to school, Rachel walks into the living room with a camera, a large notepad, and pens.

The past few days have been rocky, especially when I had the panic attack yesterday, and Rachel teased me about having a thing for Easton. Since then, it's been bothering me. Maybe I'm not hiding my feelings as well as I thought.

Seeing it's just the two of us, I move closer to her and ask, "Um, do I give off any vibes that I have a thing for Easton?"

Rachel lifts her head from where she's fiddling with the camera and gives me a questioning look. "No. Is this because I teased you yesterday?"

I nod as I take a seat beside her. "The last thing I want to do is cross that line and make everyone uncomfortable."

Rachel stares at me for a moment, then the corner of her mouth lifts into a grin. "You have the hots for Easton, don't you?"

"No." I shake my head wildly, then I double down, "No, I don't."

She nods, her grin widening. "Yes, you do." She reaches out to me and places her hand on my forearm. "Be honest with me."

My shoulders sag, and I mutter, "Nothing will come of it, and it started way before you moved to LA, so it's not because he's famous." Needing to reassure her, I add, "Seriously. I promise it's nothing for you to worry about. I'll just have to be better at hiding it."

She keeps staring at me, then tilts her head. "Before we moved to LA? How long has it been?"

I let out a sigh, admitting, "Since we were fourteen."

She gives my arm a squeeze, then asks, "Why didn't you tell me?"

"Because he's your brother."

She lets out a chuckle. "You didn't have to hide it. It wouldn't have bothered me at all." She shrugs. "We all have crushes growing up."

I give her a sheepish look. "It's not a crush."

Surprise flits over her face, then her features soften. "You love him?"

When I nod, it feels freeing that I finally get to share my secret with her, but then I quickly add, "Please don't tell him."

"I won't." Her eyes narrow on me. "Are there any other secrets you're keeping from me?"

I quickly shake my head. "Nope."

"Good." She hands me the camera. "Point it at me and press record."

"Okay." I look for the record button, and after pressing it, I peer through the lens and make sure Rachel is in focus. "Ready."

She sits up straight, and a loving smile curves her lips. "Hi, bestie. This video is for you to watch whenever you need me after I'm gone."

Oh God.

"You're the most kindhearted person I know, and I love you so much, but you have to stop letting people walk all over you. You deserve so much better." She leans a little forward, and it feels like she's looking into my soul as she says, "You deserve to be cherished and loved, Nova. The right man will come along, and you'll get your happily-ever-after. I believe it with all my heart. When that day comes, I ask only four things of you. Accept that you're allowed to be happy, and don't forget about Lainey."

"I won't," I promise. "I will love her with all my heart."

Rachel gives me a grateful look. "Thank you." Sitting back, she continues, "The third thing I need from you is to look out for Easton. Keep him grounded and remind him to take breaks, or he'll work himself to death."

"How do I keep him grounded?" I ask, fully intent on carrying out all her wishes.

"It's the little things like making breakfast together, or having a barbeque, or just talking about the old days and reminding him where he came from."

I nod. "I can do that."

She sucks in a deep breath before continuing, "The fourth thing. I really want you to see a therapist. I don't want you getting panic attacks and living in fear of men. Okay?"

With a lump forming in my throat, I can only nod.

For a moment, she stares at me with so much love shining from her eyes it makes a tear spill down my cheek.

"You're an amazing friend, Nova. I've loved every second we've spent together. From the first day when I saw you in the classroom, I just knew you were mine."

My chin quivers as I think back on that day. I thought Rachel was the prettiest girl I'd ever seen, and I followed her around like a lost puppy.

"I don't know what comes next, but if there's a way for me to look out for you from the other side, I will."

The sound escaping from me is a cross between a sob and a chuckle. "If anyone can find a way, it will be you."

She takes the camera from me and keeps the lens on her as she scoots closer until she's pressed against my side. She wraps her arm around my shoulders and gives me a kiss on my cheek, then says, "No matter where I am, I will always love you, Nova."

I nod, and unable to stop the tears from falling, I say, "I'll always love you, Rach." I blink quickly so I can keep eye contact with her. "You're the most important person in my life."

"We got through puberty and a lot of other shit together," she says, letting out a sad chuckle. "We'll get through this as well."

I'm not so sure I'll get through it, but I'll do my best.

Rachel stops the recording, then closes her eyes, and sucks in a trembling breath.

Placing my hand on her back, I gently rub up and down in an attempt to comfort her. "If I could swap places with you, I would."

She has so much more to live for than I do.

She opens her eyes to look at me, and as tears escape her eyes, she whispers, "I know. That's why I love you so much." She takes another deep breath, then says, "Next video."

God, today might just break me.

When it's almost nine o'clock at night, Rachel says, "It's been a long day. I'm heading to bed."

I watch as she gets up off the couch. "Night. I hope you sleep tight. Wake me if you need anything."

"Good night, Rach," Easton murmurs. "I'll check in on you later."

Lainey went to bed half an hour ago, and as Rachel heads up the stairs, I consider going to my bedroom.

Before I can make up my mind, Easton climbs to his feet and asks, "I'm in the mood for a glass of wine. Want to join me?"

"Ah . . . sure."

I stand up from the couch and follow him to the kitchen. Next to the pantry, there's a wine cooler with a glass door, and I see rows and rows of bottles. He takes one out, and I practically drool over his strong hands as he pulls a cork from the bottle before pouring some of the deep-red liquid into two glasses.

Why does everything about this man have to be so damn hot?

I don't drink much alcohol, so when he hands me a glass, I take a tentative sip. It's strong and sweet all at the same time, leaving a dry sensation behind on my tongue.

"What do you think?" he asks.

"It's okay."

Chuckling, Easton shakes his head. "This bottle cost me over fifteen thousand dollars. It has to be better than okay."

Holy crap!

Shocked by how expensive it is, I glance between Easton and the glass in my hand. "I know nothing about wines. You should've saved the bottle for when you have something to celebrate."

He clinks his glass against mine. "We do have something to celebrate."

"We do?" I can't think of a single thing, especially not after making videos with Rachel all day. My heart is a pulverized mess in my chest.

"The fact that you're finally here in LA with us." Easton twirls the wine in his glass, and a serious expression settles on his face before his eyes lock with mine. His tone is deeper than usual as he says, "I'm sorry, Nova."

His sudden apology catches me completely off guard. "For what?"

"For leaving you behind in Verona." His features tighten with something akin to regret as he keeps looking at me. "I should've brought you with us."

His words hit hard, and unable to keep eye contact, I lower my gaze as I place the glass on the island in the kitchen. Shaking my head, I try to chuckle. "Don't be silly. You have nothing to apologize for." I clear my throat. "I wasn't your responsibility."

When he moves closer to me, my heart instantly beats faster, and my gaze snaps to his face. He tilts his head, and the moment he places his hand on my shoulder, a wave of tingles wars with the ever-present anxiety caused by years of abuse.

"You're family, and have always belonged with Rachel and me."

I stare at the only man who's never done anything to hurt me, and it feels good knowing I mean something to him.

"Thanks for saying that," I whisper. "It means a lot coming from you."

Easton's fingers tighten on my shoulder, and as he moves closer, he gently tugs me toward him. My heart practically explodes into a wild beat when he presses me to his chest. His arms wrap around me, and I'm engulfed in a hug that actually makes me feel safe.

I stand still, soaking in how good it feels to be held by the man who owns my heart, then he says, "It would be nice if you hugged me back."

I let out a burst of awkward laughter, doing as I'm told. After I wrap my arms around Easton's waist and flatten my palms over his back, I turn my head and rest my cheek against his chest.

It's been so long since a man showed me kindness I'm overwhelmed by how good it feels.

Unlike when Easton caught me crying and comforted me on Saturday, there's no reason for him to hold me tonight, and it makes the moment so much more special.

He's doing it because he wants to.

His arms tighten around me, and it makes me feel so safe I practically melt against him.

"You give really good hugs," he murmurs.

While I'm still trying to process how good the embrace feels, he presses a kiss to the side of my head, and it has a tear escaping.

"I'm glad you think so," I whisper, my voice a little hoarse from all the good emotions I'm feeling because of him.

When he begins to pull back, I remove my arms from around his waist. Instead of moving completely away, he keeps one arm locked around me while bringing his other hand to my face.

Oh God. What's happening right now?

He takes hold of my chin and nudges my face up until I make eye contact with him. My stomach fills with a weird mixture of anticipation and anxiousness.

"I want you to know you'll always have a home here with Lainey and me," he pauses, and there's a flash of heartache on his face before he finishes the sentence, "even after Rachel is gone."

My heart is beating so fast, and I'm embarrassed when I realize my breaths are rushing over my lips.

Either Easton is ignoring my reaction or he doesn't notice because he continues, "You're safe here, and I'll never hurt you."

My thoughts come to a screeching halt, and my gaze widens while my face practically goes up in flames.

Oh God. He knows.

When I take a step backward, he lets go of me, but as I glance away, he says, "Don't be embarrassed. And don't be upset with Rachel. I made her tell me."

"Easier said than done," I mutter, taking another step away from him.

All the good emotions I've been feeling up and vanish like mist before the sun. My anxiety skyrockets again, and being aware that Easton knows about my traumatic past has the memories creeping out of the shadows.

A memory of Trent throwing me against a wall flashes through my mind, and I quickly wrap my arms around myself.

When Easton takes a step forward, I flinch, but somehow, I manage to keep still as he takes hold of my shoulder again.

He leans in closer. "Look at me." Shame pours through me like hot lava as I reluctantly do as I'm told. "You're safe with me, Nova."

All Easton's glamour and fame fade away until I'm staring at the man I fell in love with before everybody knew his name.

He always made sure I ate plenty when I spent time at their place. I celebrated every birthday with him and Rachel. He dropped us off at school dances and was always waiting outside to take us home afterward.

The same sense of safety he made me feel as a teenager weaves around me. I didn't know how much I needed the sense of safety that comes from being with people you love until now.

Unable to control the wave of emotions hitting me, I dart forward and slam into his chest. Holding on tightly, I fight with every ounce of strength I have not to burst out in tears.

My voice quivers as I say, "Thank you."

He engulfs me in an incredible hug, and I feel his breath warm the side of my head.

I know he only sees me as a little sister, but that's something I can live with because at least he cares about me in some way. It's the best feeling I've experienced in a really long time. I let out a sigh as I soak in the safety of his arms.

God, after feeling alone and being hurt for way too many years, it feels like I'm finally home.

Chapter 11

EASTON

Sitting in the study with Sylvia, we're both staring at the laptop screen. Tim, the director of the film I'm working on, shakes his head and lets out a sigh.

After spending an hour in the gym, punching the living hell out of a bag, I've been in meetings all morning to pause my career so I can focus on Rachel.

Sylvia's doing her best to keep tempers from flaring, but goddamn, it's sickening how money-hungry some people are.

It's been almost two weeks since I found out about the cancer that's killing my sister, and with every passing day, it feels like a noose is tightening around my neck.

"We'll have to push the release date back by six months," Tim complains. "It will inconvenience everyone."

My muscles grow tense, and I clench my jaw as I stare at the man, who clearly has no heart.

"I know we're asking a lot, but we would appreciate it, Tim," Sylvia replies.

I turn my head and lift an eyebrow at her because I'm done sucking up to the asshole. I have a fucking net worth of over seven hundred million. This movie won't make or break me.

Tim lets out another sigh, then mutters, "If we push day and night, we can wrap up filming in two months. While you deal with her death, we can edit the scenes and go ahead with releasing the movie early next spring. I have another project waiting in the wings and can't afford to waste time."

I sit frozen for a second as his words slice through me.

Push day and night. Deal with her death.

Motherfucker!

The moment I shoot to my feet, Sylvia quickly says, "I'll be in touch, Tim."

She shuts the laptop before I growl, "The fucking bastard."

"I'll take care of him." She gets up and places her hand on my arm.

I yank away from my manager's touch, and when it feels like my emotions are a second away from spiraling into complete chaos, I stalk out of the study before rushing past the gym and dining room.

"Easton," she calls after me. I hear her high heels tapping on the tiles as she tries to catch up to me. "Easton, wait."

Glancing over my shoulder, I snap angrily, "I'm not working with that fucker. I don't care how much it costs. Get me out of the fucking contract."

When I take the corner into the living room, I plow into someone, and before I can react, Nova falls against the back of the couch, and the camera she's holding skids across the floor.

"Nova!" Rachel jumps up from where she's sitting on the other couch.

Nova's dress has bunched up around her thighs, and the cardigan she's wearing has slipped off her shoulders, exposing her arms.

Seeing the light bruises on her bicep and the intense fear on her face is the tipping point for me. Rage at the bastard who hurt her flares up inside me, mixing with the anger I already feel. It all creates a potent cocktail of violent emotions in my chest.

I sink to my knees, and grabbing hold of a terrified Nova, I yank her to my chest. Glaring at Sylvia, I order, "Go and take care of the contract."

She nods quickly and hurries out the front door with the laptop under her arm.

Rachel crouches beside us, a worried expression on her face.

I turn my attention back to Nova, and feeling how she's trembling, an intense wave of guilt hits me. I hurt her. Not even ten days after promising that she'll be safe with me.

Breaths burst over her lips, and I begin to press kisses to her hair and the side of her face in an attempt to calm her down. My voice is hoarse and heavy with guilt as I say, "I'm so fucking sorry."

How many times has she heard those words from a man only for him to hurt her again?

My hold on her tightens even more, and I keep pressing kisses to the side of her face. The last one lands on the corner of her mouth, and when I feel her jerk in my arms, I pull back fast, thinking I've crossed the line.

Fuck.

I sink back on my haunches and take in the shocked expressions on Rachel's and Nova's faces.

"Sorry," I whisper, feeling downright terrible about everything.

Rachel takes hold of the cardigan and adjusts it over Nova's shoulders before asking her, "Are you okay?"

Looking like a deer caught in headlights, Nova nods while she begins to climb to her feet. "Yeah . . . ah . . . yes."

We all stand up, and I have to suppress the intense urge to hold her again.

Rachel glances at me, and coming closer, she places her hand on my arm. "Are you okay?"

No. My sister is dying. I'm angry as fuck, and like that's not enough, I've knocked Nova off her feet before kissing her.

Christ.

Not wanting to worry Rachel, I nod. "I'm good."

Nova walks to the camera, and when she picks it up, Rachel asks, "Nova, can you give us a moment alone?" She nods and quickly hurries toward the stairs. Once she's out of sight, my sister gives me a concerned look. "Talk to me."

I let out a heavy sigh. "Today just got the better of me."

She rubs her hand up and down my arm. "You're allowed to break as well, Easton. You don't have to be strong all the time."

I'll break once you're gone.

I pull Rachel into a hug and inhale a calming breath. "Don't worry about me."

After a short while, she pulls back. "So . . . you kissed Nova. Want to talk about that?"

Our eyes lock, and not seeing any judgment from Rachel, I frown. "You're not upset?"

"Why would I be?"

"Because she's your best friend."

"So?"

Surprised, I tilt my head. "You'd be okay if I started a relationship with Nova?"

Rachel shrugs. "If that's what you both want." She levels me with a serious look. "Do you have romantic feelings for her?"

I take a moment to think about how to respond before I admit, "She's beautiful and completely different from the other women in LA."

The past week and a half the attraction I feel toward Nova has been increasing at a rapid pace. Every day, I notice something new about her that makes me want her in ways I've never wanted a woman before.

She's like a mother hen around Rachel and always gives Lainey attention after school. Not once has she taken a moment for herself, and I'm pretty sure if we allowed it, she'd take over the entire household and work her fingers to the bone.

Nova is the most selfless person I know, and falling for her is as easy as breathing.

Rachel narrows her eyes on me. "You're not answering my question."

The corner of my mouth lifts. "You're like a dog with a bone." I shake my head and admit, "I'm attracted to her." I let out a breath. "A lot."

A smile begins to tug at Rachel's mouth. "Are you falling for her?"

I nod and don't have to wait long for her to respond. "Wow, my brother, who's never had a long-term relationship, is actually falling in love. I think this is a first because that model you took out a few times years ago doesn't count." An amused chuckle escapes her. "I seriously thought you'd remain a bachelor forever, but I'm glad Nova's the one who's making you reconsider your stance on dating."

I don't date for various reasons, Rachel, Lainey, and my career being the most important three. Most women just want to be seen on my arm and don't give two shits about who I really am when the camera is off.

Sure that I want more than a friendship with Nova, I ask, "Would it be okay with you if I pursued Nova?"

"It's not up to me." Rachel walks around the couch and takes a seat. "It would make me happy, though. I'd have peace of mind knowing you and Nova have each other after I'm gone." She leans against the backrest of the couch. "But at the end of the day, it's up to the two of you. She's just come out of a bad relationship, and you need to keep that in mind."

I cross my arms over my chest and glance at the stairs again. "I will."

After a short while, she asks, "What's going on at work?"

I let out a disgruntled huff. "The director is a fucking asshole, but Sylvia will deal with him."

"Now would be a good time for you to take an extended break from filming. You've been working nonstop since your career started. Take some time off, Easton."

"Everyone will lose their shit," I mutter, and I don't want to let down Robert, the producer, because I like working with him. That's why I wanted the postponement, but with Tim's shit, I'm out. I refuse to ever work with that bastard again.

"They don't matter," Rachel argues. "The only people who matter live in this house. I need you now, and once I'm gone, Lainey's going to need you. Promise me you'll take time off."

My heart squeezes painfully in my chest. "I promise."

She pats the couch. "Come sit." I join my sister and turn my body so I can face her, then she says, "You've done so much for me, Easton. I want you to know I appreciate everything you've sacrificed to give me this beautiful life. I know you never brought a woman home because you didn't want to disrupt my life or Lainey's. You're the most incredible big brother a girl could ask for." She sucks in a shaky breath before she continues, "I want you to start living for yourself. If being with Nova will make you happy, then go for it once she's ready. But, if you have any doubts that it might not work out, then don't. For Lainey's sake. She's going to need both her godparents."

"We'll see how things play out," I reply. Tilting my head, I ask, "Do you know how Nova feels about me?"

"Oh no, my lips are sealed." Rachel lets out a chuckle. "You'll have to find that out for yourself."

Trying to get something helpful out of my sister, I ask, "Does she view me as a brother?"

Rachel pretends to zip her mouth shut. "Sealed shut."

Suddenly, a flash of pain tightens her features, and it has me climbing to my feet. "Headache?"

When she nods, I hurry to the kitchen to grab a bottle of water and painkillers. After I hand everything to her and watch her swallow the pills, I say, "Take a nap before Lainey comes home from school. All the shit must've tired you out."

"Yeah. Porsha is coming over after school so the girls can bake cookies for the sale tomorrow." She lets out a sigh as she gets up. "God, I'm dizzy. Will you help me to my room and check on Nova?"

"Sure."

I have to suppress the urge to pick her up and settle for wrapping my arm around her. Leading her up the stairs, I keep my pace slow, and when we reach the second floor, I say, "Just call me if you need anything."

She nods as we walk into her bedroom. I wait for her to lie down, then she sighs, "Thanks, Easton."

I look down at her pale face, and it hammers another nail into my heart. "Want me to stay with you?"

"No," she mumbles, a smile tugging at her mouth. "Go check on Nova."

Leaning over Rachel, I press a kiss to her temple. "Have a good nap." I leave her room and pull the door softly shut behind me. Turning, I stare at Nova's closed door, and I take a serious look at my feelings. It's only been two weeks, but I've known her for over twenty years. I think that's why I'm falling so fast for her.

Because, after everything she's been through, she's still the same kind-hearted person. She's blossomed into a breathtakingly beautiful woman, and I'd be the stupidest idiot on the planet if I let her slip through my fingers.

Now that I know it won't upset Rachel, I start to think about pursuing a relationship with Nova.

I've always had to be careful around other women because I could never be sure whether they were with me for my fame and money.

That's not the case with Nova.

We will have to raise Lainey together. Maybe if things go well and something more develops between us, Lainey won't have to be split between two homes.

My heart beats faster as the idea of building a life with Nova fills my mind.

Nova has always belonged with us. When we were younger, I didn't notice her in a romantic way because of the age gap and the crucial fact that she was a minor.

But she's twenty-eight, and our age difference doesn't matter anymore.

Yeah, but what if she only sees you as an older brother?

I take a deep breath before letting it out slowly.

If that's all she feels for me, then I'll take care of her the same way I've taken care of Rachel, and I'll probably remain single for life.

Chapter 12

Nova

Sitting on the side of my bed, my fingers brush over the corner of my mouth where Easton's lips touched mine while I stare blankly at the floor.

When Easton plowed into me, and I fell, a panic attack hit so hard that I froze, just like all the times when Trent used to beat me.

But instead of being engulfed in pain, Easton started peppering my face with kisses, shocking me to my very core.

Holy crap! Easton Rowe kissed me.

Well, partially, but that doesn't matter. His lips touched mine.

It's getting harder and harder to hide my love for Easton. We've fallen into a routine of watching TV or talking about the good old days after Rachel and Lainey go to bed. I'm getting used to having him to myself for a couple of hours every night.

A knock at my door makes my head snap up. Thinking it's Rachel, I quickly get up from the bed and open for her.

I'm surprised to see Easton. "Oh. Hey."

A smile tugs at the corner of his mouth, and it makes me think of the 'partial' kiss.

"Rachel is taking a nap," he says. When he steps into my bedroom, I quickly move backward. After he shuts the door, he asks, "How do you feel?"

My tongue darts out to wet my lips before I murmur, "I'm okay."

When he reaches for my cardigan, my heartbeat speeds up, and I'm engulfed in a hot wave of shame.

"You can stop wearing this," he says while tugging it down my arms.

I feel super self-conscious about the light marks on my bicep, but then Easton brushes the pad of his thumb over the area. I glance down at where he's touching me, and tingles rush through me.

My eyes fly back to his face when he says, "I'm sorry I made you fall."

I let out a nervous chuckle. "Accidents happen."

His thumb brushes over my skin again, and I become aware of the fact that there are only a few inches of space separating our bodies.

Needing to put his mind at ease, I add, "I'm really okay. Please don't worry about me."

Easton lowers his hand to his side and stares at me until I begin to feel incredibly awkward. Worried that he's upset about what happened, there's a tremor in my voice as I ask, "Are you okay?"

He takes a deep breath before nodding. For a moment, it looks like he wants to say something else, but then he steps away from me and opens the door again. "Let's head downstairs."

Following him out of the bedroom, I suck in a desperate breath. When we take the stairs down to the first floor, I hear Frances, the housekeeper, in the kitchen. Every time we've interacted, she's been very nice to me.

Frances smiles when she notices us. "What would you like for dinner? I can prepare the meal, then you can just warm it up when you're ready to eat."

Easton glances at me. "Any preferences?"

I quickly shake my head. "No, but Lainey mentioned she's craving pizza."

"Pizza it is, then," Frances says while letting out a chuckle. "That child would live on pizza if we gave her half a chance."

"Please make one without pineapple," Easton mutters. "I have no idea how Lainey can stomach fruit on pizza."

"You've never liked fruit," I say with a teasing tone.

"Especially not when it's warm on pizza." I'm surprised when Easton takes hold of my hand and pulls me toward the sliding doors. "Let's sit outside."

Honestly, I'll sit anywhere he wants me to.

I shake my head at my silly thoughts and take a seat on one of the lounge chairs on the veranda. Again, Easton surprises me by pulling his chair right next to mine before sitting down.

It's nice spending time with him, and even though I love him with all my heart, I know deep down there will never be anything more than friendship between us. But it doesn't stop me from cherishing these precious moments I get with him.

He turns his head to look at me. "If I'm not mistaken, Lainey starts spring break next Friday. I want to arrange a day where we do everything Rachel loves."

"I like that idea." I sit up a bit straighter and move slightly in my chair so I can face him. "What do you have in mind?"

"We can watch that movie you both loved in school. The one with the vampires."

"*Twilight*?" I let out a chuckle. "That's one of my favorites. Rachel just tolerated watching it a zillion times for me."

"Oh." His eyebrow lifts. "Let me think." His gaze drifts over the backyard before settling on me again. "We could arrange another spa day?"

I nod enthusiastically. "She enjoyed the one we had on Monday." I consider other things we could do, then ask, "Maybe a day at the beach?"

"Yes." Easton pulls his phone out of his pocket, and I notice he opens a weather app. "Sunny days for the next week. We can have a barbeque as well."

"We can end the day by playing a board game. She always loved kicking our butts with Monopoly."

"That's because she cheated," he mutters.

My eyes lock with his. "Then we let her cheat to her heart's content."

Suddenly, his phone rings, and I glance at the screen. As he accepts the call, I stand up so I can give him privacy, but his hand shoots out and grabs hold of my wrist.

"Hey, Sylvia," he answers while indicating with a nod of his head that I should sit back down again.

I do as I'm told, overly aware of his fingers around my wrist.

"I don't care what the fucker says. I refuse to work with him," he growls.

The anger in his tone has me tensing, but then his thumb begins to brush softly over the inside of my wrist. My gaze locks on where he's touching me while my heart scampers off at a crazy pace.

"No interviews. I'm spending every day with Rachel, and I'll probably take some time off so I can be there for Lainey," he tells her before listening to whatever she says.

Easton adjusts his fingers until his index and middle fingers are right over my pulse. Realizing he can feel how fast my heart is beating, I quickly pull away from him.

His eyes snap to my face as he says, "Fine. Let me know how things go."

As he ends the call, I glance at the garden and pool, feeling embarrassed and worried. I contemplate hightailing it into the house.

"Where were we?" Easton asks, and when I look at him again, it's to see him setting the phone down on his thigh. "We should ask Rachel what she'd like to do."

My voice is barely audible as I reply, "Definitely."

"Nothing else you think we should add?"

I glance down at my wrist where I can still feel his touch.

Did he notice how my heart was racing?

Maybe I'm lucky, and he didn't.

"Ahh . . ." My tongue darts out to wet my lips. "We could all tell her how much she means to us? We could share happy memories?"

"Good idea," he agrees. For a moment, his eyes drift over my face, then he places his hand on mine and asks, "You look a little tense. Are you okay sitting out here with me?"

My heart races wildly as I answer, "Yes."

With all his attention focused on me, he asks, "Do you feel safe with me?"

I don't even have to think about the answer as I admit, "You're one of the few people I feel safe with."

"That's good to hear." His voice sounds deeper and intimate, causing goose bumps to break out over my skin.

My mind is starting to play tricks on me.

His palm brushes up and down my forearm. "Are you cold?"

Oh God, he noticed the goose bumps.

It's a hot day, but I don't want him to think my reaction is because of him, so I nod. "Yeah." I clear my throat. "It's a bit cool in the shade."

The hell it's not, but please believe my lie.

"Come here," he murmurs as he lifts his arm.

"Huh?" I can only stare at him with wide eyes as he wraps his arm around my shoulders and tugs me close to his side.

"I'll keep you warm," he chuckles.

Is this really happening to me right now?

I lean against Easton, my thoughts racing a mile a minute while conjuring up hopes that have no place sprouting in my heart.

Don't, Nova. Easton is just being nice. He would've done the same for Rachel and Lainey.

"We're home!" I hear Lainey call out.

I quickly pull away from Easton and dart to my feet. Walking to the open sliding doors, I force a smile to my face and say, "Are you ready to bake?"

"Yes!"

I move closer to the girls and notice Lainey's best friend looks adorable with her pigtails.

"It's great to finally meet you, Porsha. Lainey's told me so many good things about you."

A pretty smile forms on her face. "It's nice to meet you too."

"Nova's my godmother," Lainey says with pride in her voice. "But you already knew that."

I give Lainey a sideways hug, then glance at the kitchen, where Frances is wiping down a counter. "Is there space for us, Frances?"

"Yes. The pizzas are in the fridge. When you're ready to eat, just pop them into the oven for twenty minutes."

"Thank you," I reply.

A wide smile stretches over Lainey's face. "Pizza?"

I nod as I walk toward the kitchen. "Last night, you said you're craving some, so I figured we could have it for dinner."

"You're the best!"

I notice the girls' bags lying beside the couch. "Why don't you take your bags to your room and wash up while I get the ingredients for the cookies ready?"

"Okay." Lainey's attention is drawn to Easton when he comes into the house. "Hi, Uncle Easton."

"Did you have a good day at school?" he asks.

She nods. "Only one week until spring break. I can't wait." She glances around. "Where's Mom?"

"She's taking a nap but will be up soon," Easton replies. "So be quiet while you're upstairs."

"Okay." The girls giggle as they grab their bags and head to the second floor.

I walk to the pantry, and opening the door, I gather flour, sugar, chocolate chips, and anything else we'll need to bake the cookies.

I carry my haul to the island and place it on the marble top.

Easton comes to rest his hand on my lower back and leans into me. "Anything I can help with?"

If the man keeps touching me, I'm going to start getting ideas that have no place being in my head.

I clear my throat. "Ahh . . . can you get the eggs and milk?"

"On it."

I walk to one of the drawers and take out mixing bowls before grabbing a few spoons and a whisk.

After Easton places the milk and carton of eggs on the island, he takes a seat and rubs his palms together. "What's next?"

I let out a burst of laughter. "Are you planning to bake with the girls?"

He shrugs. "I have nothing better to do."

Lainey and Porsha come back down, and each of them climbs onto a stool.

I pull the recipe closer and say, "Let's get to work. Your mom said we need to bake two hundred cookies."

We all crowd around the piece of paper with Rachel's handwriting on it. The process goes slow, and I keep having to check the recipe so we don't make a mess of things.

I'm focused on cracking an egg open when Lainey smears a streak of flour over my cheek. The girls' laughter fills the kitchen while I chuckle and try to rub it off with my shoulder.

"I've got it," Easton says. He grabs a paper towel, and coming to stand in front of me, he carefully dusts the flour off my skin.

"Thank you." I lift my gaze to his, and my heart fills with so much love I fear it might burst.

There's something tender in his expression as he replies, "You're welcome."

I'll be happy if this is all I ever get from him.

My lips curve up as we get back to work, and I relish how wonderful it feels to be a part of this amazing family after being separated from them for so long.

Chapter 13

Easton

"Are you sure we'll be able to sell all the cookies?" Nova asks while she skeptically eyes the boxes filled to the brim with bags.

"You all decided to bake enough to feed a small country. We only needed two hundred," Rachel mutters. "Whatever we don't sell, we can donate."

"You'll sell everything," I say as I pick up a box and stack it on top of another. When I carry the boxes out of the kitchen, I add, "I'm going with."

Rachel follows after me. "Are you sure?"

"Yes." I hand the boxes over to Tyler, then tell him, "Grab the rest from the kitchen and get Noah, Ryan, and Eddie. We're leaving in ten minutes."

"Yes, sir."

I turn to face my sister and place my hand on her shoulder. "With me at the table, you'll sell out quickly. I don't want you on your feet for too long."

She lets out a sigh, looking worried. "Every woman's going to swamp our table. It's going to be a stampede."

I gesture at Tyler. "Hence the guards."

"I don't know about this," she mutters as she glances between the SUV and me.

I lean a little down to catch her eyes. "I need to get involved with Lainey's school obligations."

"Nova can help with the school stuff."

"And so will I," I insist.

Rachel's eyebrows draw together with sadness, and it has me pulling her into a hug.

"Thanks, Easton," she mumbles against my chest. "I know how difficult it will be for you."

"Don't worry about me." I press a kiss to the side of her head before letting go so we can walk back into the house.

When Tyler grabs the last box, I call out, "Lainey, Porsha, Nova, let's go."

They all come rushing down the stairs, and reaching the bottom, Nova quickly tucks a curl behind Lainey's ear before asking, "How does her hair look?"

"Beautiful," I say.

Rachel smiles lovingly. "How did you get her hair to curl?"

"Patience," Nova replies. "And years of practice with my own."

"Look at my braid," Porsha says, twirling in a circle for us to see.

"It's so pretty," Rachel praises her.

"See you later, Uncle Easton," Lainey says.

"I'm coming with."

Her eyes widen, and then she practically starts bouncing up and down. "Really? Oh my gosh, we're going to make the most money."

I let out a chuckle, and when Rachel and the girls head to the front door, I wait for Nova. I place my hand on her lower back and walk alongside her.

"Things might get a bit crazy at Lainey's school," I warn her.

"How so?"

I glance down at her. "They're not used to seeing me there." Wanting her to be prepared for anything, I say, "There might be reporters, and they will notice you."

"Reporters?"

I stop by the front door and take hold of Nova's arm to hold her back, then explain, "There's a good chance you'll be photographed with me, and rumors will spread like wildfires."

She looks up, worry darkening her green irises. "What kind of rumors?"

"Anything from you being Lainey's nanny to you being in a relationship with Rachel."

She shrugs. "That won't bother me."

"And there will definitely be rumors that we're in a relationship or even engaged."

"We? Like you and me?" Her hand waves wildly between us, then she rambles, "Is there anything I can do or say to make them think otherwise? I can kiss Rachel and hold her hand. God, anything so they don't write lies about you."

The corner of my mouth lifts. "I don't mind, but whatever you do, don't kiss Rachel."

"Why?"

"The last thing I need is the media thinking you're romantically involved with Rachel."

Because then it will look weird as fuck when I eventually make our relationship public.

That's if I get a chance with Nova.

"What's wrong with that?" she asks.

Unable to tell her the truth until I'm sure about her feelings for me, I say, "I don't want to shine a spotlight on Rachel."

"Oh. Right. Of course."

"So if you get the urge to kiss someone, just lay one on me," I tease her before I continue to walk toward the SUV.

Nova lets out a nervous-sounding chuckle, and when she reaches the SUV, Rachel says, "I'll sit in the back with the girls. You take the front passenger seat."

I notice Nova's cheeks are flushed pink as she gets into the vehicle. Walking to the driver's side, I glance at the other SUV the guards will take before I slide in behind the steering wheel.

"It's been a while since we all went out together," Rachel mentions as I start the engine.

"It's going to be so much fun," Lainey adds her two cents.

As I drive behind the guards' SUV, I look at Nova, who seems very nervous.

I'm seventy percent sure she doesn't view me as a brother. Yesterday, her pulse was racing when I touched her wrist. I pretended I didn't notice when she yanked away from me, and it set her at ease again.

My love language is touch, and for the most part, it looks like she's not opposed to it. Every now and then, I catch her looking at me, and she blushes. A lot.

I have to admit her being all innocent and blushing is one hell of a turn-on for me.

But I'll take it slow so I don't overwhelm her because the last thing I want to do is to scare off Nova. And I want to be sure about my own feelings toward her, seeing as a relationship between us will affect everyone around us.

"What do you think of LA, Nova?" I ask.

She lets out a chuckle. "I haven't seen much of it."

"We can go for a drive after the fundraiser," Rachel mentions.

I look at my sister in the rearview mirror. "That's if you're not tired."

"Then you can just drop me off at home and take Nova and Lainey out."

Nova glances over her shoulder. "We'll see how things go. We might all be tired and end up watching a movie."

Lainey looks at Porsha. "Do you think your mom will let you watch a movie with us?"

Porsha shakes her head. "We're going to visit my cousins later. I'm meeting my parents at the bake sale."

"I wish I had cousins," Lainey mutters.

My eyes flick to Nova, and when I imagine having kids with her, the corner of my mouth lifts because I know she'll be an amazing mother.

When we pull up to the school, I find a parking spot next to the guards. Nova opens her door, but I quickly reach over and place my hand on her thigh. "Wait until the guards give us the sign that they're ready."

"Okay."

Tyler comes to open my door while Noah, Ryan, and Eddie open the others.

I grab a pair of sunglasses from the compartment between the seats, and as I climb out, I put them on.

"Eddie, stay with Lainey," I order. "Noah, you're with Rachel and Nova."

They all nod, and we each grab a box of cookies. As we walk toward the baseball field, where all the tables and gazebos are set up, Tyler takes the lead, and Ryan sticks to the right of me.

"Oh my God!" a woman screams, and I let out a groan. "It's Easton Rowe."

It always amazes me how quickly a group of fans forms. It's never just one at a time.

Within seconds, they flank us from all sides, screaming my name. The guards do their work and keep them back while Tyler shouts, "No signatures or photos . . . Give Mr. Rowe and his family privacy . . . No photos . . . Stay back."

"Holy crap," Nova whispers behind me. "This is insane."

"You'll get used to it," Rachel tells her. "Don't make eye contact with anyone and keep walking."

Sylvia's probably going to lose her shit when she hears about this.

Finally reaching the table, I move behind it so I can use it as a barrier between me and the crowd.

"Just one photo, Easton," a fan begs. "Pleeeeease!"

I take a step back so Nova and Rachel can unpack the boxes, then Rachel shouts, "Unless you're buying cookies, please leave. My daughter would like to start her sale."

Just like I thought, they all line up to purchase cookies.

Nova moves backward to place an empty box beneath the table and accidentally bumps into me. I grab hold of her hips to keep her standing, and it has half the women in the crowd screaming their heads off.

"He's touching her!"

"Who is she?"

"God, please tell me you're not dating!"

"I wish I was her."

"This was such a bad idea," Rachel mutters while she grabs a ten-dollar bill before shoving a bag of cookies at the woman.

Nova looks completely rattled, and wanting to get the sale over as quickly as possible, I take off the sunglasses. "This is a fundraiser, right?" I pick up the black marker from the table and scribble my signature on the bags. "The price just went up to a hundred dollars a bag."

"Give me two."

"I want three."

The bags sell as fast as Rachel and Nova are able to move, and we're sold out before the principal even makes it to our table.

"Mr. Rowe," Principal Barnes says, holding out his hand as he approaches us.

I nod at Tyler to let the man through, and when I shake his hand, I say, "Quite the successful fundraiser my sister organized."

"Yes." He grins from ear to ear. "Since Rachel joined the PTA, everything's been running smoothly. It's such an honor to have you here today."

"Just supporting my niece."

"Would you like to join me in the teachers' lounge?" he asks, then he leans in closer. "You'll have more privacy there."

"There's Porsha's mom," Lainey says. "Can I stay with them? I want to look at the other tables."

"Sure." I glance at Eddie. "Don't let Lainey out of your sight."

"Yes, sir."

"You coming?" I ask Rachel.

"Definitely."

Walking with Principal Barnes toward the teachers' lounge, Nova still looks stunned out of her mind, so I take hold of her arm and tug her closer to me.

"Good Lord," Nova whispers when the fans follow after us, constantly taking photos and calling my name in the hopes of getting my attention.

Principal Barnes lets us walk into the building while he hangs back to tell the crowd of fans, "Go support the fundraiser."

Knowing Ryan and Noah will keep them from coming into the building, I let out a breath of relief.

When we walk into the lounge, Rachel heads to a fridge, where she helps herself to three bottles of water.

She gives me and Nova each a bottle before she drinks half of hers. Letting out a breath, she says, "You can go home if you want to, and I'll stay with Lainey for an hour or so."

"I'm not leaving you alone," I mutter as I glance around the lounge.

Suddenly, Rachel's bottle drops to the floor, and the next second, she starts to convulse. I toss my water to the side and grab hold of her just as her body tenses and her eyes roll back in her head.

"Rach!" Nova shrieks, coming to grab hold of Rachel's hand.

I quickly lower my sister to the floor, then I hear the principal ask, "Does she have epilepsy?"

"No!" I glance around us, then shout, "Tyler!"

He appears in the doorway. "Yes."

"Bring the car to the front. Now!"

My bodyguard runs off, and I turn my attention back to Rachel. As I take in her clenched jaw and the uncontrolled movements, my heart fucking breaks. So far she's only been tired and had headaches. This seizure shines a bright light on the fact that Rachel is dying.

Ryan and Noah come rushing into the room. Tyler must've told them to check on us.

Even though the seizure only lasts a few seconds longer, it feels like an hour before my sister stills.

"Rachel?" I brush my palm over her hair as I cradle her head to my chest.

It looks like she's passed out, and my eyes flick to Nova, who's ungodly pale. "Go get Lainey. Take Ryan with you, and he can bring you to Cedars-Sinai. It's the hospital I'm taking Rachel to."

"Okay." She darts up from the floor and runs out of the room with Ryan right behind her.

Adjusting my arms beneath Rachel, I lift her to my chest as I climb to my feet before looking at Principal Barnes, "Where's the front exit?"

"This way."

I follow him with Noah hovering behind me, and when we rush out of the front door of the office building, it's to see Tyler bringing the SUV to a screeching halt.

Noah runs ahead to open the back door, and I quickly climb in, cradling Rachel on my lap.

"Cedars-Sinai," I order Tyler, who waits for Noah to jump into the passenger seat before he floors the gas, speeding away from the school.

Staring at Rachel, I brush my hand over the side of her face and whisper, "Wake up." I press a kiss to her forehead, and closing my eyes, I beg, "Please wake up. It's too soon. Please, Rach. You can't leave me yet. Not today. Not like this."

Chapter 14

Nova

I search frantically through the crowd for Lainey, and not seeing her, I whimper, "Where is she?"

"I don't see her," Ryan mutters.

"Hey, aren't you that woman who was with Easton Rowe?" some random lady asks.

"No," I mutter before darting to my left to get away from her. The last thing I need is a crowd storming me because they think I know Easton.

"There's Eddie," Ryan exclaims, and he grabs my arm in a tight hold as we run in the other guard's direction.

I'm incredibly uncomfortable with Ryan touching me, but it takes me a few seconds before I pull my arm free from his hold.

Lainey comes into view, and when I reach her, I grab hold of her hand and say, "We have to go, my sweet girl. There's an emergency."

Her eyes grow wide as saucers, and she glances behind me as if she's searching for someone. "Mommy?"

I nod and pull her in the direction of the parking area. I hear Ryan informing Eddie that we're going to Cedars-Sinai as we rush across the field.

When we climb into the back seat of the SUV, Lainey asks, "What happened to Mom?"

God, it's not my place to tell her.

Worried out of my mind, I struggle to think straight and end up lying, "I'm not sure. We'll find out at the hospital."

The drive is excruciatingly long, and when we finally reach Cedars-Sinai, I ask Lainey, "Do you have Easton's phone number so we can find out where in the hospital they are?"

"Tyler told us where to go," Ryan informs me, shoving his door open to get out of the vehicle.

Not caring about waiting, I quickly climb out, and once Lainey is standing beside me, I take hold of her hand again. We follow Ryan into the building, but when we have to wait for an elevator, I feel like bursting into tears.

Please let Rachel be okay.

I watch the numbers count down, and the instant the doors open, I dart inside. I move my hands to Lainey's shoulders and keep her pinned against my side.

Feeling how she's trembling, I hug her tightly. "It's going to be okay."

She nods, but her face is torn with fear.

The elevator stops, and we hurry after Ryan as he leads us to a room. When we step inside, there's an empty bed and a small sitting area. It's unlike any hospital room I've ever seen.

Easton's pacing up and down, gripping a fistful of his hair.

"Is she okay?" I ask stupidly because it's clear she's not.

Nothing will ever be okay again.

"Uncle Easton," Lainey cries, and pulling her hand free from mine, she runs to him.

He opens his arms, catching her in a tight hug while his eyes lock with mine. "They're doing an MRI on her."

I nod and fidget with my hands, feeling restless because there's nothing I can do.

Easton walks to me, opening one of his arms, and I dart forward. I wrap my arms around him and Lainey and bury my face against his chest.

Please, God.

I don't know what I'm praying for because swapping places with Rachel isn't a possibility.

What do you beg for when the most important person in your life is dying?

My breaths become choppy, and tears mist my eyes.

Please make me stronger so I can be what Rachel, Lainey, and Easton need.

I fight for control over the devastating emotions, and when I feel a little calmer, I pull back and brush my palm over Lainey's hair while I look at Easton. "Can I get you anything?"

"A glass of water."

I nod, and turning away from them, I walk to the small round table, which has two glasses and a pitcher with water and ice on it. I quickly pour some water into a glass before carrying it to Easton.

While he quenches his thirst, I lean down and tuck strands of Lainey's hair behind her ears.

Her gaze darts between me and Easton. "Is Mommy going to be okay?"

I glance at Easton because I don't know what to say.

When he holds the glass out to me, I straighten up and take it from him. He picks Lainey up and walks to a chair, where he takes a seat. I grip the glass tightly as he positions her on his lap.

"What I'm about to tell you isn't easy," he says to her, his features strained with heartache. "Your mom is very sick, Lainey. She has cancer."

Lainey's chin quivers, and her voice is small and vulnerable as she asks, "Is Mommy going to die?"

Easton sucks in a shuddering breath, and my heart breaks for the millionth time when he says, "Yes, sweetheart." He takes another breath, and his voice cracks. "I'm so sorry."

"No." Lainey's face crumbles, and as the first tear rolls over her cheek, my own tears begin to flow again.

Easton holds Lainey tightly. "Christ, I wish there was something we could do, but you have me and Nova. We love you very much."

"I don't want Mommy to die," she cries while throwing her arms around her uncle's neck. "It's not fair."

"No, it isn't," he whispers.

Somehow, I manage to place the glass on the table before taking a seat beside them. I lean into them and press a kiss to Lainey's hair while rubbing my hand up and down her back.

Hoping I'm not wrong, I say, "We still have time with your mom. We'll spend every second with her and make her happier than ever."

Lainey nods, but her sobs come faster as she cries her little heart out.

It feels like hours have passed by the time her tears slow down, her face all blotchy and looking feverish.

Climbing to my feet, I say, "Let's wipe your face before they bring Mommy to the room."

Lainey nods, and after climbing off Easton's lap, she takes my hand and presses close to my side. I lead her into the restroom, and grabbing hold of her hips, I help her to sit on the counter.

Getting some toilet paper, I gently wipe the tears from her cheeks.

Locking eyes with my goddaughter, I promise, "I'll be here every step of the way, and I'm never leaving you. Okay?"

Her voice is hoarse from all the crying. "You'll stay with me forever?"

"Forever, my sweet girl." I hold up my pinky, and she hooks hers around mine. We both lean forward and kiss our hands, then I say, "I love you very much."

Her chin quivers again as she whispers, "I'm scared."

I wrap her in a tight hug and press kisses to the side of her head. "Me too. But we'll find a way through this. You, me, and Uncle Easton."

She nods, and pulling back, her gaze finds mine again. "Will it hurt?"

"What, my sweet girl?"

"Will it hurt Mommy when she dies?"

Oh God. I have no idea, and I tried not to think about Rachel's last days. Not knowing what else to say, I shake my head. "No. She'll sleep a lot until she doesn't wake up again."

We hear movement coming from the room, and I quickly pull Lainey off the counter and help her onto her feet. Her hand instantly grips mine as we rush out of the restroom.

Rachel is in a wheelchair, looking exhausted as hell. Easton picks her up, and I wait for him to place her down on the bed before I move closer. Lainey presses into my side as I glance between Easton, a nurse, and a man who I assume is the doctor.

Easton brushes his hand over Rachel's forehead and leans over her. "Hey, Rach."

She stares at him for too long, and intense worry pours into my soul.

When her lips part, her words are slurred and slow, "Take . . . me . . . home."

Easton's head snaps to the doctor, and it has the man in the white coat explaining, "The tumor has grown and is affecting Rachel's motor skills and the right side of her body." He steps closer to us. "She's also experiencing double vision, so it will become significantly more difficult for her to move around."

NoNoNo. I'm not ready!

I glance wildly at everyone, and I grip Lainey's hand tighter.

"I've already spoken with Rachel, and I've advised her that we contacted hospice to help make things easier for you." The doctor delivers another punishing blow. "I'm afraid at the rapid pace the tumor is growing, it won't be long now."

Pins and needles spread over my body, and my tongue goes numb from shock.

With a grim expression, Easton nods, and I don't know how he does it, but his voice sounds calm as he asks, "Can I take my sister home?"

"I recommend that she stays a few days so we can monitor her," the doctor answers, which has Rachel shaking her head.

"She wants to go home," Easton insists.

"Okay," the doctor agrees reluctantly. "I've prescribed medicine to help with the seizures and any pain she might experience. It will make her comfortable. Hospice will be in touch with you over the next forty-eight hours."

Easton nods again. "Thank you, doctor. Bring the medicine and any documents I need to sign. I'd like to leave as soon as possible."

"Of course." The doctor looks at the nurse. "Get everything ready for the patient to be discharged." Then, he focuses his attention on Easton again. "Is there anything else I can do, Mr. Rowe?"

Easton shakes his head. "Thank you for everything."

"You're welcome." The doctor hesitates for a moment, then adds, "Call me day or night if I can help. Hospice will come to your house to set up everything, which will make things easier for you."

When he leaves the room, we all stand frozen until Lainey pulls her hand from mine.

"Mommy?" she whispers as she cautiously takes a step forward.

The heartache on Rachel's face is the saddest thing I've ever witnessed, but she starts to pull herself up into a sitting position. I notice how she favors her left side, and Easton quickly moves closer to help.

When she's propped up against pillows, I help Lainey onto the bed. She quickly scoots closer to Rachel and carefully wraps her arms around her mother's neck.

Rachel is only able to put her left arm around Lainey, and I don't even think twice as I help her wrap her right arm around her daughter. I keep my hand pressed to her forearm to hold it in place.

"Mommy," Lainey cries, and her body shudders violently.

"I'm so sorry, sweetheart," Rachel slurs, and it becomes impossible not to cry with them.

"I already told Lainey about the cancer," Easton says.

Rachel gives him a thankful look before turning her attention back to her daughter. "I'm sorry . . . I hid it . . . from . . . you, Lainey. I wanted . . . more time with . . . you . . . and . . . didn't know how to tell . . . you."

"I don't want you to go," Lainey sobs, tears rolling down her cheeks.

Needing to do something, I grab a couple of tissues from next to the bed and pat Lainey's and Rachel's cheeks dry.

The nurse comes back into the room, and while Easton is signing papers, Rachel tells Lainey, "I don't want to . . . leave you, but when I do . . . I want you to know . . . a part of me . . . will always . . . stay with you."

God. My heart can't handle this. It's brutal.

The nurse gives Easton the prescribed medicine, which he holds out to me. "Will you hold this?"

Nodding, I take the bag from him.

"Let's go home," he says while he lifts Lainey off the bed. After he sets her down on her feet, he pushes his arms beneath Rachel's back and knees and lifts her to his chest.

"You can use the wheelchair," the nurse mentions.

Easton shakes his head. "Thanks for everything."

He walks toward the door, and I quickly move around the bed to take hold of Lainey's hand. We stick close behind Easton as we make our way out of the hospital, and I hate how people stare at him. Most have their phones out, shamelessly taking photos. Some have the decency to whisper, while others talk loud enough for us to hear.

"It's Easton Rowe!"

"Isn't that his sister? I wonder what's wrong with her."

"Who's the other woman with his niece?"

We can't leave the hospital quickly enough, and when we reach the SUV, I climb into the back so Rachel can lean her right side against me while Lainey sits on her left.

Easton gets into the passenger seat, and Tyler slides behind the steering wheel.

As we drive away from the hospital, I'm struggling to accept the fact that the tumor is growing fast, and we're running out of time.

Chapter 15

Easton

Carrying Rachel into the house, I head straight for the nearest couch, where I carefully lay her down.

Lainey sits beside Rachel and lies over her chest, then starts to cry hard.

Rachel brushes her palm over the back of Lainey's head as she breaks down as well, and in one of the darkest moments of our lives, we're all at a loss for words, forced to face the harsh reality that awaits us.

I say one of the darkest because I know the worst is still to come.

Needing comfort, I move closer to Nova, who looks utterly lost. I wrap my arms around her and grip her hard to my chest while I bury my face in her hair, needing all the comfort I can get from her.

When she hugs me back, my body shudders, and I struggle to fight the tears that are threatening to fall.

If I begin to cry, I'm not sure I'll be able to stop, so I use all the strength I have to rein in my emotions.

Instead of breaking down, Nova's hold on me tightens, and she whispers, "I'm here for you. We'll get through this. Somehow."

I nod because we have no choice but to power through the hell. There's no way around it.

When Lainey seems to calm down, I pull away from Nova.

I crouch and place my hand on Lainey's back. "Let's make your mom more comfortable."

"I'll get her pajamas," Nova says before rushing off toward the stairs.

"Will you get a bottle of water?" I ask Lainey.

Even though she nods and walks to the kitchen, she keeps looking at Rachel as if she's afraid her mother will up and vanish any second.

I turn my attention to my sister, and seeing how weak she is stomps all over my already-crushed heart.

Keeping my tone gentle, I ask, "How do you feel?"

She tries to smile, but the fear on her face makes it goddamn impossible. "I'm okay."

Christ.

I sit down beside her, and bracing my forearm above her head, I lean in close and say, "You don't have to be strong for us. All that matters right now is you, Rach. Don't hide your feelings from us. If you need to be angry, then be angry. If you need to break, then break. We are all here for you."

I haven't noticed Nova's come back until she says, "I think we should all just scream our heads off."

I sit up to give her a what-the-hell look, but Rachel begins to nod.

Lainey brings the bottle of water, and wanting her to be prepared, I ask, "Are you going to scream with your mom and aunt?"

She nods.

"On three," Nova says. "One. Two. Three."

When they all let out heartbreaking screams, I almost close my eyes as the most intense wave of sorrow hits me, but my gaze is locked on my sister as her voice gives out and sobs rip from her.

Lainey throws herself over Rachel, and I quickly place my hand on her back in an attempt to comfort her.

I turn my attention to Nova, and I watch as her breath hitches, but again, she somehow reins in her emotions.

Rachel is the next to calm down, but Lainey remains inconsolable.

I pull my niece onto my lap and begin to rock her gently while murmuring, "It's okay, sweetheart. Shhh . . . it's okay."

Nova glances at us. "Do you mind leaving the room so I can help Rachel change into her pajamas?"

With Lainey in my arms, I climb to my feet and walk to the sliding doors. Stepping out onto the veranda, I take a seat on one of the chairs and hold Lainey while I just stare out over the garden, not taking in any of the scenery.

Rachel is going to die, and there's nothing any of us can do to stop it.

My mind races, and I think about pulling Lainey out of school so she can spend as much time with her mother as possible before the end. Or maybe I should let her go to school so she gets a breather from all the heartache that's going to fill the house.

Fuck. What will be best for Lainey?

Keeping one arm locked around my niece, who's stopped crying and is lying against my chest, I pull my phone out of my pocket and send Sylvia a text to find the best therapist for Lainey who's willing to make house calls. I feel Lainey would be more comfortable here at home than in some random office.

Not even a minute after sending the text, she replies.

Sylvia: I'll find a therapist ASAP. How are you all holding up?
Easton: Not good. The tumor is growing fast, and we've been told to prepare for the end.
Sylvia: I'm so sorry, Easton. Let me know if there's anything I can do to help.
Easton: Thanks.

I tuck the phone back into my pocket, then hear Nova say, "You can come in."

Lainey scrambles off my lap and runs into the house. As I climb to my feet, my eyes lock with Nova's.

There's a worried expression on her face as she asks, "Do you need anything?"

"A hug," I mutter as I walk toward her.

She meets me halfway and doesn't hesitate to wrap her arms around my waist. Her hand brushes up and down my back, her touch soothing. I let out a heavy breath while folding my body around hers.

Holding Nova, a calmness begins to slowly settle inside me, and it feels as if she's passing some of her strength to me. I press my mouth to her temple and keep it there, taking deep breaths of her soft floral scent.

She pulls her arms back, and just as I think I'm not ready to let go, she moves up on her tiptoes and wraps her arms around my neck. Her hand settles on the back of my head, and it feels as if she's trying to cradle me to her. Then she kisses my jaw, and for a split second, everything feels a little brighter.

"I'm here for you," she whispers before giving me another kiss. "I'll always be here for you."

I lift my head to look at her, and when our eyes lock, I swear I see love shining in her green ones.

Warmth pours into my heart from the way she's looking at me, and it makes me want to hold onto her and never let go.

She moves her palms to the sides of my jaw and says, "You can lean on me. Okay?"

The urge to kiss her builds in me, but instead of claiming her mouth, I nod. My voice is rough from all the emotions warring in my chest. "Thanks, Nova."

She pulls away from me and glances through the open sliding doors into the house. "Do you think I should make something to eat?"

I shake my head. "We can think about food later."

When she heads toward the open doors, I follow her into the house.

Lainey's lying beside Rachel, who gives us a weak smile. "I think . . . she's asleep."

"Should I move her?" I ask.

My sister shakes her head. "I want . . . to hold . . . her."

Fuck, the slur in her speech is killing me.

I move closer and sit down on the side of the coffee table. Keeping my voice soft so I don't wake Lainey, I ask, "How's your vision?"

"Blur . . . comes . . . and . . . goes." She sucks in a deep breath. "I want to . . . talk . . . about my . . . funeral."

God help me.

Nova comes to sit on the floor beside my legs and gives Rachel a loving smile. "What do you want us to do?"

"Fireworks." Rachel lets out a soft chuckle, which makes Lainey curl deeper into her. "Cremate me . . . and shoot my . . . ashes . . . up in fireworks. I want to go . . . out . . . with a . . . bang."

A sad smile tugs at the corner of my mouth as I nod. "Whatever you want."

"I've made a . . . video. Watch it before . . . the fireworks." She takes another breath, and when she talks again, there's no slur, "I only want the three of you at my funeral." Her gaze widens, and she looks at Nova. "Get the camera from my bedroom so you can record me. Hurry!"

Nova runs out of the living room, and Rachel locks eyes with me. "I want a day where I have all my lasts. Help me walk. Have Nova help me shower. I want to eat a steak you made on the grill and to drink a glass of our most expensive wine."

I make mental notes of everything.

"I want to see the ocean and watch Lainey build a sandcastle."

I nod. "When?"

"Tomorrow."

I start to shake my head, saying, "You're not dying tomorrow."

She gives me a pleading look. "I can have another seizure that might make it impossible for me to do any of those things."

"Okay," I agree. "I'll arrange everything for tomorrow."

Nova comes flying down the stairs. "It's recording!"

Rachel shakes Lainey. "Wake up, baby."

"Mommy?" my niece asks as she lifts her head.

"Listen to me, sweetheart. Quickly," Rachel hurries to get the words out before the slur returns. Lainey sits upright, then my sister gives all her attention to her daughter. "I love you so much! You are the greatest joy of my life. Things might get bad for a little while, and after I leave, Uncle Easton and Nova will take care of you."

When Lainey begins to cry, Rachel uses her left hand to wipe her daughter's tears away. "And even when I die, I'll still be here." She places her palm over Lainey's heart. "Right here forever and always. Okay? I'll watch over you every second of every day. I'll cry with you when your heart hurts, and I'll laugh with you when you're happy. I love you so, so, so very much, Lainey."

"I love you, too, Mommy," my niece sobs. "Does it hurt?"

Rachel shakes her head. "Not at all. When I go, it will be like falling asleep."

Lainey lets out another sob. "What happens to you afterward?"

"I'll go to be with the angels, where I can watch over you."

Her left hand cups Lainey's cheek. "I love you unconditionally, Lainey. You are the most beautiful, bravest, and smartest daughter ever. Don't let anyone tell you differently. You deserve the world." Rachel takes a deep breath. "I . . . love you."

Her hand slips away from Lainey's cheek, and she stares blankly ahead of her for a few seconds.

"Shit." I grab hold of Lainey and move her off the couch right before Rachel starts to seize.

"Mommy!" my niece cries.

Nova drops the camera and grabs hold of Lainey before rushing out onto the veranda with her.

I lean over my sister. "I'm here. You're okay. I'm here, Rach." Digging my phone out of my pocket I hurry to find the number for the doctor and press dial.

"Dr. Barlow," he answers.

"It's Easton Rowe. Rachel is having another seizure."

"Make sure there's nothing near her that can hurt her."

"Done."

"There's nothing you can do but wait for it to pass. When she's coherent again, give her the prescribed medicine."

"That's it?" I bark.

"Unfortunately, there's nothing else we can do. I've contacted hospice, and they'll send a nurse out first thing tomorrow morning. The only thing I can suggest is that you bring Rachel to the hospital where we can make her comfortable and care for her until the end."

"No. I want her to stay at home."

"Okay. I wish there was something we could do, Mr. Rowe, but it's out of our hands now."

"Thank you," I bite the words out through a clenched jaw. I end the call, forced to watch as Rachel shakes uncontrollably. When it finally stops, I feel completely defeated. I brush her hair out of her face and whisper, "Rach? Can you hear me?"

She blinks a couple of times, and when she tries to talk, her words are garbled. Tears flood her eyes as they lock on me.

I get up, and finding the prescription bag on the island, I tear it open and look through the bottles for the right medicine. I shake two pills into my palm and hurry back to the couch.

Placing my hand behind her head, I bring my palm to her mouth and feed her the pills. I quickly grab the bottle from the table and take off the cap so she can have a few sips of water.

"It will help with the seizures," I say. I lean over her again and brush my hand over her hair as I lock eyes with her. "I love you, Rachel. Everything I've ever done has been for you, and I wouldn't change a single thing." Tears blur my sight, and I blink them away. "I will give Lainey the world and make sure she never forgets you."

She nods, then manages to say, "Lasts."

"We'll do everything tomorrow. Just give the medicine time to work."

She nods again before her lashes drift shut, and it looks like she's fallen asleep.

"Is it safe?" I hear Nova ask.

"Yes."

She comes back into the living room with Lainey, and panic laces her words. "How's Rachel?"

"I've given her medicine, so she'll sleep for a while."

I only realize it's getting late because Nova switches on the light in the kitchen. "I'll make Lainey a sandwich. She hasn't eaten all day."

"Good idea."

What a fucking day.

I get up, and grabbing a blanket that's draped over the back of the couch, I spread it out over Rachel.

When I turn around, Lainey's just standing and staring at her mother. I take her hand and lead her to the kitchen, where I grip hold of her hips to set her down on a stool.

Taking a seat beside her, I wrap my hand around the back of her neck and ask, "How are you doing?"

Her bottom lip juts out. "My heart hurts."

"I know, sweetheart." I lean closer and press a kiss on her forehead. Worried about what this will do to Lainey, I ask, "Do you want to stay with Porsha and her family for a little while?"

She quickly shakes her head. "I don't want to miss any time with Mommy."

Unable to hide the brutal reality that's become our lives, I say, "Mommy will only get sicker until she passes away. I'm not sure you should see that."

"I'm staying," she snaps, then her face crumbles. "Don't send me away. Please, Uncle Easton."

I pull her onto my lap. "Okay. I won't. Shh. It's okay."

Nova gives me a compassionate look, then says, "I'll make sure to leave the room with Lainey if something happens that she shouldn't see."

I nod. "Thanks, Nova."

Holding my niece, I glance at the couch, not sure how we're all going to get through the next few weeks.

That's if we're lucky. We might only have days left.

Chapter 16

Nova

Last night, Easton told me about Rachel's request, so we're all getting ready to go to the beach.

I braid the last of Lainey's hair and tie it at the end before saying, "Let's go downstairs."

When we leave Lainey's room I glance into Rachel's bedroom. Yesterday, when I went to grab her pajamas, I found most of her clothes packed in boxes. There was also a stack of letters, memory cards, and important documents on her dressing table. She even thought to make a list of all the phone numbers we might need after she's gone.

I think every night when she went to bed early, it was so she could prepare everything for her death to make things easier for us.

We walk down the hallway, and taking the stairs down to the first floor, we see people carrying a hospital bed into the living room. The couches have been moved to the side to make space for everything Rachel will need.

Easton notices us and says, "Hospice just arrived. Give them a few minutes, then we'll get going."

"No rush," I reply. "Where's Rachel?"

"Out on the veranda with Frances."

I walk to the sliding doors and exit the house. "Easton says we'll leave soon."

Rachel struggles to lift her head but manages to look at me. When she sees Lainey behind me, a weak smile forms on her face. "B-beautiful."

My goddaughter puts on a brave face as she walks to her mom. "Nova braided my hair so it won't get in the way when I build you the biggest sandcastle you've ever seen."

A soft chuckle escapes Rachel. "V-very big."

Lainey nods and places her palm against Rachel's cheek. Her tone is too serious for a ten-year-old as she says, "I love you the most in the world, Mommy."

Rachel basks in her daughter's touch. "L-love . . . you."

Easton comes out accompanied by a woman who seems to be in her forties and says, "This is Harlow. She's a nurse and will be with us during the days to help."

I give the nurse a welcoming smile. "Hi, Harlow. I'm Nova, and this is Lainey."

Harlow has a kind face, and her smile is warm as she says, "It's nice to meet everyone." She stops in front of Rachel. "Hi, Rachel, I'm here to help make things easier for you."

My best friend nods. "Going to . . . beach."

"Yes." Harlow's smile widens. "I hear we're going to have a fun day. I didn't bring my swimsuit, so I'll just hang out with you if that's okay?"

Rachel chuckles softly. "Okay."

"Frances, will you let the people from hospice out when they're done setting up?" Easton asks as he comes to pick up Rachel.

Frances doesn't hesitate to answer. "Yes."

"Let's go," Easton says.

"I'll grab the wheelchair and anything else she might need," Harlow mentions as we all head into the house.

I stop to get the camera and tuck it into my handbag before I catch up to Lainey.

Just like yesterday, we take two SUVs. One for the guards and one for us. I sit in the passenger seat again and glance over my shoulder at Rachel, who's positioned between Harlow and Lainey.

I want to spend every waking moment with my best friend, but it's no longer about me and what I want. Lainey comes first.

As Easton follows behind the guards' SUV, I glance at him and notice the lines etched into his face.

Not thinking, I reach across the console and place my hand on his thigh. It's meant to be a quick, comforting touch, but before I can pull back, he places his hand on top of mine. His fingers curl around mine, and he gives me a grateful look before turning his attention back to the road ahead.

I feel a little self-conscious, but thinking he needs the comfort, I push my own feelings aside.

After a few minutes, Easton lets go of my fingers so he can take a turn, but the moment I start to pull my hand back, he shakes his head. "Don't."

Leaving my hand on his thigh, I shoot a glance over my shoulder only to see a smile on Rachel's face as her eyes move between Easton and me. I shake my head so she won't get any ideas, but it only makes her chuckle.

His hand settles over mine again, and he lets out a slow breath as if he finds my touch soothing.

I glance out of the window at the passing scenery, but I don't focus on anything around me except for the way Easton's hand feels on mine.

All the little touches and hugs he's given me have helped so much, and they mean the world to me. I just have to keep reminding myself not to read too much into it because he sees me as a sister or maybe a friend.

But that's all it will ever be.

Seeing how those women lost their minds at the school made it very clear that Easton can have any woman in the world, and little old me doesn't stand a chance.

I'm okay with that. I get to love him every day, and that's enough for me.

Besides, I promised Rachel I'd see a therapist. I'll have to heal from the trauma I've suffered before I can think of ever having another relationship.

When Easton brings the SUV to a stop, I see a gazebo has been erected on the beach. There are also lounge chairs and a table, and a grill stands to the side. A spacious area has been taped off around everything, and Sylvia walks toward us.

Easton gives my hand a squeeze before he lets go so he can climb out of the car.

While I watch as Harlow and Lainey get out, Easton glances at Sylvia. "Thanks for getting everything ready."

"You're welcome."

She waits while Easton picks up Rachel, then she steps forward to give Rachel's arm a squeeze. Unable to say anything, she quickly rushes away to where her car is parked.

We all head down to the beach, and after Easton sets Rachel down on a lounge chair, Harlow covers her with a blanket.

For a moment, I stare at the waves rolling in, then I say, "Come, Lainey. Let's build the castle."

I kick off my shoes and put my handbag down before pulling my dress over my head, revealing my only one-piece swimsuit. After I fold my clothes neatly, I dig the camera out of my bag and glance at where Harlow and Easton are sitting with Rachel.

Today is for her.

Walking to where buckets and shovels are lying on the sand, I sink down to my knees and ask Lainey, "Where do we start?"

"The foundation. We have to make the sand smooth and hard."

I watch for a moment as Lainey pats the sand, and I do the same until we have a big square ready.

"You can load sand into the buckets while I build a wall," Lainey orders.

I glance at Rachel and notice all her attention is focused on her daughter. Taking hold of the camera, I press record and focus the lens on Rachel. I zoom in to capture the look of pure love in her eyes before recording Lainey for a little bit as she concentrates on constructing the wall.

When I point the camera at Rachel again, she notices, and weakly lifting her left hand, she gives me a wave.

She actually looks happy right now, and I'm glad I captured this moment for Lainey. I press stop and glance at the waves again, appreciating the beautiful day we get to spend with Rachel.

Suddenly, the camera's grabbed from my hand and dropped on the sand before I'm hauled into the air by Easton.

Hanging over his shoulder, I let out a shriek, but then I realize he's running toward the waves and quickly say, "I can't swim."

"Don't worry." As he plows into the waves, he brings me down the front of him, and all I feel is warm skin and hard muscle.

Holy hotness.

My brain completely short-circuits.

A wave slams into the back of my legs, shoving me hard into Easton's chest.

Thanks, Mother Nature. You won't hear me complain.

His arm wraps around me, and holding me tightly to his body, he moves us deeper until the water reaches past my thighs.

Another wave knocks into us, and Easton falls backward, letting me use his body like a surfboard while the water pushes us back to the shore.

Laughter explodes over my lips, and even though I swallow some of the salty water, I couldn't care less.

"It's my turn," Lainey calls out as Easton helps me to my feet.

With a wide smile around my mouth, I look up at him. "That was fun."

There's a hot smirk on his face, and drops of water run down his body. "Yeah?"

Oh yeah. My eyes rake hungrily over every hot inch of him. *Definitely yeah.* Like a lovestruck fool, I stare at all his bare skin, my hands splayed over his pecs.

"Watch out," Lainey shouts, laughing.

Another wave plows into us, making Easton hold me tighter, and we stare at each other for the longest minute. It feels super intense, and I'm unable to gather enough brain activity to pull away.

"My turn," Lainey says behind us, and only when Easton glances at her am I able to let go of him. Confused with what just happened and totally overwhelmed by the fluttering in my stomach, I quickly walk away and head straight for Rachel.

I grab a towel and wipe my face before wrapping the fabric around my body. Sitting down, I just stare at my best friend while my mind catches up to what happened.

She grins at me, a mischievous light in her eyes. "Fun?"

"Yeah." My head bobs up and down, then I lean forward and whisper, "I'm trying not to see things that aren't there, but it's hard."

"Not . . . imagining."

What?

She reaches her left hand out to me, and I take hold of it. "Good . . . for . . . him." She gives me a pleading look. "You . . . belong . . . with them."

Knowing Easton is with Lainey, I pull my chair closer before sitting down again. Staring at Rachel, I ask, "How are you doing?"

She shrugs. "It is . . . what it . . . is." She lets out a soundless chuckle. "At least . . . there's a . . . silver lining. I get . . . to kill the . . . tumor . . . when I die." The corner of her mouth lifts. "And . . . I can . . . rest . . . knowing you're . . . with Easton . . . and Lainey."

"I'll stay with them as long as they'll let me," I assure her.

She nods, and sucking in a deep breath, she looks at where they're playing in the waves.

Within seconds, Rachel falls asleep, and I take the time I have to just stare at her.

Harlow comes to adjust the blanket over Rachel and checks her pulse.

"Will she feel any pain?" I ask, my tone brimming with fear.

The nurse shakes her head, then meets my eyes. "You should prepare yourself. It won't be long now."

"How long do you think we have?"

"Days. She knows, and that's why she wanted to give you all today. I don't think she'll be able to leave the house again, and we can't stay out here too late."

Even though I nod, I struggle to accept what Harlow's telling me. Getting up, I keep the towel wrapped around me while I walk down the beach until I can't hear Lainey's laughter anymore.

I stop, and staring at the ocean, I let my tears fall.

I need more strength, Lord.

Much more.

Chapter 17

Easton

"Are you sure you don't want me to stay?" Harlow asks as I walk her to the front door.

She's asked me the same question every night for the past nine days, and I appreciate it. Giving her a smile, I nod. "I'll call if we need you."

"Okay. Have a good night."

I shut the door behind her and head back to the living room. Even though Rachel sleeps most of the time, I turned her bed so she can see the TV.

Lainey's watching a fantasy movie while Nova's making coffee.

I sit down on the armchair I've placed next to the bed and take hold of Rachel's hand. Leaning back, I let out a sigh while I stare at my sister.

"Here you go," Nova says, holding a mug out to me.

I take the beverage and give her a grateful smile.

Nova goes to sit down beside Lainey again, and while she drinks her coffee, she draws patterns on my niece's back.

I sip on the beverage, my attention divided between my sister and the movie. Every now and then, I catch myself staring at Nova, her mere presence bringing me a sense of calm I desperately need.

Rachel's fingers stir in mine, and my eyes snap to her face. She looks very weak and slowly blinks.

When I lean closer, she barely manages to whisper, "T . . . im . . . e."

"Nova!" I snap.

While Lainey turns off the TV, Nova comes to press a kiss to Rachel's cheek, and I hear her whisper, "I love you, Rach." She gives her another kiss, then makes space so Lainey can stand beside her mother.

Nova places her hands on Lainey's shoulders as my niece whispers, "I love you, Mommy."

I set the coffee down on a table, and moving to sit beside Rachel on the bed, I lean over her. Staring at her with every ounce of love I feel for her, I say, "I remember the first time Mom and Dad brought you home. God, I was so happy to finally have a sibling." She blinks slowly. "You were everything I wished for."

When she blinks again, I know it's for the last time.

Lifting my head, I glance at Nova, who immediately steers Lainey back to the couch. My goddaughter curls against her aunt's side and begins to cry silently.

I look at Rachel again, drinking in her peaceful features for close to an hour before she exhales, and as her final breath leaves her, tears fall from my eyes.

Every memory I have of Rachel flashes through my mind, and I keep staring at her face, which looks like she's sleeping.

I suck in a deep breath as I move my fingers to her pulse, and not feeling anything, I pull my phone out of my pocket and dial Harlow's number.

"Should I come back?" she asks as she answers the call.

My voice is hoarse as I say, "Yes."

"Okay."

I end the call and drop the device on the armchair before looking at Rachel again. I brush my hand over her hair, and leaning forward, I press a kiss to her forehead. "I'll miss you."

When a sob bursts from Lainey, I get up and rush to her. I crouch down and pull her into my arms. "It's going to be okay, sweetheart."

Not today and definitely not tomorrow, but one day.

Nova gets up and walks to Rachel, where she presses another kiss to her cheek. After being so strong the past few weeks, her shoulder begins to shudder.

I move to sit on the couch with Lainey on my lap, then say, "Come here, Nova."

Her breathing starts to come in choppy puffs, and she looks at Rachel for a little longer before she rushes to me. I quickly open one of my arms for her, and when she falls down beside me, I pull her into my side.

She wraps her arm around Lainey, and burying her face against my chest, she breaks down.

With Nova and Lainey weeping in my arms, I stare at Rachel's peaceful face until Harlow comes rushing into the house.

I shut the front door and lean my forehead against the frosted glass.

Watching the coroner take Rachel's body was unbearable. I'm so fucking glad I told Nova to wait upstairs with Lainey so they didn't see it.

My legs feel numb, and sitting down flat on my ass, I lean back against the door while staring at the vase of flowers on the glass table.

Rachel chose that table, and she always made sure there were fresh flowers in the vase.

I glance over the living room.

Rachel chose everything because I wanted it to be the home she always dreamed about having.

A groan ripples from deep in my chest, and my shoulders start to jerk.

I cover my face with my hands as the tears come, and I'm not strong enough to stop them.

In the darkest moment of my life, arms wrap around me, and Nova's soft scent envelops me. I rest my head against her chest, and gripping hold of her arm, I hold onto her as I break.

"I've got you," she whimpers before she presses kisses to my hair. Her voice is hoarse with tears as she keeps murmuring, "It's okay. I'm here."

I nod and take every ounce of comfort she offers me.

Sitting on the tiles, we hold each other for the longest time, and only when I manage to calm down do I think to ask with a gravelly voice, "Where's Lainey?"

Nova pulls back. "She fell asleep on Rachel's bed." Lifting her hand to my face, she brushes her thumb over my cheeks to remove the tears.

Feeling a little embarrassed, I try to joke. "If you tell anyone I cried like a baby, my career as an actor is over."

She shakes her head, a serious expression on her face. "All your secrets are safe with me." Her palm settles against my jaw. "You're important to me, and I'll always be here for you the way Rachel was there for me."

Taking hold of her shoulder, I pull her to me so she leans into my side. I let out a heavy breath, then admit, "You're important to me too. I'm going to need you more than ever now that Rachel is gone."

She nods as she wraps her arm around my waist.

I rest my chin on the top of her head and close my eyes. We sit still until my ass begins to hurt, then I mutter, "Let's get up."

Nova climbs to her feet and holds her hand out to me. I take hold of it and let her help me up.

Glancing at the empty hospital bed, I say, "Hospice will collect everything tomorrow, and I need to make arrangements for the fireworks Rachel wanted."

"I can make the calls," Nova offers.

I shake my head. "I'll ask Sylvia to help."

I need to send her flowers or a gift because she's gone above and beyond the duties of a manager.

Nova stops in the middle of the living room and looks around. "It feels like I should be doing something."

"Wine," I say, changing direction to the kitchen. "We're both going to have the rest of the bottle Rachel had me open."

Nova scrunches her nose. "Is it still good to drink?"

I let out a chuckle. "You really don't like wine, do you?"

She shakes her head.

"Fine, I won't make you drink it." I decide to pour myself a tumbler of bourbon instead, and carrying it out to the veranda, I take a seat on a chair, and stare at the backyard that's lit up with garden lights.

When Nova comes out of the house, I quickly grab hold of the other chair and pull it right next to mine. "Come sit."

She sighs as she takes a seat, and pulling her knees against her chest, she rests her cheek on them and looks at me.

I take a sip of the amber fluid, then ask, "How are you holding up?"

"It feels unreal," she whispers. "I don't think it's sunk in yet."

I nod before drinking more of the bourbon.

We're quiet for a while, then I murmur, "For twenty-eight years, everything I did was for Rachel."

"Now everything you'll do will be for Lainey," she says, reminding me that I have a little human to take care of, to love, to live for.

Thinking Nova might need to have the conversation, I ask, "You're going to continue living here, right?"

Her teeth tug at her bottom lip. "Only if you're okay with it."

I hold my hand out to her, and when she places her palm on mine, I wrap my fingers around her, saying, "Yes, I'm okay with it. Like I said earlier, I'm going to need you."

Relief flashes over her beautiful features. "I'll stay as long as you let me."

Brushing my thumb over her fingers, I stare into her eyes. "We'll get through this together."

She nods as she lifts her head, and staring at the garden, she says, "For Lainey."

And for us.

We continue to sit outside, and when I'm done with my drink, I set the tumbler down on the ground. Leaning back in the chair, I link my fingers with Nova's and look at our joined hands.

"It happened so fast," Nova murmurs. "We were supposed to have more time."

I know.

I watch as the blow knocks the air from her when it sinks in that Rachel's gone.

Pulling at her hand, I say, "Come here."

Nova gets up as her chest heaves, and taking hold of her hips, I tug her down onto my lap. When I wrap my arms around her, she presses her face into the crook of my neck. It sounds like her sobs are being ripped from the depths of her soul.

After a few minutes, she calms down enough to say, "I already miss her so much."

"Me too."

Nova rests her cheek against my chest, and just like she did earlier with Lainey, I draw random patterns on her back.

I have no idea how much time passes, but I become aware of her snuggling into my chest before she stills.

Realizing she's fallen asleep, I press a kiss to her hair and whisper, "Sleep tight, beautiful."

At least one good thing has come of the past few weeks, and it's that Nova feels safe enough with me to sleep in my arms.

Chapter 18

NOVA

The past three days have been a blur. I've spent most of my time consoling Lainey, and I think I've run out of tears to cry. I feel kind of numb as Easton pushes the spikes of the four rockets containing the fireworks into the lawn.

To our right is a big white screen that Sylvia arranged so we can watch Rachel's farewell video to us. We found a short letter with it that said we also need to play a specific song when we light the fireworks.

Once everything is ready, Easton comes to stand beside Lainey. He presses play, and the projector throws Rachel's smiling face onto the screen.

My heart clenches painfully, and my throat already starts to strain.

"Hey, guys," her voice echoes around us. "You are the best family any girl could ask for. I leave knowing I was loved and cherished. I don't want you to mourn me, but instead, celebrate the wonderful life I got to live. I want to become your favorite memories. I want you to share jokes about me at barbeques." Her smile is filled with love, and she looks so healthy. "Now light those fireworks, and let me go out with a bang." She blows us a kiss, and we watch as she stops the recording.

"I don't know any jokes about Mommy," Lainey sobs.

"Your mother once made me eat a mud cake, telling me it was chocolate," Easton says, his voice tense with grief.

Remembering the day, I chuckle softly. "You brushed your teeth twice."

"Eww." Lainey also manages to chuckle, then we watch as Easton walks to the fireworks.

I connect my phone to the Bluetooth speaker and press play on the song Rachel selected. When the lyrics to "Forever & Always" by Written by Wolves begin to fill the air, Easton lights the first rocket.

It shoots high into the air and explodes into bright-pink sparkles. Another goes up, filling the sky with blues, then the third adds purple before the last rocket ends with a bright green that lights up the entire area.

I'll remember you forever and always, Rach. You were the best part of my life.

My sight blurs, but I blink the tears away, and walking back to Lainey, I place my hand on her shoulder, and ask, "Are you doing okay?"

She tries to nod, but then her face crumbles. "It was so pretty. Just like Mommy."

"Yeah," I agree as I pull her into a hug.

When the song's last notes fade away, I let go of Lainey so I can disconnect my phone from the speaker.

A heavy wave of grief rolls over me, and it feels like it's trying to crush my chest.

"Can we watch the video again?" Lainey asks, her voice fragile.

"Of course," Easton answers. He fiddles with the projector, and we watch it two more times with Lainey, then he rubs her back gently and says, "It's time for you to get ready for bed."

"I'll get the bath ready." I smile at my goddaughter. "Do you want bubbles?"

She nods, and we all head upstairs. When I open the faucets in the tub, Easton presses a kiss to the top of her head before leaving the bathroom.

I check the temperature constantly, making sure it's not too hot before I shut off the faucets.

"Will you stay with me?" Lainey asks as she pulls her shirt over her head.

"Of course." I take a seat on the closed toilet lid, and when she climbs into the tub, I ask, "Is the temperature right?"

She nods, scooping some bubbles into her hands. Her sad gaze darts to me, and I can see she wants to ask something.

"You can talk to me about anything," I encourage her.

"You didn't have a mom, right?"

"Yeah, mine left when I was four years old."

"Did it hurt?"

I nod but then say, "Not for long, though. My mother wasn't as amazing as yours."

"Who took care of you after she left?" Lainey asks.

The years after my mother left were hard. I had to learn very quickly to take care of myself because my grandfather didn't give two damns about me. I was always told to stay out of his way, and I think he only enrolled me in school so he'd be rid of me during the days.

A sad smile tugs at my lips. "When I met your mom, she took care of me."

"You have me now, Nova."

I move off the lid to sit on the floor right beside the tub and give her a grateful smile. "I love you, Lainey. Like you're my own, but I'll never try to replace your mom. Okay?"

She nods. "I love you too." Her face starts to crumble under her grief as she adds, "I'm so glad you came to live with us."

I brush my hand over the back of her head. "Me, too, my sweet girl."

A tear rolls down her cheek. "I don't want to sleep."

"Okay." I keep brushing my hand over her hair. "We can watch a movie until you're tired."

She nods, her chin quivering and her eyes sparkling with tears.

I gesture with a nod at the water. "Wash up so we can go snuggle on the couch."

"Can we have popcorn and chocolate and watch *The Golden Compass*?"

"Sure." I climb to my feet. "Let me grab your pajamas, and then I'll make the popcorn."

"I want my pink ones," she calls after me as I leave the bathroom.

I open her chest of drawers and grab the set she wants, along with underwear. Heading back to the bathroom, I place the clothes on the counter. "See you downstairs."

"Okay."

I shut the door behind me, and as I walk to the kitchen, I try to breathe through my own sorrow.

I don't know how any of us will get through this.

I see Easton sitting on the couch, his forearms resting on his thighs, while he stares down at the floor.

"Are you okay?" I ask.

His head snaps up, and he nods. "Yeah." Climbing to his feet, he asks, "How's Lainey doing?"

"As well as can be expected." I grab the popcorn from the pantry and place it in the microwave. "She wants to watch *The Golden Compass*. Want to join us?"

"Sure." He takes a seat at the island and stares at me.

I feel a little awkward and ask, "What?"

"I'm just thankful you're here."

His words soothe my broken heart, and I give him a warm smile. "I'm glad to be here."

"I've arranged for a therapist to meet with Lainey," he informs me.

"That's good."

I'll have to find one as well.

It's only then that I think about how much it will cost, and I begin to worry that I won't be able to keep my promise to Rachel.

As if Easton can read my thoughts, he asks, "Would you like to meet with one too?"

Embarrassed to admit the words out loud, I say, "I'll have to get a job first. Right now, I don't have money for a therapist."

He tilts his head. "I'll pay." When my lips part, he holds up a hand to stop me from declining. "I want to, Nova. It's the least I can do to repay you for everything you've done for us."

I'll be able to keep my promise to Rachel.

Even though I feel uncomfortable, I nod. "Thank you, Easton."

"I'll ask Sylvia to find you a good therapist."

A grateful smile wavers around my mouth while I glance at the fridge where I've stuck the piece of paper with all the important phone numbers written in Rachel's handwriting. I glance over all of them, and when I see she's listed a number for a therapist right at the bottom, my heart clenches painfully.

"Rachel already found a therapist for me." I gesture at the list. "Right at the bottom."

Easton is quiet for a moment, then he whispers, "She thought of everything."

My throat strains as a wave of tears threatens to overwhelm me, but I blink them away when the microwave beeps. I take the bag out, and finding a bowl in the cupboard, I pour the popped kernels into it before I look at Easton again.

"We should probably talk about how we'll share responsibilities where Lainey is concerned," I mention.

"How do you want to do it?" he asks.

I shrug as I carry the bowl to the island and reply, "I can handle everything school-related." I think for a moment, then add, "I'll also handle anything where she has to be out in public because you get swarmed, and honestly, it's a little distressing."

He lets out a chuckle. "You'll get used to it."

I shake my head. "I don't think so. At the bake sale, it looked like those women were a second away from tackling you to the ground."

"For the most part, they keep their distance."

"For the most part?" My eyebrows pull together as I give him a worried look.

Letting out a sigh, he climbs to his feet. He comes around the island, and taking hold of my arm, he pulls me into a hug that feels both comforting and intimate.

I've noticed he's touching me more and more. The other night, I fell asleep on his lap, and he didn't move until I woke up much later.

I also don't tense up around him anymore.

Easton's body curves around mine, and it feels unbelievably good. Moments like this are what's getting me through the heartache.

"Don't worry about me," he murmurs, his tone so deep it sends tingles rushing through me.

"I'll always worry," I whisper.

Because I love you.

Easton pulls back a little, and with our faces only inches apart, his eyes lock on mine.

"I appreciate that you worry about me," he says, and the way he looks at me makes me feel special.

His arms are still wrapped around me, and we're standing so close together it has my heart setting off at a crazy pace and my mouth instantly going bone dry. I can clearly see the light- and dark-gray areas in his irises and every inch of his attractive face.

Nerves and a fluttering of anticipation make my insides quiver.

He begins to lean down, and I hold my breath.

What's happening?

"I love the smell of popcorn," Lainey suddenly says as she comes down the stairs.

My face goes up in flames as I yank away from Easton. Grabbing the bowl of popcorn, I carry it to the coffee table in the living room. Feeling utterly confused and rattled, I rush back to the kitchen to get a chocolate.

"What do you want to drink, Lainey?" I ask, and when my voice sounds hoarse, I clear my throat. It only adds to my embarrassment.

He was probably just leaning in to kiss me on the cheek or forehead. He's done that plenty of times before.

God, I'm seeing things that aren't there.

And now I'm running around like a headless chicken.

"Um . . ." Lainey opens the fridge and looks inside before grabbing a juice box. "I'll have this."

"Great." I walk back to the living room and take a seat on the couch while reaching for the remote. Finding the movie, I wait for Lainey to get comfortable beside me before I press play.

"Scoot up," Easton says, and I move to the middle of the couch.

While he sits down beside me, Lainey turns her body so she can lean back against me while draping her legs over the armrest.

"Comfortable?" I ask.

She nods, then looks at the table. "Can you pass me the popcorn, please?"

Easton picks up the bowl, and leaning into me, he places it on her lap. When he rests his arm on the back of the couch behind me, the side of his chest presses against my bicep and shoulder.

I'm practically squashed in between Easton and Lainey. Completely focused on every movement and breath from Easton, I have no idea what's happening in the movie. I'm dying to steal a glance at him, but he'll definitely notice.

My thoughts turn to earlier in the kitchen, and I replay the moment over and over.

Even though I love him and would give anything for a chance to be with him, I'm not sure I can handle a romantic relationship right now. It's only been a month since I broke things off with Trent, and with everything that's happened, I haven't had any time to deal with the trauma he inflicted on me.

Feeling more and more confused by the minute, my thoughts are a jumbled mess.

Easton's arm moves from the couch to my shoulders before wrapping around the side of my neck while his other hand takes hold of my chin. He nudges my face up so I'll look at him, then he whispers, "Are you okay?"

Crap, he noticed.

Trying to cover up that I'm anything but okay, I lie, "Yes. Why? Don't I look okay?"

He lets out a chuckle. "You look fine. You just seemed deep in thought."

Just trying to figure out my chaotic emotions.

"I'm totally fine," I whisper. "Well, as fine as I can be under the circumstances."

Easton leans in again, and my heart all but stops in my chest, but then he presses a kiss to my forehead.

Ugh, I need to stop seeing things that aren't there.

I turn my attention to Lainey when she snuggles into my side, and noticing she's fallen asleep, I whisper, "We should take her to bed."

Easton climbs to his feet. "I'll carry her."

When he picks her up, she mumbles, "I want to sleep by Nova."

He gives me a questioning look as I stand up, and I quickly nod. "Sure. Let's take her to my room."

"Will you switch off all the lights?" he asks as he heads toward the stairs.

"Okay." I pick up the bowl, uneaten chocolate, and empty juice box and carry them to the kitchen. Before I switch off the lights, I glance through the living room. "Night, Rach."

My heart squeezes painfully in my chest, and I suck in a shuddering breath.

God, I miss you so much. I don't know if I can get through this.

I wait for a minute or so for the blow of grief to lessen before I head up the stairs. When I walk into my bedroom, Lainey's already tucked into bed and fast asleep. I stare at my goddaughter for a few seconds, thinking how amazing she is.

Just like her mother.

My heart clenches again, and letting out a sad sigh, I walk to the closet to get a pair of leggings and a T-shirt. Heading to the bathroom, I quickly brush my teeth and wash my face before changing into my pajamas.

While I take a moment to pull a brush through my hair, my thoughts turn to the beautiful fireworks earlier.

It's hard to accept Rachel is gone.

A lump forms in my throat, and it takes a minute or so for me to fight back the urge to cry. Sucking in a deep breath, I leave the bathroom only to come to a stop right outside the door.

Easton's sitting on the edge of the bed, and when he looks at me, there's a sad pull around his mouth. He's only wearing sweatpants, which makes it really hard for me to focus on anything.

Unable to stop myself, my gaze drifts over his bare chest, and my abdomen clenches at the sight of all his tanned skin and muscles.

"Mind if I sleep here as well?"

I somehow manage to walk toward the bed as I whisper, "Not at all. Get in."

I hope I don't have a nightmare tonight. The last thing I want to do is upset Lainey and Easton.

"You take the middle," he says, and as I crawl onto the mattress, he switches off the light.

I lie down facing Lainey, and my muscles are tense as I listen to Easton coming closer. The bed dips beneath his weight, and then my eyes go wide as saucers when he wraps his arms around me. His chest presses against my back, and I feel his breath stir in my hair every time he exhales.

"You okay?" he whispers.

"Uh-huh. You?"

His body presses harder against mine, and his arms tighten around me, then he lets out a sigh and replies, "Yes."

He's only holding you for comfort. Don't overthink things.

Lainey turns on her side and snuggles closer to me, and once again, I end up being sandwiched between them.

I lie awake for a long while before exhaustion finally drags me into a dreamless sleep.

Chapter 19

Easton

Over the past week, we've fallen into a routine where we all snuggle together while watching one movie after the other. I know things need to change, and we have to move forward, but fuck, it's hard.

Poor Nova hasn't had her bed to herself since Rachel's memorial service. Lainey and I never give her a moment's peace, but she hasn't complained once.

You're becoming a needy bastard.

Chastising myself doesn't work because I'm already using all my self-restraint not to do all the things I want to do to Nova. Every night, when I feel her body pressing against mine, my control slips more and more, and the only thing keeping me from crossing the line is the fact that I don't want to scare her off.

There are moments when I'm sure Nova's interested in me, but most of the time, she treats me like a friend.

I'm one hundred percent certain I want more with Nova, but if I make my move and she just sees me as a brother, it will fuck things up badly.

My phone rings, pulling me out of my thoughts, where I'm sitting at the island with my smoothie forgotten in front of me.

I pull the device out of my pocket, and seeing Sylvia's name on the screen, I answer, "Hi, how are you?"

"I'm good. How are you all doing?" she asks.

"We're managing," I reply. "What's up?"

"I hate to do this to you, but we need to have a press conference. Rumors are spreading, and there are all kinds of articles being printed."

Nova and Lainey come down the stairs, and I watch as Nova toasts a few slices of bread.

"What kind of rumors?" I ask. When Nova points at the toaster, giving me a questioning look, I nod.

Lainey climbs onto the stool beside me while Sylvia mutters, "There are photos of you with your hands on Nova's hips, so everyone is speculating that you're dating."

"Don't worry about those," I tell her.

"There are also photos and videos of you carrying Rachel out of the hospital," she informs me.

I let out a sigh. "I'm not doing a press conference, but I'll meet with one reporter. What do you want me to say during the interview?"

"You need to tell everyone Rachel has passed away and that Nova is nothing more than a close family friend and Lainey's godmother."

I climb to my feet and walk toward the sliding doors as I say, "I'm fine with the first part but not the last bit." Only when I'm outside do I add, "She is more than a friend."

"Oh." Sylvia's quiet for a moment, then she asks, "Are the two of you dating?"

"Not yet." I keep glancing at the doors to make sure I'm alone. "I'm giving Nova time to get used to me before I begin a relationship with her."

"Okay . . . um . . . then we'll just tell the public what I said. There's no need to give them something more to speculate about."

"Fine."

"But you need to let me know the moment you start dating. I want to be prepared for the shitstorm the news will unleash."

"Okay," I agree. "Is that all?"

"No. We have to agree on a time that I can bring Mark from *The Hollywood Reporter* over to your place for the interview."

Taking a deep breath, I think for a moment before replying, "How about four this afternoon?"

"Works for me."

"Is that all?" I ask again.

"For now. Bobby also gave me a bunch of scripts for you to look at. I'll drop them off when I see you for the interview."

I let out a heavy sigh before I drop the bomb on Sylvia, "I'm going to take some time off."

"How long?" she asks.

"I don't know." I suppress an annoyed huff. "I haven't taken a break since I started acting. Lainey and Nova need me."

"I understand, but at least look at the scripts. Okay? Maybe you'll change your mind after a month or two. Most producers will wait two months if it means you'll star in their movie."

"Fine," I agree, because she's right. I might get bored after a while and return to work sooner. Only time will tell.

"Thank you, baby Jesus," she mutters.

"Sylvia," I say while I head back into the house, "thank you for everything you've done for me. I really appreciate it."

"You're welcome." I'm just about to pull the device away from my ear when she says, "Oh, I almost forgot. I've made an appointment with the therapist for the day after tomorrow at ten a.m. Her name is Eden Dungey, and she comes highly recommended."

"Thank you." I walk back into the house and head for the fridge, where the list of phone numbers is. "I'm going to give you a number. Can you call the therapist and make an appointment for Nova?"

"Sure."

"Her name is Regina Davis." I recite the number quickly.

"Got it. I'll let you know when the appointment is. See you at four."

I end the call and sit down beside Lainey again. She sinks her teeth into the cream cheese smeared over her slice of toast.

"What do you want on your toast?" Nova asks.

"Same as Lainey's, please." I love the light-yellow dress she's wearing. "Sylvia will make an appointment with Regina Davis for you."

A nervous look ghosts over her face. "Thank you."

I wait for Nova to set the plates down on the island, and when she takes a seat, I say, "A reporter is coming over at four to do an interview. I need to make a statement about Rachel."

"Oh." She stares at me, then asks, "Will you be okay doing an interview about her?"

"I hate reporters," Lainey mutters, her chin quivering.

I rub my hand up and down her back to comfort her. "I do, too, sweetheart, but the sooner I get it done, the better." Glancing at Nova, I add, "There are also rumors spreading that I have to address."

"On no," Nova exclaims, a worried expression tightening her beautiful face. "What kind of rumors?"

I'm not going to lie. As much as the circumstances suck, I love how much she worries about me.

"Everyone thinks you and Uncle Easton are dating," Lainey mutters. "I've read about it online, and kids at my school have been texting me to ask if it's true."

"Oh my God!" Nova's eyes widen, and she looks visibly rattled. "I'm so sorry, Lainey."

"Turn off your phone for a while," I tell Lainey. "I don't want anything else upsetting you right now."

Lainey nods, and lowering her head, she lets out a shuddering breath before tears spill over her cheeks.

I wrap her up in a tight hug, and only when she seems to feel a little better do I pull back. "The reporter will be here at four. I want you to stay upstairs so they don't get a photo of either of you."

"Okay," Lainey agrees.

"God, I'm so sorry about the mess," Nova whispers, still trying to recover from everything Lainey said. "Maybe you can tell them I'm your cousin or something?"

"Fuck no," I mutter before thinking to censor my words.

"Uncle Easton!" Lainey exclaims before letting out a burst of laughter. "Mom would slap you upside the head."

The moment the words leave her mouth, her expression grows sad, and the next second, a sob bursts from her again. She drops the toast onto her plate, and before she can climb off the stool, I grab hold of her and haul her onto my lap.

Holding my goddaughter, I rock her while saying, "It's okay, sweetheart." My eyes meet Nova's as she rushes around the island to pat Lainey's back. "I think you and Lainey should go out this afternoon. It will do you good to get out of the house a bit."

"I don't want to go out," Lainey whimpers between sobs. "I want to stay at home with you and Nova."

"Okay," I agree. When she calms down, I tilt my head to see her face. "Better?"

She nods, then asks, "Can I invite Porsha over?"

"Of course." I look at Nova. "Can you call Charlotte and see if it's okay if Porsha comes to visit?"

Nova nods. "I'll call her right now."

When she heads to the stairs to get her phone, which is probably in her bedroom, I turn my attention back to Lainey and say, "Go change out of your pajamas."

"Okay." She climbs off my lap, and I end up staring at the slice of toast on my plate while I think about Lainey's and Nova's reactions to the rumors that we're in a relationship.

I'm not sure how Lainey would feel about me dating Nova. Fuck, I'm not even sure how Nova would feel. No one has ever confused me as much as she does. Does she hate the idea of dating me, or was she scared I'd be upset about it?

I let out a sigh while I pick up the toast and bite into it.

Besides everything else we're dealing with, Nova's still recovering from her abusive ex. I just need to be patient.

When Nova returns to the kitchen, I watch as she checks the list of phone numbers before programming one into her phone and pressing dial. A moment later, she says, "Hi, is this Charlotte?" She glances nervously at me, then continues, "I'm Nova Allen, Lainey's godmother. Lainey would like to know whether Porsha can come over this afternoon. Maybe she can spend the night, and the girls can have a sleepover?" She listens for a while, and her features grow sad, then she murmurs, "Thank you. I'll tell Easton. See you at two." She ends the call, then says, "Charlotte gives her condolences and said she'll drop Porsha off."

I nod and gesture at her toast. "Come eat."

When Nova takes her seat across from me, I say, "With everything that's happened, we haven't spoken much about you. How are you holding up after . . ." I try to search for the right words but end up muttering, "breaking things off with the abusive bastard?"

She looks startled by the question, but it's quickly followed by her cheeks turning pink with embarrassment. "I'm good. There hasn't been much time to think about that part of my life. I'm only seeing the therapist because I made a promise to Rachel."

"Have you heard from the asshole since you left Verona?"

She nods, and I'm just about to get angry when she says, "There were only a few messages, and he called once, but after that, I haven't heard from him again."

"Good," I mutter. "If he contacts you, let me know." She nods again, just holding the toast in her hand, which has me reminding her, "Eat, Nova."

We finish our breakfast in silence, and when I get up to collect the plates, I say, "Even though Frances doesn't need much supervision, will you deal with her? Rachel always took care of the staff."

"Sure."

"Just tell her what to make for lunch and dinner, and if we run out of anything, let her know so she can go shopping," I mention.

"And the groundkeepers?" she asks.

"They'll ask if they need anything."

"Okay."

Remembering Nova's truck that's been standing at the side of the house, I ask, "How do you feel about selling your truck?"

She thinks for a moment. "I haven't used it since I've been here, but I'll need it soon." Her teeth tug at her bottom lip. "I haven't started it in a while. That's going to be a problem."

"Why would you need it?" I ask. "You have access to Izak and the SUVs."

An awkward expression tightens her features. "As much as I like staying here, we both know at some point I'll have to get my own place."

Not liking where this conversation is heading, a frown forms on my forehead, and I set the plates down again. "There's no reason for you to get your own place."

She glances down at the marble top and starts to wipe invisible dust from the surface. "One day, you might meet someone and decide to get married, and she won't like having me around."

My heartbeat speeds up when the thought of Nova marrying another man flashes through my mind.

"That won't happen," I snap, my tone too harsh.

Her eyes jump to my face, and her features tighten with fear. "I didn't mean to upset you." I hate how her shoulders curl forward as if she's trying to protect herself.

Fuck.

I step closer and wrap her up in a hug. Feeling how she's trembling, I keep my tone soft as I say, "I'm sorry for snapping." I press a kiss to her hair. "Don't be scared of me."

Nova nods against my chest.

"I don't want to talk about me marrying some random woman or you moving out. You belong here with Lainey and me," I say, so there are no misunderstandings between us.

"Okay." She wraps her arms around my waist. "I'm sorry."

I press another kiss to her hair and tighten my hold on her. "You have nothing to apologize for."

"I just don't want to make life harder for you," she admits, her voice sounding too fragile.

"You're not. You've been amazing, and we're lucky to have you, Nova."

Her cheek rubs against my chest, then she pulls away from me, and I have no choice but to let go of her.

Avoiding my eyes, she murmurs, "Thank you for being so nice to me."

Before I can respond, Lainey comes down the stairs and says, "Porsha told me you called her mom, and she can come over."

I take a seat at the island again, and while Nova clears the plates, I keep stealing glances at her.

I hope the therapy will help her heal and that she'll be open to dating again.

Otherwise, I'm fucked.

How do I live in a house with the woman I'm falling in love with and pretend we're just friends?

Chapter 20

NOVA

While Lainey and Porsha are playing in her bedroom, I stand at the top of the stairs and shamelessly listen to the interview happening downstairs.

"We're sorry for your loss, Easton," the reporter says, his tone professional.

Easton clears his throat before he replies, "Thank you, Mark."

"Do you plan to take some time off?"

"Yes. I'm sure my fans will understand that I need to spend time with my niece," Easton answers.

"I'm certain you've been too busy to hear about the rumors, but you've been seen with a certain redhead, and everyone's wondering who she is."

Oh God.

I lower my face into my palm.

"Her name is Nova Allen. She's a close family friend and Lainey's godmother."

"Oh. Do you share custody of Lainey?" the man asks.

"Yes, we've decided to coparent her." A moment later, Easton mutters, "No more questions about my niece, or this interview ends right now."

"I apologize, Easton." A few seconds pass, then he asks, "Are you working on any movies your fans can look forward to?"

"Not at the moment."

"I think we got everything," the reporter says, not sounding very happy. "Thank you for your time, Easton."

I listen to everyone moving around downstairs, and just as I'm about to head to Lainey's bedroom to check on the girls, I hear Sylvia say, "I get that you're going through a hard time, but you could've smiled more."

"Next time you arrange an interview, make it clear that I won't tolerate questions about Lainey," he snaps angrily. "She's off-limits!"

Instinctively, my body tenses.

Sylvia's voice is much more demure when she replies, "I understand. At least it's over and done with." I hear papers rustle, then she says, "I've made an appointment with Regina Davis for Nova on Thursday morning at nine. And here are the scripts. Please look at them."

"Okay."

"There's also a Dior ad for you to consider. It's shirtless."

Easton makes a noncommittal sound, and I don't hear anything else for a while.

I slowly creep down the stairs, and when I see him standing by the island looking at a stack of papers that's piled on the marble top, I quickly glance at the living room and foyer.

"Can I come down?" I ask, my tone filled with caution.

His head snaps in my direction. "Yes."

Keeping my distance, I ask, "Are you okay?"

He nods, then lets out an annoyed huff. "I hate interviews."

My need to soothe him beats the apprehension I feel because of his anger, and I slowly move closer until I'm able to place my hand on his back. "I'm sorry you have to deal with all of this."

He opens one of the scripts and looks at the sticky note that's stuck to the page.

Kate Phillips has been cast in the lead role.

"Fuck no," he snaps, anger tightening his voice once more.

My body jerks, and I quickly pull away from him.

Easton grabs the script and furiously throws the pile of papers into the trash, making me wrap my arms around myself, my head ducking low.

A fine layer of sweat beads over my skin, and fear floods my veins. My breaths burst over my lips, and they're so loud it's all I can hear while my vision blurs.

Every muscle in my body locks up, and my feet refuse to move.

"You expect me to eat this shit?" Trent shouts as he throws the grilled cheese sandwiches in the trash. "You fucking lazy bitch! Is it that hard to make a decent plate of food?"

It's all I could afford to buy with the last money I had.

I don't bother defending myself and keep my lips pressed together while staring down at the floor.

"You're fucking pathetic!" Trent's fist connects with my cheek, sending me falling to my side. Before I can catch my bearings, his foot connects with my stomach, and all I can do is gag through the intense pain. "You will make a decent dinner!" he roars before kicking me again.

A soothing voice breaks through the panic, and I desperately latch onto it.

"No one's going to hurt you. You're safe. Christ, Nova! I'm so fucking sorry."

I manage to suck in a full breath of air, but a second later, I'm hit with a wave of destructive emotions, and I can't stop from bursting out in tears.

A cool palm cradles my cheek, and I hear Easton say, "Open your eyes, baby. Look at me."

It takes a while for the wave of emotions to begin lessening, and I begin to feel a little calmer. When I open my eyes, it's to see Easton's features drawn tight with worry.

"I'm so sorry," he groans before he presses a kiss to my forehead. "I didn't mean to trigger you."

It feels like there's an elephant parked on my chest, but with every breath, the pressure eases. When I realize I'm sitting on Easton's lap,

I lower my gaze, feeling super self-conscious. I quickly move off to sit beside him and wipe the tears from my face.

Crap, I just had one hell of a panic attack in front of Easton.

Feeling miserable, my voice quivers as I whisper, "I'm sorry."

"There's nothing for you to apologize about," he says, his tone gentle. When he lifts his arm, I flinch, and it has him slowing his movements as he brushes his hand over my hair.

"I will never hurt you, Nova," he whispers.

I nod, and still not able to look at him, I reply, "I know." Wanting to direct the attention away from me, I ask, "Why did you throw that script away?"

"I refuse to work with Kate Phillips," he explains.

"Oh?"

He wraps his arm around my shoulders and tenderly pulls me into his side. "She once spread rumors that I made a sex tape with her."

"That's awful." I suck in a deep breath of his woodsy cologne, the scent soothing my nerves.

"Yeah, so she's on my shitlist for life."

"Now she's on mine too," I mutter.

Easton lets out a burst of laughter. "Yeah? You have a shitlist?"

I nod, my cheek brushing against his shirt. "It's short and only reserved for the worst people."

"Do I know anyone on the list?"

The corner of my mouth lifts slightly. "Kate."

"Let's get something to drink."

We get up, and as we walk to the kitchen, I pat my hand over my hair to make sure there aren't any strands sticking up.

Easton grabs two bottles of water from the fridge and hands one to me before asking, "Who else is on your shitlist?"

I shrug while I admit, "My mother, my grandfather, and the idiots I've dated."

"Idiots? Plural?" A frown forms on his forehead. "How many have there been?"

I hold up two fingers.

His frown darkens. "And both were abusive."

Shame washes over me, and I lower my head again. "They weren't in the beginning. If I had known they'd hurt me, I wouldn't have dated them." I try to defend my stupid actions of the past that put me in harm's way.

Easton takes hold of my arm and leans down in an attempt to get me to look at him, but I keep my gaze lowered.

"I'm not blaming you." He rubs his palm up and down my arm. "It just fucking sucks that the two relationships you've had were with bastards who hurt you."

I gather my courage and lift my head while trying to force a smile to my face. "It's in the past."

"I don't think so," he disagrees. "You have an appointment with Regina Davis on Thursday at nine a.m. I really hope she'll be able to help you."

I nod before taking a sip of water.

Easton inhales deeply before asking, "Are you comfortable with me?"

My head bobs up and down. "Yes. I know you won't hurt me."

A smile tugs at the corner of his mouth. "Good. It's important to me that you feel safe with me."

I tilt my head and hesitate for a moment before I admit, "You're the only man I feel safe with. I've known you for over twenty years, and you've never done anything to hurt me." I hesitate again before I take the only chance I might ever have to say the words to him. "I love you for it."

I almost let out a massive sigh of relief for finally getting to express in some way how much he means to me, but I manage to suppress it.

He pulls me to his chest and hugs me tight. "It makes me happy to hear you say that."

I take a deep breath of his addictive scent while a sense of peace settles in my heart.

Yeah, I'll be happy with just having Easton as a friend. It's so much more than I ever could've wished for.

He pulls back, then says, "While we're tackling serious topics, we need to discuss finances."

"Oh. Yeah, sure." I take a step backward and fidget with the bottle in my hands. "It's probably time for me to get a job."

He shakes his head. "I'd prefer it if you stayed at home to take care of Lainey. I don't want her routine changing too much."

"Okay." I give him a confused look because I'm not sure I'm following.

He pulls his wallet out of his pocket, and after removing a credit card, he places it on the island. "This is for you."

"What?" I gasp, my gaze flicking between the black card and Easton's face.

"The credit card is yours to use for anything you and Lainey need." When I keep staring at him, he gives me a pleading look. "Please let me take care of you."

Oh my God.

"Easton," I breathe his name like a prayer. "I can't let you do that. What will people think?"

"I don't give a shit about what other people think. I promised Rachel I would take care of you, and I have every intention of keeping that promise."

My heartbeat speeds up as I move closer to the island, and when I see the name *Easton Rowe* printed on it, my stomach flutters.

"Please, Nova." Placing his hand on my lower back, he leans down to catch my eyes. "Take the card." I reach for the credit card, and when I pick it up, he presses a kiss to the side of my head and murmurs, "Thank you."

"I'm the one who should say thank you," I mutter. "You already do so much for me."

The corner of his mouth lifts. "You can thank me by actually using the card. There's no limit on it."

My forehead wrinkles with a frown. "I need a limit."

"Let's make it twenty thousand. Once you get used to it, we can up it."

My eyes widen again, and I almost choke on a random drop of spit. "That's too much!"

He shakes his head. "You're Lainey's guardian, and soon, everyone will know you're living with me. I understand it's going to take some time for you to adjust to this new life, but trust me when I say twenty thousand is nothing in my world."

Holy crap. I'll never be able to spend so much money in a month.

My cheeks grow warm, and I struggle not to smile because never in my wildest dreams did I think I'd live in the same house as Easton and have him take care of me. It feels like we're becoming a family.

Giving him a grateful look, I stand on my tiptoes and press a kiss to his jaw before saying, "Thank you so much, Easton. I have no words to describe how much I appreciate everything you do for me."

"It's just money, Nova. You do so much more for us." He shrugs, and a sad expression creeps into his eyes. "Besides, Rachel was right, you deserve the world."

My heart clenches painfully in my chest, and a wave of sorrow rolls over me.

Lainey and Porsha come flying down the stairs wearing their swimsuits. "We're going to swim."

The girls don't even stop and run out of the house, and the next second, we hear splashes as they jump into the pool.

"I'll keep an eye on them," I say.

"You can't swim, so you won't be of much help to them." Easton chuckles, then adds, "Let's sit outside. It's a nice day, and I can do with a relaxing afternoon after the interview."

When we take a seat on the lounge chairs, I watch as the girls pretend they're mermaids.

My thoughts turn to the past month and how my life has completely changed.

I'm too scared to believe that things will stay like this forever. Rachel's death has taught me that life can flip on you at the drop of a hat.

But right now, I have Easton and Lainey, and until things change, I'm going to appreciate every day I have with them.

Chapter 21

Nova

Lying alone in my bed after sharing it with Easton and Lainey for the past few days, it's hard for me to fall asleep.

I'm glad Lainey's spending time with her best friend, but I miss being sandwiched between her and Easton.

I miss feeling his arms around me, and I'm scared the nightmares will return. Especially after the panic attack I had earlier.

Sighing, I climb out of bed and sneak into the hallway. I tiptoe down the stairs so I don't wake anyone else. The house is so quiet it makes me feel a little on edge. After I take a seat on one of the couches, I pull my legs up to my chest and rest my chin on my knees.

I wish you were still here, Rach. Everything feels empty without you.

A breath quivers over my lips, and I don't bother wiping away the tear that escapes.

Easton said I could stay, but I can't help wondering what would be best for Lainey in the long run. We can't live like this forever, and at some point, he might meet someone and get married.

I should get a job, right? Then I'll be able to rent a place that I can make home for Lainey. She can live with me when Easton has to travel for work.

God, what would you do, Rach? I should've talked to you about this while you were still here.

When I don't find any answers for my worries, I let out a sigh and grab the TV remote. Switching the device on, I make sure it's muted before I spend ten minutes looking through all the movies. I'm hoping watching some TV will make me feel sleepy.

Two of Easton's movies pop up, and I quickly glance over my shoulder before I press play on the one that has a rare kissing scene in it.

The first time I saw it, I was surprised because Easton mostly stars in action movies, and even though I don't like seeing him kiss another woman, I can't stop myself from watching it.

I fast forward to the scene where the kiss is about to happen, and even though I've seen it a thousand times, I still get butterflies when he stalks toward the actress with a determined expression.

God, I wish I was her.

Even though nothing romantic can ever happen between us, a girl can still dream.

Easton shoves the actress up against a wall and kisses the living hell out of her.

Giving in to my guilty fantasy, I imagine I'm the woman he's pinning to the wall, and tilting my head, I tug my bottom lip between my teeth.

"Caught you red-handed," Easton suddenly says.

"Oh my God!" I dart to my feet, turn the TV off, and throw the remote somewhere on the floor.

Crap!

Taking a few steps closer to where he's standing at the foot of the stairs, I say, "I'm so sorry. It's not what it looks like."

It's precisely what it looks like. I was drooling over Easton, and he caught me. Dear God, please let the ground open up and swallow me whole.

"I couldn't sleep, and when I put on Netflix, I saw the movie, and it's really good, so I thought I could watch it again because you're asleep, which you clearly aren't, and you're seriously a good actor." I point at the TV, then ask the worst question I can possibly ask under the current circumstances,

"How difficult is it to kiss someone like that? Do you have to like the woman, or do you just go wham-bam-thank-you-ma'am?"

Dammit, Nova! For the love of all that's holy, please shut up.

"It's all an act," he chuckles, sounding amused with me.

At least he's not angry.

"Want me to show you?" he asks.

Not understanding his question, I grunt like an idiot, "Huh?"

He shrugs as he moves closer. "I can show you."

"How to act?" I ask, my tone way too high-pitched.

"No." He takes another step closer to me, and the light coming through the sliding doors makes everything suddenly feel intense and intimate. "How to kiss like I do in a movie."

I tilt my head sharply, thinking I must be fast asleep and this is turning into the best dream I've ever had.

Easton lifts his hand and wraps his fingers around the back of my neck, and I swear, my heart sets off at such a crazy pace there's a strong possibility it might beat right out of my chest.

"Ready?" he asks.

I have zero brain function to say anything, and not thinking about the repercussions, I nod.

Easton's features tighten until he looks at me as if I'm the only woman who matters to him.

Holy shit.

There's an intense fluttering in my stomach, and my breaths come in shallow, quick puffs.

His grip on the back of my neck tightens, and as his face comes closer to mine, my heart all but stops. I hold my breath, and the moment his lips touch mine, every single one of my senses zooms in on him.

Yes. Oh God, yes.

The feel of his mouth pressing against mine is overwhelmingly glorious, and I don't even care about the needy moan drifting from me.

His tongue brushes along the seam of my lips, and it sends shock waves of good feelings rushing through me as I open for him to enter.

A deep groan rumbles from Easton, then I'm yanked flush with his body. His tongue plunges into my mouth, and a powerful tremble rocks my body.

Somehow, I grab hold of his sides, and it's only then I realize he's not wearing a shirt. Feeling his skin beneath my palms and having his mouth on mine is the most intense thing I've ever experienced.

A gasp bursts from me, and the next second, the kiss spirals into a wild war of desire and desperation to taste as much as possible of each other.

At least, that's how it feels for me.

It's like Easton is trying to devour me as he lays claim to every inch of my mouth. Utterly consumed with the man I love more than anything, I lift my arms and wrap them around his neck, clinging to him as if my very life depends on him.

I lift onto my tiptoes in an attempt to get as close as possible to him. With every stroke of his tongue and nip of his teeth, tingles crash over me like waves until I'm a breathless, needy mess who's willing to do anything for him not to stop.

Easton's hands glide down my sides, and when he reaches my butt, he grips me tightly, and I'm lifted off my feet. Without breaking the kiss, he takes a few steps until my back is pressed against the nearest wall.

Holy crap, this is a dream come true.

One of his hands moves to the back of my thigh, and he lifts my leg. I quickly hook it around the back of his, then the meager air I'm able to breathe in between kisses explodes from me as he thrusts against the overheated spot between my thighs.

He feels incredibly hard and big, making a fire ignite in my abdomen.

So good.

Easton moves his hand from behind my neck, and he grips a fistful of my hair. My head is tugged back, and I lose his mouth to my throat, where he bites and sucks at my sensitive skin.

"Easton," I moan, my hands coasting over his shoulders before settling on his muscled chest.

He leaves a trail of kisses up my throat and jaw, then his teeth tug at my bottom lip before his tongue drives back into my mouth again.

God, how have I survived so long without experiencing this kind of kiss?

The heat and hunger coming from Easton shine a stark light on the barren life I've lived up until this moment. All the loneliness, feeling like I never belonged, settling for bastards who abused me—it all feels so cold and brutal now that I get to experience the real thing.

Only, it's not the real thing.

Feeling like I'm doused with a bucket of ice, I rip my mouth away from his and push against his chest. I quickly pull myself out of the space between his body and the wall and hurry toward the kitchen.

Breathless and shocked, I struggle to cope with the fact that I got carried away. Yanking the fridge open, I grab water and take a few desperate sips before placing the bottle on the island.

"Nova?"

Act like your life depends on it.

"I can see why you won an Oscar," I say, injecting lightheartedness into my voice. "You're a good actor."

Shit.

I place my hand on my stomach as it bottoms out.

What did I do? How do I fix it?

My mind races while my emotions spiral out of control.

"Hey." Easton places his hand on my shoulder, but I quickly step away from him and put a safe distance between us.

Forcing myself to chuckle, I hope it sounds natural. I walk to the stairs, saying, "Thanks for showing me. Sleep tight."

Thanks for showing me? Really?

I rush up to the second floor and dart into my bedroom, but as I begin to shut the door, Easton pushes his way inside before closing it softly behind us.

With the lights on, there's no mistaking the worried look on his face as he says, "We aren't sleeping until we've talked about what just happened."

"Nothing happened," I lie, doing my best to keep my voice steady but failing miserably. "You showed me how you k . . . what you do in movies. It was good . . . I mean, you were great."

With my heart thundering in my chest and embarrassment heating my face, I move backward.

There are harsh lines cut into his face, and it's clear he's upset, which only makes everything so much worse.

I can't believe I messed up like this!

Hating that I've put us in this awful situation and made him angry, I whimper, "I'm sorry."

My breathing keeps speeding up until nothing but puffs of air burst over my lips. My chest tightens, and I grip the fabric of my shirt as a panic attack rips through me.

"Christ, Nova," Easton exclaims, darting forward to close the distance between us. "You did nothing wrong. Calm down for a second so we can talk. Okay?"

Unable to control the trembling in my body, his words don't sink in. All I can think about is that I've ruined everything.

My skin grows clammy as I try to slow down my breaths.

Easton lifts his hands to my face, framing my cheeks, and looking deep into my eyes, he says, "Just breathe. It's okay. Shh. Deeper breaths."

Somehow, I manage to calm down enough to stop the panic attack. Feeling rotten, I pull my face free from his hold and take a few steps away.

Trying to do some damage control, my voice is hoarse as I say, "I'm sorry I got carried away. It was . . ." my mind races to come up with a valid excuse, "a spur-of-the-moment thing and won't happen again." My eyes dart to Easton's worried face before lowering to the plush carpet. "I'd appreciate it so much if you could pretend tonight didn't happen, and we can go on as normal. If not for me, then for Lainey's sake." Desperate to fix things, I keep rambling, "Because of the relationship I just got out of and losing Rachel, it's hard to think clearly. I'm so sorry."

Easton stares at me for so long I can't keep from whimpering, "Please, can we forget tonight happened? I promise nothing like that will ever happen again."

I'm confused when he looks disappointed. "Is that what you really want?"

Yes. I just want things to return to normal.

Sucking in a deep breath, I give him another pleading look. "Please. Lainey's going through enough, and I don't want my stupid actions upsetting her more." I quickly gesture at him. "I also don't want to upset you."

His eyes narrow on me. "I'm the one who initiated the kiss." He folds his arms over his chest. "I'm sorry I crossed the line."

His words sink in, and I realize we were both at fault.

"You're under a lot of pressure," I say to stop him from feeling bad.

He shakes his head, and uncrossing his arms, he pushes his fingers through his hair before locking eyes with me and admitting, "I kissed you because I wanted to."

I've been trying not to dissect the kiss, but now that he's said the words, it's impossible to ignore the fact that Easton kissed me with so much passion it ignited a fire between us.

He begins to move closer to me but stops and shakes his head again. "Christ, Nova. I'm falling head over fucking heels for you, and I thought you felt the same. Did I read things wrong between us?"

Easton is falling for me?

My lips part in shock, and I'm stunned for a moment before my emotions spiral out of control as happiness and worry war inside me.

Even though I love Easton, I can't take a chance on the only dream I've ever had. I have to put Lainey first. If Easton and I get romantically involved and things don't work out, it will disrupt Lainey's entire life.

And I'll lose him.

The thought of losing Easton and Lainey is unbearable, and I begin to shake my head. "It doesn't matter how we feel. Lainey comes first."

"I'm pretty sure she'll be fine with us dating," he says, his eyes not leaving my face for a second.

I shake my head again. "If we get romantically involved and it doesn't work out, it will disturb Lainey's life." My chin quivers, my emotions completely out of control. "And I'll lose your friendship. I'm not willing to take the risk." I give Easton a pleading look. "This is the first time I feel like I belong somewhere and I have a purpose."

Easton sucks in a deep breath before letting it out slowly. He turns his head and stares at the dressing table for painfully long minutes before he looks at me again.

"Are you attracted to me?"

My tongue darts out to wet my dry lips before I whisper, "It doesn't matter how I feel."

His features tighten, and his tone is tense as he asks, "Are you attracted to me, Nova?"

I feel like bursting out in tears, but I manage to keep control over the urge as I nod. "But—"

He takes a step toward me. "Do you love me?"

Oh God.

Trying to diminish my feelings for him, I reply, "Of course. I've known you all my life."

When it looks like he's going to fire another question my way, I hold up a hand. "Stop, Easton," I beg, my heart thundering in my chest. "I just got out of a horrible relationship. We lost Rachel. Lainey needs us." My voice cracks because I can't have the one thing I've wanted for so many years. I can't be selfish. "I just want . . ." I swallow hard as I force the lie over my lips, "I just want to be your friend so I can be there for you and Lainey."

Sadness creeps into his eyes, and it takes a brutal swing at my heart. "If that's what you really want."

Unable to force the words over my lips again, I can only nod.

Easton turns around, and as he leaves my bedroom, my heart clenches painfully in my chest.

My hands fly up to cover my mouth so I can smother the sob as it escapes me.

No matter how badly I want Easton, I can't be selfish. This is what's best for everyone.

Chapter 22

Easton

After a shitty night's sleep, I lie on my bed staring up at the ceiling.

I've gone over the kiss and conversation a million times, wishing things had played out differently.

Everything she said made sense. She just got out of an abusive relationship, and we have to think about Lainey.

The bastard in me was hoping Nova wanted me as much as I wanted her.

But damn, it sure felt like she wanted me when I kissed her.

She admitted to being attracted to me, and my gut tells me she loves me.

She just needs time.

My mind races to come up with a plan until I finally decide the only thing I can do is go on as usual.

I'll show Nova that I'm in her life to stay and that we're meant to be together.

Nova

Lying on my stomach, I hold the pillow tightly as the memories of last night keep playing on repeat in my mind.

Easton catching me in the living room while I was watching his movie.

Him kissing me, and how amazing it felt.

The horrible talk that followed.

Letting out a sigh, I check the time on my phone, and when I see it's already past eight in the morning, I know I can't keep lying here. I have to face whatever awaits me today.

Climbing off the bed, I walk to the closet and grab a dress before heading to the bathroom.

The heartbreak caused by last night's disaster makes my grief feel a million times heavier and the pit in my stomach bottomless.

While I go through my morning routine, my anxiety grows until it feels like I've swallowed a swarm of bees.

God, I'm so nervous. How do I act this morning?

I should wait to see what he does and follow his lead. Right?

What if Easton is angry?

Suck it up and just power through it.

As I'm brushing my teeth, my thoughts keep jumping from one thing to the next until they settle on the kiss. In the stark reality of daylight, I have to wonder whether Easton didn't act out of grief. It's only been a week since Rachel passed away.

Maybe he just needed comfort, and things escalated. This morning, he might've realized I did the right thing when I said we could never get romantically involved.

I let out another sigh as I rinse my mouth. After patting my face dry, I hang the towel on the rail before reluctantly leaving my room.

Whatever happens, you'll deal with it. Lainey comes first.

When I reach the top of the stairs, I hear Lainey say, "Can I have another piece of bacon, please?"

"Sure," Easton replies.

I slowly head down, the aroma of bacon and eggs hanging in the air. When the kitchen comes into view, I see Lainey and Porsha sitting at the island, and Easton's back is turned to me.

My hands grip the sides of my dress tightly, and my stomach feels like it's stuck on spin cycle.

Lainey glances over her shoulder, and a sad smile tugs at her lips. "You're up. We're having breakfast."

I take a few steps closer. "Morning."

"Morning." Easton glances at me before he places more bacon on Lainey's plate. "Do you want more, Porsha?"

"No, thank you."

God, I desperately need caffeine.

I make a beeline for the coffee machine, and as I grab a mug from the cupboard, Easton murmurs, "Sit with the girls. I'll bring your coffee when it's ready."

I glance at him as he moves closer, but before he can reach me, I walk to the island and sit down across from the girls.

I clear my throat and place a hand on the anxious knot where my stomach is supposed to be. Forcing a smile to my face, I ask, "Did you both sleep well?"

Lainey nods. "Yes, but Porsha woke up at the crack of dawn."

"Only because your hair was in my mouth," Porsha complains.

Lainey giggles before taking a bite of her bacon.

Easton places a steaming mug of coffee down in front of me, and I dare a quick look at his face. "Thank you."

"Want some breakfast?" he asks.

Unable to stomach food right now, I shake my head. "Just coffee."

When he walks away from me, I take a couple of sips while trying not to analyze every single move he makes.

Looking at the girls, there's a punch to my heart because it reminds me of when Rachel and I were younger.

After their parents died, I spent an entire week at their house. I heated the food the neighbors brought over and made sure they ate.

I also kept the place clean and did everything I could to make things easier for them.

"Until what time can Porsha stay?" Lainey asks.

"Her mom's coming to get her at twelve," I answer.

Lainey's face instantly falls. "I wish you could stay longer."

The next instant, she bursts out in tears, and I quickly get up and rush around the island.

Wrapping my arm around Lainey's shoulders, I hug her and coo, "I'm sorry you're hurting, my sweet girl. Shh. I'm here."

"C-can Porsha stay longer?" she asks through shuddering sobs.

"Of course," I answer while slightly pulling back. "I'll call her mom."

Lainey's tears lessen, and when I'm sure she's calming down, I quickly head upstairs to grab my phone. Once I have the device, I press dial on Charlotte's number while walking back to the kitchen.

"Morning," Porsha's mom answers cheerfully.

"Morning. I'm calling because the girls would like to hang out for a while longer."

"Sure. What time should I pick up Porsha?"

Unsure, I ask, "Maybe before dinner?"

Lainey's expression fills with hope.

"Great. I'll be there around six tonight," Charlotte says.

"Thank you."

As I end the call, I inform the girls, "Porsha can stay until six p.m."

Porsha takes hold of Lainey's hand and asks, "Do you feel better?"

Lainey nods and leans her head on her best friend's shoulder. "Yeah."

When I sit down at the island again and pick up my cup of coffee, I ask, "Why don't you change out of your pj's? Then you can lie on the couch and watch your favorite movies?"

The girls nod, and slipping off the stools, they head up the stairs.

When Easton's hand settles on my back, I'm startled, and my body jerks. He quickly pulls away, and his features grow tense with a worried expression as he sits down beside me.

"Everything okay?" he asks.

I nod, and noticing my hand is trembling, I set the mug down and grip my hands tightly together on my lap. I take a fortifying breath before forcing a smile to my face. At least, I hope it looks like a smile, as I ask, "Did you sleep okay?"

God, my nerves are killing me.

He tilts his head, and instead of answering me, he asks, "Are we okay after what happened last night?"

Nope. Not by a long shot.

I quickly nod. "You?"

Easton glances at the living room while saying, "I'm fine."

It's clear as daylight we're both lying.

Lifting my hand, I brush the pad of my finger over the handle of the mug, then I whisper, "I just want what's best for you and Lainey."

It takes a long moment before Easton asks, "And what about what's best for you?"

What I want doesn't matter.

Turning my head, I meet his gray eyes that seem stormy this morning. "Getting to be here with you and Lainey makes me happy."

The corner of his mouth lifts slightly. "As long as you're really happy."

I force another smile to my lips. "I am."

Changing the subject, he says, "Remember, the therapists are coming tomorrow morning."

I nod, and when he gets up and reaches for the girls' empty plates, I say, "You made breakfast for them. I'll clean up."

"Just put everything in the sink. Frances will be in any minute." He seems to hesitate for a moment before starting to walk away. "I'll be in the study reading through the scripts."

"Okay."

With a heavy heart, I stare after Easton, and once he's out of my sight, I let out a miserable sigh.

Maybe I can talk to the therapist about Easton and me. I sure could use some advice right now.

God, I miss you, Rach. You'd know exactly how to fix this mess I've created.

Sitting on the couch, my knee bounces nervously as I wait for the therapist to finish meeting with Lainey.

My first session went as okay as can be expected. Regina seems nice, and she assured me she's helped many people deal with past trauma, the loss of a loved one, and the uncertainty of the future.

It took her mere minutes to pick up on my anxiety, and we touched lightly on everything I'm struggling with. She mostly asked questions, which I answered as honestly as possible.

We'll meet on a weekly basis until I've learned to cope better with everything. Before our session ended, she recommended that I try meditating, practicing mindfulness, and breathing exercises to ease my anxiety.

Noticing I'm wound tight, I force my leg to stop jumping and suck in a deep breath before letting it out slowly.

One breath at a time.

One thing at a time.

One day at a time.

"Is Lainey still with Eden?" Easton suddenly asks from behind me.

"Yes." I check the time on my phone. "They're running a little late."

Movement from outside draws our attention as Eden and Lainey get up from the chairs on the veranda. Easton darts forward to open the sliding doors, and as they step inside, he asks, "How did it go?"

"I'm going upstairs," Lainey says, her eyes red and swollen from crying.

I quickly look at the therapist, and once Lainey is out of hearing distance, she says, "Lainey is an amazing little girl, but she's struggling to cope with the sudden loss of her mother. It's going to take a few sessions to help her work through the complex emotions." Eden pulls her phone out and looks at it, then says, "I'd like to see her on a weekly basis. Once she returns to school, we can move the session to the afternoons or have them on Saturdays."

"Afternoons will be better," Easton replies. Worry creases his forehead as he asks, "Will she be okay, though?"

Eden gives us a reassuring smile. "Everyone deals with grief differently, and I can't say how long it will take before she feels better, but she'll get there eventually."

Easton nods. "Thank you for coming." His eyes only touch on me briefly. "I'll check on Lainey."

"I'll walk you out," I tell Eden and head in the direction of the front door with her. "Thank you again for coming over."

"Enjoy the rest of your day." She smiles politely as she walks to her car and climbs into the driver's seat.

Letting out a sigh, I head back into the house, and when I look at all the bouquets that were sent to Easton after Rachel passed away, I notice the flowers in the vase are wilted and need to be replaced. It's something Rachel insisted on doing on a weekly basis.

"I need to get fresh ones," I whisper to myself before I go upstairs to check on Lainey as well.

Chapter 23

Nova

Since the kiss and therapy sessions, things have felt awkward.

I honestly don't know what to do to make things better between Easton and me, so I focus all my attention on the household and Lainey.

Exhausted because I had a nightmare last night and struggled to fall back to sleep afterward, I head down the stairs.

Easton comes into the living room from the opposite direction, looking all hot and sweaty. The T-shirt he's wearing sticks to his muscled chest from the workout he must've just done in the gym.

Don't drool.

Noticing my handbag, he asks, "Going somewhere?"

"The flowers in the foyer are wilting, so I'm going out to get fresh ones." I glance at Lainey, where she's sitting on the couch, playing a game on her phone. "Lainey, do you want to come with or stay at home?"

"I'll come with," she answers.

Easton pulls his cell phone out of his pocket and types something on it, then says, "Izak will be ready in ten minutes."

"Oh." I hold up my truck's key. "I was thinking about taking my truck. That's if it will even start. I might have to get a new battery."

He shakes his head and comes to take the key from me. "There's no way I'm letting you drive around in that unreliable thing. You need to sell it." When my lips part, he gives me a serious look. "You're Lainey's godmother, Nova. How do you think it will look if you're seen driving her around in a beaten-up truck?"

"I wasn't going to argue," I mumble. "I'll sell it this week."

"Oh." He visibly relaxes. "Good. Let me know if you need help."

I just nod before walking away from him. "Come, Lainey."

"See you later, Uncle Easton." She falls in beside me, then asks, "Can we stop at The Sweet Spot for milkshakes?"

"Bring me a strawberry one," Easton calls after us.

"Okay," Lainey replies.

When I see Izak already waiting out front, I give him a polite smile. "Hi. Thank you for driving us around today."

Returning the smile, he nods. "We're just waiting for Tyler, then we can leave."

I forgot we have to take a guard with us. No one will recognize me, but Lainey draws attention wherever she goes.

Rather safe than sorry.

We climb into the back of the SUV, and while we wait, I check my wallet to make sure I have the credit card Easton gave me.

It's the first time I'm going to use it, and the thought makes me feel nervous.

You're getting things for the house.

Tyler joins us, and as he climbs into the front passenger seat, I say, "Hi, Tyler."

"Afternoon," he greets us.

Izak slides behind the steering wheel, and starting the engine, he asks, "Where to?"

"The flower shop we always go to just off Sunset Boulevard," Lainey answers.

"I'd also like to stop at a Walmart to get some groceries," I add.

"We can go to Ralphs. It's closer." Lainey grins at me. "And then The Sweet Spot for milkshakes."

During the drive, I look at my goddaughter and ask, "Is there anything you'd like to do for your last two days before you go back to school?"

She shrugs. "I don't know." She thinks for a moment. "Porsha and I can go to the spa for manis and pedis." Lainey's gaze drops to my hands, then she adds, "Maybe you should come with."

I chuckle. "Is that your way of telling me my hands look bad?"

"No. But your nails would look pretty with some nail polish on."

I glance down at my short nails and scrunch my nose. "Okay. Give me the name of the spa, and I'll make an appointment for us." My gaze returns to Lainey. "Do you think I should invite Porsha's mom?"

She nods. "You could get to know her better."

"I'll put in more effort with Charlotte for you."

Izak parks the SUV on the side of the road, and we wait for Tyler to open the back door before we climb out.

I walk with Lainey into a cute little flower shop and glance at all the pretty arrangements.

"Hi, Lainey," an elderly woman says as she comes out from behind the counter. "I haven't seen you in a while." Her eyes flick to me, then she asks, "Where's your mom?"

Shit.

My heart squeezes painfully in my chest, and I instantly worry about Lainey.

I quickly place my hand on her shoulder and tug her against my side before I say, "I'm Nova, Lainey's godmother." I hold out my hand to the woman, and after we shake, I explain, "We lost Rachel recently."

"Oh no!" A shocked expression ripples over her face. "I'm so sorry to hear that. She was such a lovely person."

Lainey turns her body into mine and wraps her arm around my lower back.

"We're just here for some fresh flowers," I mention so we can get out of here.

"My name is Esther." She gives us a compassionate smile, then gets to work. "I just got the most beautiful pastel-colored roses and peonies in." She points at a bunch of buckets containing the flowers.

"They are lovely." I nod.

"Good. The usual amount?" Esther asks as she takes one bunch after the other from the buckets.

"Ah . . . please. That would be great."

While she's busy, I brush my hand over Lainey's braid and whisper, "You okay?"

Her eyes are brimming with tears as she asks, "Can I wait in the car?"

"Sure." I glance at Tyler, who immediately steps closer when Lainey walks in his direction.

As soon as she gets into the back seat, Esther says, "Such a sad thing. What happened?"

God.

My voice is hoarse with sorrow when I murmur, "She had cancer."

Esther wraps newspaper around the stems. "You had to have known her well to be Lainey's godmother."

"Rachel was my best friend," I reply.

She shakes her head. "So young."

I know.

I let out a breath of relief when she's finally done, and I get to pay. I quickly swipe the credit card before loading all the flowers into my arms. "Thank you!" Rushing out of the store, I head to the trunk that Izak already has open and carefully place the flowers in it.

When I climb into the back seat, I reach for Lainey and pull her into a sideways hug. "I'm so sorry, my sweet girl."

She brings her knees up and curls against me, crying her heart out. My own tears trickle over my cheeks as I try to comfort Lainey as best I can.

"I'm here," I murmur, rubbing my hand up and down her back. "I've got you."

Izak steers the car away from the curb and asks, "Should we go home?"

Lainey pulls away and wipes the tears from her face. "No. Go to Ralphs."

"You sure?" I ask as I pat my cheeks dry.

She nods and lets out a quivering breath. "Yeah, I'm okay."

I suck in a calming breath and press a kiss to the side of her head. I hope nobody else brings up Rachel while we're out.

When we get to the store, Tyler sticks close behind us as we grab a cart.

"Is there anything you want?" I ask Lainey.

"We're out of juice boxes and string cheese."

I've noticed she likes snacking on them. "We'll get some."

I glance at the shelves as we head down the first aisle. There are all kinds of magazines, and Lainey grabs one for teens.

When she places it in the cart, a magazine catches my eye. I stop dead in my tracks, and it takes a moment to realize I'm staring at a photo of me and Easton splashed all over the cover. It's from when he had his hands on my hips after I accidentally bumped into him at the bake sale.

The headline has the blood draining from my face.

> Gold digger preys on Easton Rowe in his darkest time.
> Does the A-list star need saving?

My gaze darts over the other magazines, and seeing one headline after the other, my breaths speed up as horror crashes through me like a tidal wave. Then I see a photo of Easton and me on the beach, where I'm staring up at him like a lovesick puppy.

> Hollywood star involved in sordid fling while

abandoning his dying sister on hospice doorstep. Where is Lainey Rowe? Already shipped off to a boarding school while mother's best friend marries Easton Rowe in shotgun wedding?

"Nova?" Lainey takes hold of my hand and tugs on it. "Stop looking at them. It's stupid fake news."

Realizing Lainey has seen the godawful headlines, I grip her hand and rush down the aisle to get away from the magazines.

Tyler brings the cart, and I try to act calm while we continue to shop.

Oh my God. How . . . ? Why . . . ?

Lainey tugs on my hand to get my attention. "Nova?"

My heart lies heavy in my chest as I glance down at her. "I'm so sorry you had to see that."

She shakes her head at me, her eyebrows drawn together. "Are you okay?"

I force a smile to my face. "Yes, don't worry about me. I'm fine."

Rattled out of my mind, I struggle to focus and only get half the groceries I came for.

It's only the beginning, and God knows what lies they'll continue to spew about me and Easton.

Chapter 24

EASTON

Not long after Nova and Lainey left, I got a text from Sylvia saying she's coming over.

After taking a quick shower, I head to the office to grab the scripts I looked through. Just as I reach the kitchen and place the stack of scripts down on the island, Sylvia rushes into the house. "Easton!"

"Kitchen," I mutter, turning to look at her.

When she sees the stack of papers, she waves her hand. "Don't bother with those. I have good news."

I lift an eyebrow at her. "Yeah?"

"Robert fired Tim!" She lets out a bark of laughter. "He sent him packing when he heard you refuse to work with Tim."

A smile curves my lips, and I'm not going to lie, it feels good knowing justice has been served to the bastard.

"That is good news," I chuckle.

"Robert refuses to lose you. He said they'll shoot all the scenes in New Zealand while you take personal time. Then, once they're back at the studios, they can shoot your scenes."

I cross my arms over my chest, my smile growing wider because Robert is a brilliant producer, and I love working with him. "That will be so much better for me."

"Right!" she screeches. "You can still complete the film and be close to Lainey. I don't know who the new director will be, but at least we're rid of Tim."

"While you're here . . ." I smile as I shove one of the scripts across the marble top. "This one sounds good."

She blinks at me for a moment. "Are you pulling my leg?"

I shake my head. "I like working with Steven."

For a moment, it looks like Sylvia's going to burst into tears, but then she closes the distance between us and gives me a hug. "Thank you! God, thank you." She pulls away. "I was so worried about your career."

"I figured the sooner I get back to work, the better." Shrugging, I glance around the living room. "Doing nothing will drive me crazy."

She grins from ear to ear. "Today is a day that just keeps giving." She glances around. "Where are Lainey and Nova?"

"Out shopping." I point at a stool so she'll sit down. "Can I get you something to drink?"

"I'll help myself," she replies. Walking to the fridge, she opens it and grabs a can of soda. After she takes a seat, she sighs. "Heads up. The press is printing all kinds of shit."

"What kind of shit?" I ask.

Sylvia shakes her head. "The kind you don't want to know about."

"Fuck. I hope Nova and Lainey don't see any of it while they're out."

"You need to prepare them, Easton. You know how brutal the paparazzi can get."

Trust me, I know.

Sylvia pulls the script closer and pages through it. "This is a great choice. I've only heard nice things about Emma Thorne."

"Talking about the female lead," I mutter. "Do you think you can get me a no-kissing clause?"

Sylvia lets out a groan. "God, I knew my luck was too good to last."

"I star in actions and thrillers, not romances," I remind her.

"Still, you have a large female audience."

I let out a heavy sigh. "They watch my movies for the action."

Sylvia glances at the ceiling as if she's sending up a silent prayer for strength.

"There are other ways we can make it look like I'm kissing the female lead. Or we can use a double to stand in for me," I mention.

She perks up, clearly liking the options I just gave her, but then worry tightens her features. "Have you already shot the kissing scenes for *The Eradicator*?" When I nod, she lets out a huge breath of relief. "Thank God." She spreads her hands open over the script in front of her. "I'll have Robert send over a new schedule so you can plan ahead. In the meantime, I'll talk to Steven and see what he says about the no-kissing thing."

"Thanks. I appreciate it."

She shakes her head. "This is why I get paid the big bucks."

Frances comes down the stairs after packing away our clean clothes, and she gives my manager a friendly smile. "Hi, Sylvia. Will you be staying for lunch?"

Sylvia shrugs and looks at me. "Am I?"

Chuckling, I nod. "Of course." I glance at my housekeeper. "What are we having?"

"Garlic butter chicken with zucchini and corn."

"Sounds yummy," Sylvia replies.

I climb to my feet. "Let's go sit out on the veranda so Frances can have the kitchen to herself."

As soon as we take our seats in the lounge chairs, Sylvia asks, "How are you holding up?"

I take a deep breath before answering, "The grief comes in waves. Having Nova here helps a lot."

"How are things between you and Nova?"

I shake my head and glance out over the manicured garden. "It's going slow. She's not ready for a relationship yet."

"But you still plan on dating her?" Sylvia asks. When I nod, she continues, "You've managed to remain single for so long. What is it about her that changed your mind about being the most eligible bachelor in Hollywood?"

"Everything." A soft smile plays around my lips. "She's selfless and unbelievably good with Lainey. There's just something about her that calms me, but at the same time, she gets my heart racing just by blushing." Sylvia stares at me for so long that I mutter, "What?"

"I've never seen you in love before. It's kind of . . . weird."

Laughing at her, I shake my head. "Weird?"

"In a good way. You look happy, though, and it's all that matters at the end of the day." She glances at the pool. "How do you think Lainey will feel about you and Nova dating?"

"I think she'll be happy." I pause for a moment before adding, "Nova is hesitant about us dating because she's scared we might break up down the line, and it will hurt Lainey."

Sylvia raises an eyebrow at me. "She has a valid point."

"I understand her worry, but you know me. I won't start a relationship with someone if I'm not one hundred percent sure. I've known Nova for over two decades. I'm certain we can make it work."

"Yeah, but does Nova know that?"

I'm not sure.

"Uncle Easton," Lainey calls from inside the house.

"I'm on the veranda."

When she comes out of the house carrying a milkshake, I remember I asked for one.

"Oh, hi, Sylvia," Lainey greets her as she hands the milkshake to me.

"Hi." Sylvia gives her a smile. "How are you doing, kiddo?"

Lainey shakes her head, and it looks like she's about to cry. "Not good."

"Oh no." Sylvia takes hold of Lainey's arm and pulls her into a hug. "I'm sorry, kiddo."

I set the milkshake down on the ground beside the chair.

Lainey's tearful eyes meet mine. "Nova saw magazines, and they all had the worst things printed on them about you and her."

Fuck.

"I'm already dealing with them, but they'll keep printing fake news as long as people keep buying them," Sylvia replies.

Knowing Sylvia is comforting Lainey, I get up from my chair. "I'll be right back," I say before walking into the house. I glance around and see Nova standing by the glass table in the foyer.

Walking closer, I take in every inch of her face. Her cheeks are flushed, and there's a frown line between her eyes, but other than that, she seems okay.

"Hey," I murmur as I get close to her.

She glances at me quickly before looking down at the stems she's cutting. "Hey."

"Lainey told me what happened with the magazines."

She doesn't stop cutting the stems but instead works faster.

I come to a standstill beside her and lean my head down to try and catch her eyes.

She glances at me again, but then a flash of pain flits over her face, and she mutters, "Dammit!"

When the scissors drop on the glass table, my eyes flick down, and the moment I see the blood on Nova's finger, I grab hold of her hand.

"It's just a little cut," she says, her voice strained. She yanks away from me and rushes to the guest restroom.

Setting after her, I follow her into the restroom, shutting the door behind us.

Nova shoves her finger under cold water and stares at the sink.

"Want to talk about it?" I ask.

She shakes her head, then her breath hitches, and her face crumbles. "They're saying the meanest things about you." A tear spirals down her cheek, and she looks heartbroken when her eyes meet mine. "The one headline said you dumped Rachel at hospice." Her tears fall faster, each one taking a swing at my heart. "Why do they have to be so cruel?"

"It's just a bunch of shit to make money." I pull her against my chest and press a kiss to her hair. "I'm sorry you had to see it."

She lets out a quivering breath, and when she pulls back, I reluctantly lower my arms.

I shut off the faucet and take a look at the tiny cut on the side of her finger. "It doesn't look too bad." I duck my head to catch her eyes again. "In the future, don't look at any headlines or articles about me."

She nods. "I'll avoid the magazine aisle like the plague."

"Good girl," I murmur before pressing another kiss to her forehead. "Sylvia's here, and she's staying for lunch."

"Oh! And here I am, crying like a baby." She rushes to open the door.

When we walk through the living room, I say, "Frances, can you take care of the flowers, please?"

"Sure."

I place my hand on Nova's lower back and walk out of the house with her.

"Hi, Sylvia." She gives my manager a friendly smile. "I'm so sorry I didn't come to greet you immediately."

"Don't worry about it," she replies. "Lainey's been keeping me company."

Sylvia's phone rings, and she quickly digs it out of her handbag. "It's the producer." She answers the call. "Hi, Robert. I'm here with Easton. Good news. He's on board again."

I take a seat and pull a chair closer to mine while looking at Nova. "Come sit."

As Lainey heads back into the house, Sylvia says, "Hold on while I check with him." She mutes the call before glancing at me. "Word has spread that you're no longer starring in *The Eradicator*. Robert wants to arrange a convention so everyone can see you're still in the movie. It will only be for an hour or two. Sign a few photos. Smile at fans. Answer a couple of questions. You know the drill."

"I'm good with that," I reply.

She unmutes the call. "Easton is on board. Let me know when . . . Okay . . . You have a good day." She drops the phone back into her bag.

Wanting to bring Nova up to speed with what's happening, I say, "I'm continuing with *The Eradicator*, but we'll film here in LA, so I don't have to travel."

Nova nods. "That's good to hear. I'm glad you can work close to home."

Sylvia glances between us before she says, "Now that Nova is living here and she's Lainey's guardian, we need to talk about a few things. Are we signing an NDA?"

"No," I mutter. "I trust Nova."

"Okay." Sylvia pulls her phone out again and opens an app where she can make notes. "Nova, you're from Verona, right?"

"Ah . . . yes," Nova replies.

I frown at Sylvia. "What are you doing?"

"Just getting some info so I can be prepared for anything. The press is bound to start sniffing around Nova's past." She lifts her head and looks at Nova. "Is there anything I should know that can reflect badly on Easton? Drug use? A family member in prison? Police record? Naked photos? Sex tapes?"

Jesus Christ.

"I don't know who my father is, and my mother left when I was four, so I don't know anything about them," Nova answers. "No drugs, and I've never broken the law." Her teeth tug at her bottom lip. "I was in a relationship where the police were called out for domestic disturbance."

My heart clenches, hating the hell Nova was forced to endure.

"I'm sorry to hear that." Sylvia makes a note, then asks, "What kind of disturbance? Was it a verbal fight, or did it get physical?"

"Sylvia," I mutter.

Her gaze flicks to me. "I need to know if there are photos out there of Nova with a black eye. You know, if the press gets a hold of something like that, the headlines will say you beat the shit out of her."

"Oh God," Nova groans beside me. "There are photos. The police took them, though. And it was more than a year ago."

"You'll be surprised at what the press can dig up," Sylvia grumbles. "Anything else I should know about?"

Nova shakes her head. "No. I've lived a pretty quiet life."

"That's about to change," Sylvia says.

"Lunch is ready in the dining room," Frances informs us from the open sliding doors.

Climbing to my feet, I mutter, "Let's eat." As we head into the house, I glance down at the nervous expression on Nova's face and say, "Don't worry."

"Easier said than done," she mumbles.

It's going to take some time for Nova to adjust to the limelight, but I'll be there to help her every step of the way.

Chapter 25

Nova

Watching as Charlotte and Porsha walk toward us, I feel a little nervous as I stand beside Lainey at the entrance to the spa.

Charlotte is wearing a stunning long silk dress and high heels, and her blond hair is styled in a short pixie cut.

I should've put more effort into my appearance.

"Morning," Charlotte greets us with a warm smile. "I'm so glad we're doing this."

"Hi." A smile curves my lips. "I thought it would be nice for the girls, and Lainey mentioned my nails are in desperate need of attention."

She lets out a chuckle. "You're going to love the manis and pedis here. It's so relaxing. Sometimes I fall asleep."

We head into the building, where peaceful music is playing in the background.

Stopping at the counter, I say, "I made a booking for four under Allen."

The lady smiles widely. "Let me take you to the back. We've seated you all together."

"Thank you."

Black leather chairs line both sides of the room, and while Charlotte and I take our seats on the left, Lainey and Porsha sit across from us.

After the beauticians greet us and get to work, Charlotte looks at me and asks, "What are you going to do once Lainey returns to school?"

"Honestly, I haven't thought about it," I admit.

She seems to hesitate for a moment before she says, "Rachel used to help with fundraisers and organizing food drives for orphanages." She reaches across and places her hand on my arm. "No pressure, though, but you're always welcome to join us. See if it's something you'll enjoy doing. Right now, there are four of us. Myself, Jamie Bridges, Jane Carlson, and Tori Douglas. Just a bunch of moms trying to do some good."

Moms.

I turn my attention to where Lainey is talking with Porsha, and I realize I'm the closest thing she now has to a mother.

Without having to think about it, I answer, "I'd love to help. Just let me know when and where, and I'll be there."

"Great!" She pays attention to what the beautician is doing, then glances at the girls. Leaning closer again, she says, "Lainey seems to be doing okay under the circumstances."

Not wanting to talk about our grief, I only nod.

Charlotte reaches for my arm again. "How are you holding up? Your whole life must've changed. I can't imagine how difficult it has to be."

My heart clenches painfully, and I'm hit with an intense wave of sorrow.

Avoiding talking about myself, I say, "I love being here with Lainey and Easton. I'd move heaven and earth for them."

Charlotte's expression softens. "I can see why Rachel made you Lainey's godmother. I have a feeling we're going to become good friends."

No one will ever be able to replace Rachel, but for Lainey's sake, I'll try my best to become friends with Charlotte.

Smiling at her, I murmur, "I'd like that."

She lets out a contented sigh when the beautician begins to massage her feet. "If I fall asleep and drool, just pretend you don't see anything."

I let out a chuckle. "You've got it."

We talk about random things, and when there's a nice shiny coat of pink on my nails and I feel completely relaxed, I say, "This can become a bad habit."

"Not a bad habit but a must," Charlotte corrects me. "We can make it a set date every two to three weeks."

"That would be nice," I agree, deciding to give my appearance more attention. I'm no longer just a girl from a small town in the Sugar River Valley but Lainey's guardian and connected to Easton. I'm going to have to adapt to how things are done here in Beverly Hills.

After we've paid and we're walking toward the cars, Charlotte says, "The girls are having so much fun. Maybe Lainey could spend the night at my house for a sleepover with Porsha, seeing as she'll be back at school on Monday. That's if you don't have plans?"

"Lainey," I call out to get her attention. When she stops walking, I ask, "Do you want to have a sleepover at Porsha's house?"

"Oh my gosh! Yes."

"Let me just check with your uncle," I say while digging my phone out of my handbag.

"Don't worry about calling him. I can follow you home because you'll have to pack a bag for her anyway."

"Right." I give her a quick wave as I head to the SUV where Izak and Tyler are waiting. "See you at home."

When Lainey and I climb into the back seat, she says, "I'm actually enjoying today."

"I'm happy to hear that, my sweet girl."

"Do you like Charlotte?" she asks.

"I do. She seems really nice."

A smile curves Lainey's lips, and I take today as a win.

Izak hardly has time to stop the SUV completely when Lainey jumps out and runs into the house. I follow her inside and hear her asking, "Can I sleep over at Porsha's house? Nova already said yes."

"Sure," Easton answers from where he's sitting on the couch and reading through a script.

"Do you need help packing an overnight bag?" I ask.

Lainey shakes her head. "I'll be right down."

I hear movement behind me and turn to smile at Charlotte and Porsha. "Lainey's just grabbing her bag."

Easton stands up and gives them a friendly smile. "Did you all have fun?"

"Yes, and we've decided to make it a standing date every two to three weeks," Charlotte replies.

Placing my handbag on the island, I ask, "Can I get you anything to drink, Charlotte?"

"No, thanks."

Lainey comes flying down the stairs. "Bye, Uncle Easton." She gives him a quick hug, then rushes over to me for a hug. "Bye, Nova."

"Have fun," I say while chuckling. "What time should I pick Lainey up tomorrow?"

Charlotte shrugs as she follows the girls out the front door. "Let's play it by ear."

"Okay." I stand on the front steps and wave at Lainey. "Be good."

"I will," she calls out. "Love you!"

"Love you too."

When I head back into the house, Easton's waiting for me with his arms crossed over his chest. "Lainey seems a little better."

"Yeah. Spending time with Porsha is good for her."

He tilts his head. "Did you enjoy the outing?"

I nod. "Charlotte seems nice." I move away from him and walk to the couch where the script is lying. "Have you been working while we were out?"

"Yes. I'm just going over my lines so I'm ready when filming starts at the studios."

I pick up the stack of papers. "Can I look?"

"Sure."

I glance over the page he's currently on, and I grin when I picture him saying the words. Seeing a part where he has to leap over rooftops, I say, "I've read you do your own stunts. Is that true?"

"Yes."

My head spins to him. "So you jumped out of that moving car in *The Elimination Project*? They said you broke your leg."

"Jumped out, yes. Broken leg, no." He comes closer. "I did sprain my ankle, though."

With wide eyes I stare at him. "Isn't it dangerous doing your own stunts?"

He just shrugs. "There's a whole medical team on standby should something go wrong."

I hesitate for a moment before asking, "Have you ever thought about acting in a romance?"

Easton moves closer, and taking the script from me, he drops it on the couch. "I'll never act in a romance. I've actually asked Sylvia to include a no-kissing clause for future projects."

"Oh." It suddenly sinks in that we're alone for the first time, and the thought instantly has nerves spinning in my stomach.

Easton tilts his head. "Just so you know, I wasn't acting with you."

My gaze flies to his, and unsure how to respond, I can only stare at him.

Luckily, Easton changes the subject by asking, "What are your plans for tonight?"

"I'd like to take a shower," I say as I start to walk toward the stairs. "My feet feel like slippery eels from all the lotion they put on."

God, things feel super awkward.

When I reach my bedroom, I let out a sigh, wondering if it's a good idea for me to stay in the mansion after the kiss.

It feels like I'm fighting a losing battle, and I'm being torn in all kinds of directions. I love Easton, and now that I know he's attracted to me, it makes it really difficult to ignore the sexual tension between us.

Lainey should be my only priority.

After grabbing clean underwear, a pair of leggings, and a T-shirt, I head into the bathroom. Opening the faucets, I let the water warm while I get undressed.

My reflection in the full-length mirror against the one wall catches my eye, and I stare at my body. This is the longest I've been bruise-free in years.

No broken ribs. No busted lips. No black eyes. No angry handprints.

I notice that I've even picked up weight.

Only six weeks with Easton, and I look healthy.

I don't have to worry about scrounging money together for rent.

I don't have to worry about where my next meal will come from.

I don't have to worry that I'll be beaten.

Even though my emotions are a mess and my grief for Rachel is still raw, a sense of safety wraps around me, and it's all thanks to Easton.

I step into the shower, and the warm water feels soothing. While I wash my body, I replay the kiss and conversation that followed for what feels like the millionth time.

My resolve falters, and I wonder if I'm making the right decisions.

I wish Rachel were here.

I close my eyes against the wave of sorrow hitting me square in the chest. With no one around, I give in to my grief and let my tears mix with the water. Every memory I have of Rachel flits through my mind. It's still hard to believe she's gone.

Eventually, my tears dry up, and I shut off the faucets. While I'm drying my body, I try to push all my emotions down.

God, I'm tired of overthinking everything.

My next session with my therapist is in a few days, and I plan to talk to her about my current circumstances. Maybe she'll be able to give me some guidance.

Chapter 26

Nova

When I'm done showering and I step out into the hallway, I glance at Rachel's bedroom.

Taking a deep breath, I walk inside, and when I smell her scent lingering in the air, my heart constricts.

Hi, Rach.

I walk to her dressing table and look at all the flash drives. Just needing to be close to her, I sort them into neat little stacks before I look through the envelopes.

Lainey's 1st birthday without me.

Lainey's 1st Christmas without me.

Lainey's 12th birthday.

There are letters going up until Lainey turns twenty-one, and ones for when she starts dating, her prom, her wedding, and when she has her first child.

Rachel thought of everything.

When I look at the next envelope, it's addressed to Easton, and the last one has my chin quivering.

Nova. Open after I've self-destructed.

I let out a sputter, something between a burst of laughter and a sob.

God, I miss your sense of humor.

With the letter in my hand, I walk to her bed and sit down on it. Folding my legs beneath me, I reach for the bedside table and grab the box of tissues. I place it on my lap before I open the envelope. My hands tremble as I unfold the page, and then I can't read the words fast enough.

> Hi bestie,
>
> I'm sorry for the epic disappearing act I threw on you.
>
> Trust me, I didn't want to leave you.

I suck in a quivering breath while blinking like a crazy person to keep my sight from blurring.

> I need you to listen to me. Okay?
>
> I know your love language is acts of service, but girl, you need to start putting yourself first. Please. Do it for me.
>
> Don't weave your entire life around Lainey. I want you to love my daughter and be a mother to her, but I also want you to be happy.
>
> If you haven't yet, go to Easton and tell him you love him. I promise your heart will be safe with him. He'll never hurt you, and he'll give you the life you deserve.

A sob bursts over my lips, and I have to stop reading for a moment.

I've been wishing that I could talk to Rachel because I knew she would tell me what to do, and all this time, this letter has been lying on her dressing table.

Rachel understood me so well.

And while I'm asking favors, can you do me a big one? Can you always show Easton and Lainey to appreciate the little things so they don't get swept up in all the glam?

Love them, Nova. Love them for both of us.

Also, you'll see I've packed all my clothes. You're welcome to take whatever you want. Especially the Dolce & Gabbana dress I wore to the Oscars when Easton won Best Actor. It's my favorite, and I think you'll look beautiful in it.

And for the love of God, please use my handbags. I spent a lot of time building the collection. Just let Lainey have the first pick, then you can go crazy. I hope you'll think of me when you wear my clothes.

I think that's everything.

If there is a way for me to watch over you, I'll find it, so if you feel a sudden burst of love, that's me hugging you.

I love you, Nova.

Thank you for being my best friend until the end.

Rach.

With tissues squashed to my nose, I reread the letter over and over while I sob my heart out.

I lie down on her bed and press my face into her pillow. Smelling Rachel, a sense of calm washes over me, and my sobs eventually lessen.

I promise I'll live every day to the fullest in memory of you, Rach.

I take a few more breaths of her scent before I sit up again. I carefully tuck my letter back into the envelope. Climbing off the bed, I grab Easton's letter and leave the room.

I head downstairs, and when I get close to the couch, Easton glances up. Instantly, worry tightens his features. "What's wrong?"

I hold the envelope out to him. "Rachel wrote you a letter. I was going through the flash drives and envelopes when I found them."

"Them?"

"She wrote one for me as well, hence my swollen eyes."

He sets the script down, and while he takes the envelope, he stands up. "Thanks, Nova."

I watch as he walks out onto the veranda before I take a seat on the couch.

Easton

I stare at Rachel's handwriting, trying to build up the courage to read her last words to me. Over the past few weeks, I've done my best not to break down because I know she would have hated it.

I open the letter, and the instant I begin to read, my jaw clenches hard, and tears prick my eyes.

> Hi, Easton.
> I know I've said it a million times before, but damn, I totally won the lottery in the brother department. You are such an incredible man that you made it impossible for me to find love.
>
> I compared every idiot I dated to you, and obviously, they paled in comparison. I want you to teach Lainey everything you taught me. Don't let her settle for anyone who doesn't measure up to your standards.
>
> Now, let's talk about Nova. Don't let our world dim her light.

And for the love of God, if you haven't told her how you feel about her yet, then get a move on. Life is too short to wait for the perfect moment.

Nova loves you. I'm breaking my promise to my best friend, but I feel it's something you need to know. She'll be scared to start a relationship with you, and she'll put Lainey first. It's Nova's nature to sacrifice her own happiness for others, and it's up to you to make sure she doesn't.

I hate to admit it, but I'm pretty sure she loves you more than me and Lainey combined. Don't let her slip through your fingers, or I swear, I will haunt you.

Shocked, I reread the words. I know Nova is attracted to me and she cares, but reading that she loves me is the final push I needed.

Come hell or high water, I'm going to keep fighting for a relationship with Nova.

Let's get back to you. I wish you everything that's beautiful in this life. I hope you get to become a father and hold your own baby in your arms. (Even better if Nova's the mother)

PS. You're not getting any younger. Just thought I'd remind you.

God, what else can I tell the man who's taught me everything I know? Who's given me the world? Who's loved me so unconditionally since the day I was born, I'm sure I'll still feel it in the afterlife?

Thank you isn't enough.

It will never be enough.

I love you, Easton.

Your baby sister, Rach.

I let out a shuddering breath and wipe the tears from my cheeks before I glance out over the yard that's lit up with garden lights.

I love you, Rach.

A breeze plays around me, and I inhale a calming breath. Exhaling slowly, I fold the letter and tuck it back into the envelope.

Thinking about what Rachel wrote to me, I'm sure she wrote something similar for Nova.

God, I hope so. If there's one person Nova will listen to, it's my sister.

Climbing to my feet, I head back into the house. Nova's sitting on the couch, her eyes instantly locking on my face. "Are you okay?"

"Yeah." Instead of grabbing Nova and kissing the ever-loving shit out of her and forcing her to agree to dating me, I take a seat on the other couch. "Want to watch a movie? Maybe *Twilight*?"

She lets out a chuckle. "You're willing to sit through *Twilight* with me?"

The corner of my mouth lifts as I look at the woman I love. "Only if you make popcorn."

"It's a deal."

I watch as she gets up and walks to the kitchen. Her body seems tense, and she keeps shooting glances my way.

"Everything okay?" I ask.

Her eyes flit to me again. "Yes. Of course." The moment she's done answering me, she looks away.

She's nervous.

Once Nova heads back to the living room with the popcorn, I grab the remote and switch on the TV. She holds out the bowl to me, but I ignore it and take hold of her arm so I can tug her down beside me.

The moment her butt touches the couch, I wrap my arm around her shoulders and pull her closer so she'll lean against me. "Try to relax."

"I am relaxed," the words burst from her.

No, you're not, beautiful, but it's something I'll work on with you.

I press play, and as the movie begins, I grab some popcorn from the bowl. When I bring a kernel to Nova's mouth, her eyes dart to my face. Her lips part, and getting to feed her makes me grow hard at the speed of light.

Desire ignites in her eyes, but she tries to hide it from me by focusing on the movie.

It's only a matter of time. You're already mine. You just need to realize it.

It takes more restraint than I thought I possessed not to take what I want. Instead, I settle for wrapping my arm around Nova's front and pulling her back until she's leaning against my chest. I brush my fingers up and down her arm while fighting the urge to kiss my way up her neck.

The memory of kissing Nova fills my mind, and remembering her moans and how she said my name like it was a prayer has me growing even harder.

Jesus, I'm going to die of blue balls at this rate.

I suck in a deep breath and try to watch the movie, but it's impossible.

Holding Nova and not acting on my desire and feelings becomes the sweetest torture I've ever had to endure.

Chapter 27

Nova

Lying in bed, thoughts of the night fill my mind.

I paid no attention to *Twilight* because I was overly aware of Easton.

The way he held me.

His fingers brushing up and down my arm.

His breaths stirring in my hair.

Holy crap. I've never felt this hot and bothered before.

Turning onto my other side, my thoughts drift to what Rachel said in the letter.

Deep down, I know I'm safe with Easton and he'll never hurt me intentionally, but am I willing to take the risk and get romantically involved with him?

God, I'm scared.

What if we date and I somehow ruin things?

What if, down the line, I annoy him the way I annoyed John and Trent?

Staring into the darkness around me, my teeth tug at my bottom lip.

What if . . . my failed relationships weren't my fault?

What if Easton is the man I should be with, and we actually make things work?

My heartbeat speeds up at the thought.

What if we get married, and we're able to create a stable family life for Lainey?

Don't think so far ahead. One day at a time.

Closing my eyes, I focus on taking deep breaths while stilling my mind. It takes a little while, but I'm finally able to drift off to sleep.

Walking into the mansion, everything feels out of place, and I suddenly find myself in the small house I shared with Trent.

Angry people crowd the windows, and I somehow sense they're Easton's fans.

All of a sudden, I'm standing in the middle of a field, and huge skyscrapers move across the plains while tornado sirens blare around me.

Intense panic burns through me, and I start to run. Seeing a pool, I dive into the water but then fall onto a hard wooden floor.

"You're not good enough," Trent sneers, his foot connecting with my side. "You'll never be good enough for him."

Dark and suffocating emotions fill my chest.

"Easton!" I cry while I try to crawl away from Trent. The wood turns to sludge, making it difficult to move, and when I begin to sink into the dark and sticky liquid, I scream, "Easton!"

I dart upright and slam into a solid wall of muscle. My eyes pop open as I desperately gasp for air, and seeing Easton, I throw my arms around his neck and begin to sob.

His body practically engulfs mine, and I shudder as the remnants of the nightmare ripple through me.

"You're safe. I've got you," Easton murmurs, and when he picks me up bridal style, I bury my face in his neck while trying to regain control over my chaotic emotions.

He carries me to his bedroom, and after placing me on his bed, he lies down and pulls me back into his arms.

"Shh . . . I'm here," he says, his tone tender and comforting.

I press as close to him as I can get, and taking deep breaths of his woodsy scent, I finally start to calm down.

Feeling bad for waking him, I whisper, "I'm sorry."

"There's nothing to apologize for," he assures me. "Nightmare?"

I nod, my cheek brushing against his bare chest.

"Want to talk about it?"

"I can't remember much of it," I reply. "Just a field with tornado sirens. Trent was kicking me, and I couldn't get to you."

Easton's hold on me tightens even more, and he throws one of his legs over mine, his body caging me to the bed in the best way possible. "I won't let anyone ever lay a finger on you again."

My left arm is pinned between us, but I'm able to cling to him with my right. With every passing minute, I feel a little better, but I doubt I'll be able to fall asleep again.

"What's the time?" I ask.

"Around three a.m."

Easton rubs my back, and at some point, he slips his hand beneath my shirt and draws random patterns on my skin.

Just like earlier, when we were watching TV, I become overly aware of him, to the point where the world can go to hell around us, and I won't notice.

I have no idea how much time passes, too consumed with the man I love more than life.

Unable to stop myself, I flatten my palm on his back and slowly explore every swell and dip of his muscles.

My breathing speeds up, then he shifts until we're lying face to face. His hand is still brushing up and down my back, and as our breaths mingle, he slowly drags his fingers over my ribs.

My lips part, and placing my hand on his forearm, I drink in the feel of his warm skin as my palm moves up to his shoulder.

I want him more than I want my next breath.

His face moves a little closer, but then he pauses. When I place my hand on his jaw, he groans, "I can't take much more."

My breaths are coming in quick puffs, and unable to fight the sexual tension between us a second longer, I give in and press my mouth to his.

Another groan rumbles from Easton, and I feel the intense desire coming off him in waves as he starts to kiss me. His tongue drives into my mouth, and using his body, he pushes me onto my back.

Our tongues twist, and I get lost in the addictive taste of Easton.

His hands feverishly start to explore my body, and it feels as if he can't touch me enough, drawing a satisfied moan from me. His mouth dominates mine until my lips are swollen and tingling. My fingers tug at the strands of hair, every nerve in my body alive for him.

God, I want all of this man. I've waited so long that asking me to wait another second might just be the end of me.

Every touch and kiss from him sets me on fire and makes me feel super emotional because I'm finally getting to experience the only dream I've ever had—for Easton to love me the way I've loved him the past fourteen years.

"Easton." I want to beg him to touch me harder, to kiss me deeper, to take my body and make it his.

"Christ, Nova," he groans before he pulls away so he can tug my leggings and underwear off. I quickly grab hold of my T-shirt and pull it over my head.

"Tell me I can fuck you," he orders, his tone rough with hunger. He sounds so damn hot it makes my abdomen tighten and heat flood my core.

While he switches on the bedside lamp, I nod frantically, my gaze glued to his face as his heated gray irises burn over every naked inch of me.

"So fucking perfect." He climbs back onto the bed, and settling between my legs, he leans forward and presses a kiss to my hip before his head dips lower.

The instant his tongue brushes over my clit, my eyebrows fly up, and my lips part on a gasp.

Oh wow.

Intense pleasure ripples through me with every swipe of his tongue, and when his lips close around me and he sucks, my body arches, and I let out a cry.

Goose bumps scatter over my skin, and his response to my cry is to lick and bite the sensitive bundle of nerves between my legs until I'm nothing more than a whimpering mess who can't stop moaning uncontrollably.

A man has never gone down on me, and having Easton be my first makes all the sensations so much more intense.

"Easton," I cry, pleasure threatening to overwhelm me. I've never felt anything this powerful before.

I arch my back more, and every muscle in my body tenses when he starts to circle my opening with the pad of his finger. "Oh God," I whimper. "Please."

The moment he pushes his finger inside me, my entire world splinters into paralyzing ecstasy. Pure bliss overwhelms me, and I let out a hoarse cry, my body convulsing as if I'm being electrocuted.

He drops kisses on my abdomen, my stomach, and between my breasts. When his mouth takes mine in a wild kiss, he pulls his hand from between my legs.

Easton's lips worship mine for long, delicious minutes before he lifts his head. He looks at me with so much love and desire that my heart swells to twice its size with happiness. Then he growls, "You taste so fucking good."

I bring my hands to the sides of his neck before I admit, "That was a first for me and totally mind blowing."

"Good," he mutters all possessively. He lowers his head to my chest, and his teeth tug at my nipple before his lips close over the hard bud. Alternating between my breasts, he gives them both attention until they're sensitive, and I'm all hot and bothered again.

"I need you inside me," I beg, my body squirming beneath his.

Easton moves away from me, and I watch as he climbs off the bed. When he pushes his sweatpants off, my eyes widen at the sight of his long, hard manhood. The two men I've been with weren't even half his size, which makes me worry that it will hurt.

Opening the drawer of the bedside table, Easton removes a condom from it. His eyes flick to me as he rips the foil open with his teeth.

Holy hotness.

When he rolls the condom over his hard length, the sight of him touching himself is one heck of a turn-on.

Knowing what's about to happen, anticipation and nervousness tremble inside me. With bated breath, I watch him crawl back onto the bed. He grips hold of my right thigh, and lying down on top of me, he hikes my leg over his hip. His cock brushes over my opening, making the air whoosh from my lungs.

Lowering his head, he claims my mouth in a possessive kiss, and it feels like he's trying to brand me with his tongue and teeth. He moves his hand down between us and pushes his finger inside me, pumping in and out a few times before he adds a second one.

That feels so damn good.

My hips begin to swivel, my body begging for more.

I've never come while having sex before, so feeling another orgasm starting to build in my abdomen surprises the hell out of me.

Moans and whimpers escape me, the intimate moment we're sharing forming a bubble around us. Our kisses grow even more urgent, filled with the desperate need to devour each other.

Easton pulls his fingers out of me, and positioning his hard length at my entrance, he starts to push inside me.

Finally!

Just as the head of his manhood stretches me, he pulls back before slamming into me with a single hard thrust.

Oh God.

My body bows off the bed, and I'm unable to stop the cry bursting over my lips from the sting deep inside me.

"Sorry," he hisses, dropping kisses all over my face. "Fuck, you're tight." He presses his forehead to mine, his features strained from the effort it takes to keep still.

A breath quivers over my lips, and then I realize Easton is inside me, and my emotions threaten to overwhelm me.

A frown line appears between his eyes. "Are you okay?"

I force a smile to my lips and wrap my arms around his neck so he won't pull away from me. "I'm good. Just a little emotional."

"Good emotional?" he double-checks.

"Very good." With our eyes locked, I admit, "I've dreamed about this for fourteen years."

Surprise flickers over his face. "Fourteen?"

When I nod, his expression softens, then he gives me a tender kiss. His hold on my thigh tightens, and he pulls slowly out of me. There's a slight burn, but nothing I can't handle, until he plunges back inside me and the sting returns.

Easton notices the flash of pain on my face, and when it looks like he's going to stop, I say, "Keep going so I can get used to you."

Luckily, he listens, and keeping his pace slow, he thrusts into me a few more times. His body trembles and his muscles strain, telling me it's taking a lot of self-control on his part to accommodate me.

I bring my hands to the sides of his jaw, and locking eyes with him, I say, "You don't have to hold back. It doesn't hurt anymore."

Easton's hand moves to my butt, and his fingers dig into my skin. Holding me in place, he drives harder into me. He keeps speeding up, his skin rubbing against mine and causing a world of intense sensations to build in me.

His eyes remain locked with mine, and the moment feels so intimate a lump forms in my throat.

Easton is making love to me.

"Fuck, you take me so well, baby." He groans with satisfaction when he thrusts into me again. "It feels incredible to be inside you."

I wrap my other leg around him, locking his body to mine, before I admit, "You're everything I've ever wanted."

Chapter 28

Easton

It takes more strength than I possess to not lose control with Nova. Feeling every tight inch of her wet heat wrapped incredibly tight around me makes it fucking hard to keep a slow pace.

Her skin is silky soft against mine, setting every nerve ending in my body on fire. I press my forehead to hers and watch as her eyebrows pull together and her green irises shine with unshed tears.

"You're mine," I whisper as I sink deep inside her again. Needing for her to know exactly how I feel, I say, "I will never love another woman the way I love you."

A sob bursts from her, and she wraps her arms tightly around my neck.

We're both completely overwhelmed, and it has my control slipping. My hips move faster, and I start filling her with hard thrusts. Her body rocks beneath mine, and her tears quickly fade and turn into moans of pleasure.

Fuck, this woman is my undoing.

Her body tenses even more and pushes against mine, her hips lifting to meet every powerful thrust I give her.

Nova gasps and whimpers, and I drive into her at a relentless pace until she screams my name as her orgasm hits. "Easton!"

Music to my fucking ears.

"That's it, beautiful," I praise her, my voice hoarse from the incredible pleasure and emotions I'm experiencing. "Come for me."

My hold on Nova tightens as she convulses beneath me, and hammering into her, I keep going until my own release rips the air from my lungs. My body jerks uncontrollably, a satisfied groan rumbling from my chest.

Addicted to the feel of Nova, I continue plunging into her while I come, my jaw clenched from the intense ecstasy seizing my body.

Perfect. So fucking perfect.

Once the pleasure begins to fade, I slow down until I remain buried deep inside her. Our rushed breaths warm the air between us, and for a moment, we only stare at each other.

I drink in the sight of her postorgasmic glow, loving that I'm responsible for the look of pure satisfaction on her face.

I settle all my weight on top of Nova, pinning her to the bed. Framing her cheeks with my hands, I proceed to kiss the living hell out of her. "Mine," I growl between kisses. "All mine."

It sounds like the words come from deep within her soul as she whispers, "I love you so much."

I claim every word from her mouth as my tongue dominates hers, and we spend minutes kissing before I lift my head again.

When I look into Nova's green eyes, my heart overflows with everything from possessiveness to an insane obsession to protect her from every single bad thing in this world.

"You own my heart, Nova."

She brings her hands to the sides of my neck and tilts her head as she stares up at me in absolute wonder. "I see you." She sucks in a breath, then adds, "The real you."

The words hit me square in the chest. I didn't know I needed to hear Nova say that.

My eyes search hers, then I ask, "Does this mean you're willing to give us a chance?" When she just looks at me, not answering quickly enough, I shake my head and give her a pleading look. "Don't say no. Not after tonight."

Her chin quivers, and her voice is strained when she admits, "I'm scared."

Hoping that every ounce of love I feel for her shows on my face, I ask, "Do you trust me?"

She nods, but her eyes shine with tears again, and one rolls into her hair. "I don't trust myself. What if I mess things up?"

"That's not a possibility." I catch one of her tears with the pad of my thumb. "I wish you could see yourself through my eyes."

"What if we fight?"

"Then we'll talk about the problem until it's resolved."

I watch as she thinks for a moment, then she asks, "What if your fans hate me?"

I let out a chuckle. "They're not in this relationship. This decision is between you and me." When her lips part, I quickly add, "But I'm sure they'll love you."

"And Lainey?"

"Us being in a relationship will only make the family stronger. Together, we can give Lainey a loving home." When she remains quiet, I ask, "Any other questions?"

She hesitates for a moment, then asks, "Do you really love me?"

I brush my fingers over her temple as I stare deep into her eyes. "I love you, Nova. Please let me give you the life you deserve."

An emotional smile forms around her mouth, and when she nods, intense relief pours into my heart. "Okay."

"Thank you." I pepper her with kisses. "Fuck. Thank you." Only when we're both breathless from the kisses do I push myself up, glancing down as I pull out of her. Her body shudders, making a smile tug at the corner of my mouth. "I love how sensitive you are."

Climbing off the bed, I walk to the bathroom so I can dispose of the condom. Once I'm done, I wash my hands and comb my fingers through my messy hair before I walk back into the room, only to find my bed empty.

The fuck?

Grabbing my sweatpants, I pull them on. Noticing Nova's leggings and shirt, I pick them up while wondering why the hell she'd run naked from my bedroom right after we had sex for the first time and agreed to be in a relationship.

Everything felt fine when I got up.

I stalk out of the room, and just as I turn left into her bedroom, she slams into me. I drop her clothes and quickly wrap an arm around her so she doesn't fall.

Frowning down at her, I ask, "Why did you leave?"

"I needed to use the bathroom as well."

Right. Of course.

She extracts her body from my arms, and grabbing her clothes from where they fell on the floor, she walks back into her room.

I stare shamelessly at her body as she gets dressed, thinking I'm one hell of a lucky man.

She darts into the bathroom to pull a brush through her hair, and while she's busy, I glance around the mostly empty room.

Frowning, I ask, "When are you going to make this room yours?"

She comes out of the bathroom, giving me a questioning look. "What do you mean?"

"There's nothing personal in here."

"My clothes are in the closet," she replies, then she starts to look embarrassed. "That's all I brought from Verona."

I walk to her closet, and seeing how little Nova has makes me feel like shit for not noticing sooner.

"Remember the limit I gave you?"

"For the credit card?" she asks.

I look at her where she's standing near her bed. "Up it to a hundred. I want you to fill this closet with clothes."

"What?" she gasps, staring at me as if I've lost my mind.

Closing the distance between us, I wrap my hand around the side of her neck and lock eyes with her. "One hundred thousand dollars, Nova. You better spend it all on clothes for yourself, or I swear I'll drag you to the stores myself. Then you'll just have to deal with a mob of fans following us while I make you shop until you drop."

With wide eyes that make me love her even more, she whispers, "I don't think I can spend that much money. How . . . even?"

The corner of my mouth lifts. "Take Lainey with you. She'll show you how to spend the amount in a few hours." I press a kiss to her parted lips, then add, "Oh, by the way, one hundred is the minimum amount to spend. There's no maximum. I want you to get everything your heart desires."

She takes hold of my wrist and gives me a grateful look. "Thank you, Easton." Her eyebrows draw together. "I'm not with you for money, though."

"I know." My lips curve up in a loving smile. "You've had the card for a while now and clearly haven't bought a single thing for yourself."

A shy expression forms on her face. "I paid for my nails with your credit card."

"It's your credit card now." I kiss her forehead. "Use it. Please."

She nods while she closes the small distance between us so she can wrap her arms around my waist.

I hold my woman tightly, loving the feel of her against my chest. "Rachel told me in the letter that she'd haunt me if I let you slip through my fingers."

Even though sadness trickles into her eyes, she chuckles. "If anyone can find a way to haunt you, it will be Rach."

"Right?" I tilt my head, a grin tugging at my lips. "So . . . fourteen years?"

Her cheeks flush a beautiful pink. "Yeah." She looks a little nervous as she admits, "You're my first love."

Staring deep into her eyes, I say, "I'm sorry it took me so long to realize you're the woman for me."

"I think things happened the way they did because Rachel deserved all of your attention before she passed away."

"Thanks for saying that, but I screwed up when I left you behind in Verona. I'll spend the rest of my life making it up to you."

She shakes her head. "Stop beating yourself up. You didn't do anything wrong." Her eyes shine like emeralds up at me. "I made my own choices. I could've followed you here, but instead, I stayed in Verona." A soft smile tugs at her lips. "But I'm here now, and it's all that matters."

"Right." Lifting my hand to her face, I tuck some strands behind her ear. "And I'm never letting you go."

She pulls free from my hold. "Want some coffee?"

"Sure."

I follow Nova out of the room, and when we reach the kitchen, she begins to prepare the beverages while asking, "When do you want to tell Lainey?"

"When she gets home. I think the news will be good for her."

Noticing Nova's much more relaxed, I feel a sense of relief. She brings the mugs to the island and sits down beside me.

I take a sip before I mention, "I'll have to make an announcement about our relationship."

"Crap," she mutters. "Do we have to?"

"The press has a way of finding out things. Once the world finds out about us, there will be a lot of shit printed. Don't believe everything you read."

"Okay."

Christ, she's finally mine. Nova is my girlfriend.

We stare at each other for a few seconds, then I chuckle as I admit, "You have no idea how relieved I am right now."

"I do." Her mouth curves up in a happy smile. "Trust me, I do."

"Will you come visit me on set?"

Her eyes dart to mine. "Sure. When?"

"I'm starting next week. You can bring me smoothies."

"Just show me how to make them."

I can't stop smiling as I stare at her. "Thank you for giving us a chance."

Her lips curve up. "Thank you for being patient with me."

"I would've waited forever for you if I had to," I admit.

Emotion washes over her face, and her eyebrows draw together. "Really?"

"Or at least fourteen years," I chuckle before getting serious. "You're the one for me, Nova. It will only ever be you."

She lifts her hand to my face and cups my jaw. "That's the most romantic thing I've ever heard."

Winking at her, my tone is playful. "Yeah?"

"Yeah." She leans over and presses a soft kiss to my mouth.

Once we're done with our coffee, I stand up, and taking hold of Nova's hand, I pull her toward the couch. Sitting down, I grip hold of her hips and tug her onto my lap so she's straddling me.

"That's better," I grin while I rub my hands up and down her sides.

Her tone is light and happy as she replies, "It is."

Bringing my hand to her neck, I pull her in for a kiss, which quickly gets out of control. Hard and desperate for my woman, I let out a disgruntled groan. "Condoms are upstairs."

"I have an IUD."

My eyebrow lifts as I tease her, "You could've mentioned that earlier."

She gives me a playful smile. "It was hot watching you rip the foil open with your teeth and roll the condom on."

"Yeah?" I push her backward, and as I tug her leggings down her legs, I ask, "You liked that?"

With desire darkening her eyes, she admits, "I like everything you do."

As soon as we're both naked, I pull her back onto my lap so she can straddle me before I proceed to kiss the ever-loving shit out of her.

She tastes as sweet as she is, with a hint of innocence that's downright addictive.

"Fuck, Nova," I groan as I massage her breast, which fits perfectly in my palm. "You feel so good." My tongue darts out, and I lick my way up her throat. "And you taste incredible."

"Easton." My name sounds like a prayer on her lips, and I fucking love it.

"I want to get to know every inch of your sexy body," I say, my voice deep with desire for her. "I want to find out what makes you cry for more and what makes you beg for mercy."

"You," she gasps, her fingers tugging at my hair as she grinds down on my cock. "Your mouth. Your hands. Your body."

I drop a kiss between her breasts before I move up again. Biting her jaw lightly while my hands feast on the feel of her soft skin, I say, "You're fucking beautiful."

I reach down and adjust my cock at her entrance, and as Nova takes me deep inside her, she looks fucking sexy.

Once I'm buried to the hilt, her lips part to let out a gasp.

Feeling how hot and wet she is, I groan, "You're soaked for me, baby."

Nova starts to move, her hips swiveling every time she takes me deep, and I fall irrevocably in love with the breathtaking expression of ecstasy on her face.

When I reach down and flick her clit, her body jerks, telling me she's fucking sensitive. "Christ, I'm going to love making you come," I growl before I crush my mouth to hers and I take over fucking her.

"Please," she whimpers against my lips.

I drink her whimpers and moans like a man dying of thirst, and I let out a pleased growl when her body tenses with an impending orgasm.

Breaking the kiss, I press my forehead to Nova's and watch as her features tighten. Our breaths mingle, and when I thrust harder, she lets out a cry, and I get lost in the sight of her finding her release.

"So fucking perfect," I groan before my own orgasm hits.

Chapter 29

Nova

It's been a few days since Easton told me to fill my closet with clothes, and not wanting to put it off for too long, I'm bracing to shop until I drop.

When Lainey and I enter the first store, we glance around at all the clothes that are on display.

Where do I start?

"Let's go over there. Those dresses look pretty, and they'll look gorgeous on you," Lainey says while tugging me to the left side of the boutique.

We look at a few dresses, and when I notice they're more than four thousand dollars apiece, I almost have a heart attack.

This is for Easton. You need to look good beside him. Don't look at the prices again.

Lainey shoves a bunch of dresses into my arms, then orders, "Go try them on. I want to see them on you."

"Yes, ma'am," I tease her as I walk into the fitting room.

I quickly take off my dress, which is more than five years old and showing wear and tear, then pull on the dark-blue silk fabric with stunning flowers printed all over it. I adjust the dress around my body and tighten the sash around my middle.

When I look at my reflection in the mirror, my lips curve up.

Gosh. It's beautiful.

I open the door and quickly walk to where Lainey is scrolling on her phone. She looks up, and a broad smile spreads over her face. "Oh my gosh! That one is so pretty. You have to take it."

I try on dress after dress until I'm all sweaty and tired. After we pay, Izak takes the shopping bags from us so he can put them in the SUV.

Lainey grabs my hand, and I'm hauled to the next store, where the clothes cost even more.

I decide on a cream pantsuit, saying. "Let's see how this looks on me, and then we need to take a break."

"Okay," Lainey agrees.

I walk to the fitting room and quickly try on the clothes. When I step out to show Lainey, she places a pair of heels in front of me.

"I think these would look awesome with the outfit."

I shove my feet into the shoes, then wait for her verdict.

She looks me up and down, then narrows her eyes. "Oooh! Wait a second." Darting away from me, I watch as she talks to the store assistant. A small black handbag is taken from a shelf and handed to my goddaughter, who jogs back to me. "Hold this quickly," she orders, and I hoist the strap over my shoulder.

A pleased smile spreads over her face. "Perfect. Go change so we can go to Louis Vuitton. Our appointment is in twenty minutes."

"We need to take a break," I remind her as I walk back into the fitting room.

I remove the expensive clothes and put on my dress and shoes. Gathering everything in my arms, I carry them out to where Lainey is waiting by the counter.

While the assistant rings up our purchase, I look at Lainey. "We need to slow down a little."

"After Louis Vuitton. Okay? They have the best scarves and handbags."

Unable to deny her anything, I agree, "Okay."

Usually, I grab a dress or shirt at Walmart or Target, so this is way out of my comfort zone, but I push through for Lainey, who seems to be in her element.

After the fourth store, Lainey finally pulls me toward a restaurant.

"Thank God," I mutter.

She lets out a burst of laughter. "Don't worry. You'll get used to it."

"Not in one day," I chuckle as I drop down on the chair at the table shown to us. I have to resist the urge to kick off my shoes so I can rub my sore toes.

"Do you like everything you've gotten so far?" Lainey asks as she looks at a menu.

"I love all of it." Needing something cool, I tell the server, "I'll have an iced tea and chicken salad."

"I'll have the same," Lainey mumbles. Her chin quivers, and her eyes begin to shimmer with tears.

With Lainey suffering such a heartbreaking loss, the therapist said it's normal for her to have breakdowns at random times.

Reaching across the table, I place my hand on hers. "You okay?"

She ducks her head and whispers, "I miss Mommy."

"Me, too, my sweet girl." I lean forward and tilt my head. "How about we go home, and we put on one of her videos and drown our sorrows in a pizza and a big bucket of ice cream?"

Struggling to hold her tears back, Lainey nods, and we quickly stand up. As we walk to the door, I tell one of the servers to cancel our order. When we exit the restaurant, Tyler gives me a questioning look.

"Change of plans. We're going home," I inform our guard.

We walk to the SUV, and as soon as we climb into the back seat, Lainey creeps in under my arm and presses against my side.

Sometimes, she's a real little adult, but then there are times like now when she's just a ten-year-old girl with a broken heart.

I hold her and drop kisses on the top of her head during the drive home, and when Izak stops the SUV in front of the mansion, we get out and head inside.

"Hi, Frances," I greet our housekeeper. "Sorry to do this to you on such short notice, but can you make us one of your delicious pizzas, please?"

"Sure. It will be ready in thirty minutes," she answers while giving Lainey a sympathetic look. "I'll put on extra pineapple for you."

Tyler and Izak bring in all the bags, and I say, "Can you take them up to my bedroom, please? The first room on the right."

"Sure," Tyler replies.

I place my hand on Lainey's shoulder and ask, "Do you want to change into something more comfortable while we wait for Frances to make our pizza?"

She nods, and as she walks to the stairs, I follow after her. While Lainey heads into her bedroom, I go into Rachel's. I glance through the flash drives and pick the one that's marked *Lainey 1*.

I grab the box of tissues from the bedside table and walk back to the living room.

"Brace yourself, Frances," I warn her. "We're going to watch a video of Rachel, so there will be lots of crying."

"I'll just cry with you," she chuckles sadly.

I get everything ready, and when Lainey comes into the living room wearing comfy shorts and a T-shirt, I hand her the box of tissues.

Taking a seat beside her, I pull her against me before I press play.

I actually feel pretty as I walk in the direction Izak told me to go. I washed my hair and spent an hour curling the ends, and I took my time putting on makeup.

Carrying Easton's smoothie, I glance up at the big buildings and curiously look at a group of people working in a big warehouse. I can't tell for sure, but they seem to be building a forest in there.

Izak said to take a left.

I turn up a street and hear someone call over a loudspeaker, "Action!"

Just hearing the word has a smile spreading over my face, then a man running on a roof grabs my attention, and I stop dead in my tracks.

Gunfire erupts as Easton runs while shooting at someone. He's wearing black combat clothes that look seriously hot on him.

Suddenly, he leaps into the air and lands in an expert roll on the next rooftop before he sets off running again.

Holy crap!

My attention is solely focused on him as I watch the scene play out, but when he leaps over the next rooftop, he barely makes it.

My hand flies up to cover my mouth as I cry, "No!"

Easton grabs hold of the edge of the roof, and luckily, the other actor he was chasing turns around and walks back to the edge. Instead of helping Easton up, he points a gun at him, and a shot rings out.

When Easton falls, I gasp and dart forward to get to him, but then he hits a safety net, and I instantly feel stupid as I slow down to a stop.

"Cut!" the director calls out. "Good work, Easton. I think we got the shot."

Easton climbs off the net, and I smile as I watch him walk to where the director is sitting behind the camera.

I'll wait a little. I don't want to interrupt them.

"Hey!" A man shouts behind me. "How did you get on set?"

I glance over my shoulder at the man who's holding a clipboard. He has an earpiece in, which he talks into, "Get security to the set. There's another crazy stalker."

I shake my head and let out a chuckle. "It's okay. I'm not a stalker."

With an angry expression, he grabs hold of my arm and starts to drag me away. "You're all the same. This is trespassing, lady. How the hell did you get past security?"

"Wait," I say as I pull back against his hold. "I'm Easton's girlfriend."

The man lets out a bark of incredulous laughter. "Yeah, and I'm the president."

He yanks hard on my arm, making a sharp pain shoot up to my shoulder, and it has a wave of intense panic slamming into me. A memory of Trent yanking me around flashes through my mind, and it paralyzes me for a few seconds.

My body begins to tremble, and my breaths explode over my lips.

"Please," I whimper, instinctively knowing the kicks and punches are next.

They always come next.

"Nova!" I hear Easton shout, and it rips me out of the haze of panic and has me wrenching my arm from the man's hold.

I fall to the side, and the smoothie splashes over the sidewalk.

When the man tries to grab hold of me again, Easton growls, "Get your fucking hands off her."

The next second, Easton darts past me to shove the man backward before swinging around to crouch by me.

Not wanting to cause more of a scene, I hurry to say, "I'm sorry." When I try to climb to my feet, Easton's arms slip beneath me, and I go airborne as he lifts me bridal-style to his chest. I quickly wrap my arms around his neck and bury my face against him.

Sucking in desperate breaths of his scent, I try to stop the trembling in my body so I won't cause Easton any more worry.

"Is everyone okay?" I hear a woman ask.

"I want that fucker fired," Easton snaps angrily before he stalks away with me.

I have no idea where he's taking me, but a minute or so later, he sets me down on my feet so he can open a door, and then I'm ushered into a massive trailer.

In the few seconds I get to glance around, I see gleaming wood, a table with a big mirror and bright lights where he probably gets his makeup done, brown leather couches, a small kitchen, and a bar area.

Easton yanks the door shut behind us before lifting his hands to my face. Framing my cheeks, he forces me to look at him. "Christ, Nova, are you okay?"

"Yes," I whisper, a little stunned by what just happened.

Letting go of my face, he glances up and down my body, but then he lets out a growl. He grabs hold of my hips, and I'm pushed backward until my legs bump into one of the couches, and I land with a plop on the soft leather.

I watch as he gets a first aid kit from a cupboard before he sinks down on his knees in front of me.

Seeing the anger on his face, I say, "I'm really okay."

His eyes flick to me, and without a word, he cleans the gash on my knee. I didn't even realize I hurt myself. I look at the palm I caught myself with and brush the gravel off my skin.

When Easton sticks a Band-Aid over the raw spot on my knee, his eyes flick to my face again. "I'm so fucking sorry that happened to you."

I shake my head. "Don't apologize. It's not your fault." I glance at the door. "Won't you get in trouble for being away from work?"

He lets out a chuckle while he moves to sit beside me. "If I say we take a break, then we take a break."

His eyes lower to my arm, and the lines around his mouth tighten even more as he gently takes hold of my bicep, brushing his fingers over the angry red marks. "I'm going to kill the fucker for hurting you."

"Don't do that, and don't fire him either. He was just doing his job."

"Like hell he was," Easton snaps. "Your name is on a list of people who have access. If he did his job, none of this would've happened. And even if you're a fan, yanking a woman around doesn't fly with me."

He leans down and presses a kiss to the marks on my skin. "I swear, if this leaves a bruise and you have to wear a fucking cardigan again, I'm going to lose my shit."

Lifting my hand to his face, I rest my palm against his jaw. Locking eyes with him, I give him a comforting smile. "I'm okay. I promise."

He lets out a harsh breath before crushing his mouth to mine.

God, this man makes me feel so protected and loved.

Suddenly, there's a knock at the door, and a woman calls out, "Easton, is everything okay?"

He lets out a groan as he breaks the kiss. "Yes. I'll be out in five."

"I'm leaving Nova's handbag by the door in case she needs it," the woman says.

"Thanks." Getting up from the couch, he helps me to my feet. I watch as he walks to the door to grab my handbag, and bringing it to me, he says, "There's a restroom through that door. I kissed off all your lipstick."

"Thanks." I walk into the restroom, surprised at how luxurious everything is. There's even a big shower.

Checking my reflection in the mirror, I fix my hair and lipstick before making sure nothing is out of place and I look my best.

When I exit the restroom, it's to see Easton typing something on his phone before tucking the device back into his pocket. My gaze glides over every muscled inch of him, loving the rugged look he's wearing for the scene they're filming.

He lifts his head, and the smile returns to his face. "You look beautiful, baby."

Hearing him call me 'baby' does things to my heart and abdomen.

"I like that," I murmur as I walk closer to him.

"What?"

"You calling me 'baby.'"

He presses his lips to my forehead, then takes my eyes prisoner with his. The look of pure adoration on his face makes my heart skip a beat, then he says, "I love you so much it scares me. When I saw that fucker manhandle you, I was ready to rip his head off. My feelings for you just keep growing. I'm overprotective of you. I'm overly possessive of you." His hands frame my face again. "You're ingrained into my fucking soul, Nova."

Hearing how much I mean to him has happiness flooding every fiber of my being.

Chapter 30

Easton

I memorize the expression of unadulterated happiness on Nova's face as she looks up at me with awe and love.

"Easton," she whispers, her voice filled with emotion. "Thank you for choosing to love me."

I shake my head. "I didn't have much of a choice. You walked back into my life and laid claim to my heart with your shy smiles and selfless nature. Loving you is the easiest thing I've ever done in my life. It feels natural and right, like you've always belonged with me."

"Always and forever." She says the words Rachel loved to use. Lifting herself onto her tiptoes, she kisses me tenderly before pulling back to stare into my eyes again. "You've owned my heart since I was fourteen, and it will only beat for you until the day I die. I've never loved another man. It's only ever been you."

Hearing that she's only loved me and not the other bastards she dated fills me with great satisfaction.

"The selfish asshole in me likes hearing that," I admit. I let out a sigh as I step back. "Let's head out before Amy comes looking for me again."

"Amy?"

"The set manager." My eyes glide over Nova, and I struggle to keep the anger from flaring up inside me because some fucker hurt her right in front of me. I take a calming breath, then ask, "Are you ready to meet everyone?"

When she nods, I hold out my hand to her, and the moment she places her palm in mine, I link our fingers together.

Opening the door, we barely have time to step out of my trailer before Amy hurries closer. With an apologetic smile on her face, she holds out her hand to my girlfriend. "Hi, Nova. I'm Amy, the set manager. I'm so sorry about what happened. I can assure you the problem has been dealt with. Again, please accept my apology."

As Nova shakes her hand, she says, "I'm totally okay. Please don't worry. I should apologize for keeping you all out of work."

"We were due to take a break. Can I get you anything to drink or eat?"

Nova shakes her head, then glances up at me. "I dropped your smoothie."

"Don't worry about that. I already had it cleaned up," Amy replies. "Should I have them prepare a smoothie for you, Easton?"

"No, I'm good," I decline the offer. "Let's introduce Nova to everyone."

Keeping a tight hold of her hand, I pull her toward the set where everyone is working to prepare things for the next scene.

Sean, who's playing the main villain, notices us first. Even though most of the roles he acts in are bad guys, he's a jokester at heart, and everyone loves working with him.

He's actually the closest thing I have to a friend and a total work addict like me.

"Holy shit, Easton wasn't lying," he shouts for all to hear as he saunters toward us. "Hot damn." He gives Nova a cocky grin before winking at her. "When you grow tired of Easton, I'm available."

When it looks like he's going in for a hug, there's an instant surge of possessiveness in my chest. Like a fucking caveman, I let go of Nova's hand, and wrapping my arm around her shoulders, I yank her into my side. Giving Sean a look of warning, I mutter, "No hugging."

He lets out a bark of laughter. "Okay."

I gesture at him. "This is Sean Russell."

"Hi," Nova says, her tone filled with nervousness. "It's so nice to meet you."

"The pleasure is all mine," he replies while giving her his signature smirk that usually has women falling all over themselves for him.

Jealousy surges through my body, making me tighten my hold on Nova. Steering her away from Sean, I spend the next hour introducing her to everyone. She slowly relaxes and even jokes with a few of my costars. When it's time to get back to work, Robert, our producer, has her sit beside him while Amy hands her an iced latte.

Seeing the happy smile on Nova's face eases the tension in my body left over from the incident earlier.

I walk to the safety team and wait patiently while they connect a harness to me. Checking all the clips, I make sure they're secure before giving the team a thumbs-up.

My body is hauled into the air, and when I reach the roof, I climb onto it and jog to the side where I have to start running from.

Sean's waiting down below to join the scene.

"Ready?" Martin, the new director, asks via the loudspeaker.

I give him a thumbs-up and roll my shoulders as I set my face in a grim expression.

"Action!"

I lunge forward and run to the marker before leaping off the roof. My heart pounds in my chest as I grab hold of the fire escape railing on the side of the other building before swinging my body over the steel rail and jumping down the flight of stairs.

"Motherfucker," Sean shouts, and when he opens fire on me with blanks, I pretend to dodge live rounds while jumping to the ground and rolling behind a trash can.

"Cut!" Martin shouts. "Sean, we need more rage in your voice. Easton, let's take it from where you're about to jump down the stairs."

I brush dust from my pants before I grab hold of the ladder to climb back up. While I get ready, I glance at Nova, and seeing the look of awe on her face has my chest filling with pride.

I'll never get enough of her looking at me like that.

We go through the scene again, and when Martin gives the thumbs-up, I walk to a table to grab a bottle of water.

"Easton, Sylvia's on the line for you," Amy says, bringing my phone, which she usually holds while I'm filming.

"Thanks." I take the device and say, "Hey. What's up?"

"I'm calling to let you know a date has been set for the convention. I think it will be a good time to announce your relationship with Nova."

"When?"

"The last Saturday of the month. I'll email you all the details."

I think for a few seconds, then reply, "Okay. It gives us two to three weeks."

"Enjoy them." She lets out a chuckle. "Once everyone finds out about you and Nova, it's going to unleash a shitstorm of attention."

"I know," I sigh. "Talk to you later."

Ending the call, I hand the device back to Amy and head to where Nova is sitting. Crouching beside her chair, I say, "Sylvia just let me know that we're announcing our relationship at the convention to promote *The Eradicator*. You'll need to be there."

Her eyes widen. "What will be expected of me?"

"They'll take a few photos of us, but I'll answer all the questions so you don't have to."

"Okay." She rubs her hands together before fisting them on her lap. "I might have a nervous breakdown before they get to take the first photo."

Shaking my head, I lock eyes with her. "You're going to be fine because I'll be there with you."

She nods and lets out a deep breath. "I have a few weeks to prepare." When she gets up, I rise to my full height. "I'm going to pick up Lainey from school."

"Give her a hug from me," I say before I press a kiss to her mouth. "I'll be home around ten."

"I'll miss you until then."

I watch as she walks away, and only when she's out of my sight do I turn my attention back to work.

Nova

Holding the smoothie Easton texted me to bring, I walk to where they're filming.

After spending some time with Lainey this afternoon, I decided to bring Easton a smoothie and a plate of the delicious pot roast Frances made for dinner.

If he's going to work late, I'm going to make sure he at least has something nice to eat.

This time, nothing goes wrong, and when I reach the set manager, I say, "Hi, Amy. I don't want to bother Easton. I just brought him something to eat."

"Hey, Nova. They have one scene to shoot, then Easton will be with you. Take a seat over there."

I sit down in the chair and rest the Tupperware on my lap. I see Easton where he's standing with Milla Hamilton, who's not much older than Lainey. They're both in makeup, looking like they've been through a war, with their clothes ripped and soot covering their arms and faces.

In the movie, Easton's character has to protect Milla from the villain who wants her dead because she knows something she shouldn't.

"Ready?" the director calls out.

When Easton and Milla nod, Amy shouts, "Silence on set."

I watch as Easton closes his eyes for a few seconds before he picks up Milla. He stares at her face as she goes limp in his arms.

"Action!"

Easton takes a few stumbling steps forward, and when intense sadness and shock wash over his features, I hold my breath. He drops to his knees, gripping Milla tightly to him, then he lets out a harrowing shout, "No!"

The raw sound in his voice sends goose bumps over my skin, and I lift a hand to cover my mouth.

"No," he cries, and it sounds so real my heart beats faster. "Don't die on me. Don't you dare leave me."

When he breaks down and tears leave tracks through the dirt on his face, I begin to get worried because this time, it doesn't feel like he's acting.

I stand up, gripping the smoothie and Tupperware tightly while I watch Easton let out a shuddering breath before whispering, "Open your eyes, Bella."

"Cut!" the director shouts. "Perfect!"

Easton helps Milla back onto her feet before turning around and walking away. Not wasting a second, I rush after him as he stalks toward his trailer.

I follow him inside and quickly pull the door shut before setting his smoothie and Tupperware down on the counter. He walks to the middle of the sitting area, and keeping his back to me, I hear him suck in a sharp breath.

Coming up behind him, I whisper, "Easton?"

Suddenly, he spins around and grabs me to him, and then my heart breaks all over again when he lets out a broken cry.

I hold him as tight as I can to me, brushing my hand over his back. "I've got you. Shh, I'm here."

It takes a few minutes before he's able to regain control over his emotions, but even after he calms down, he still clings to me.

"Better?" I murmur.

He nods, then admits, "I thought of Rachel to make the scene as realistic as possible."

"Oh, Easton." I keep rubbing my hand over his back and press a kiss to his hair and neck. "I could feel it."

"I'm so fucking glad you're here," he whispers before taking a deep breath.

I keep holding him as long as he needs me to, then he mutters, "That take better be perfect because I'm not doing it again."

"The director said it's perfect, so you don't have to worry." When I pull a little back and see the tear tracks on his face, I ask, "Can I clean your face, or do you have to keep the makeup on?"

"You can remove it."

After he takes a seat at the dressing table, I grab a pack of facial wipes and carefully clean his skin.

"Why did you come back?"

"I brought you a smoothie and dinner," I explain while focusing on getting all the makeup off.

He stares at me for a few minutes, then whispers, "You're so good to me."

My lips curve up. "Yeah?"

He lifts his hand, and wrapping his fingers around the back of my neck, he tugs my face closer to his. "Yeah." He presses his mouth to mine and kisses me with so much passion I swear my toes curl.

Easton doesn't break the kiss as he stands up. As we make our way to the back of the trailer, where a double bed is located, we strip off our clothes.

Needing him as much as he needs me, I push him to sit down on the edge of the bed before I climb onto his lap. Not wasting time with foreplay, I take his thick, hard length inside me, and we both groan in unison.

"So fucking good." His tone is rough with satisfaction.

Grabbing hold of my hips, he thrusts up every time I push down on him, and together, we set a wild pace. With my arms wrapped around his neck, I kiss him while relishing in the incredible feel of him moving deep inside me.

I get to comfort him.

I get to pleasure him.

I get to love him.

God, my life is becoming something straight out of a fairy tale.

Chapter 31

Easton

Lying with my head on Nova's lap and my eyes closed, I soak up the attention she's giving me. She keeps dragging her fingers through my hair while her other hand draws patterns on my chest.

I have no idea what's playing on the TV.

"This is nice," I sigh.

"It is. You've been working your butt off and deserve to rest a little. I'm glad you have three days off."

Just as I open my eyes, Nova's phone starts to ring in the kitchen. I let out a groan. "Don't answer it."

"It might be Lainey's school," she says as she pulls her thighs from under my head.

I sit up and watch Nova frown when she looks at the screen. "Hello?" Her eyes widen. "Oh, hi, Deputy Stone."

My eyebrow rises, and I climb to my feet.

"Oh my God, I'm so sorry. Ah . . . can you hold for me quickly?" Nova covers the phone with her hand, then says, "The deputy sheriff found my grandfather walking in town, and it sounds like he was confused and didn't know where he was. Will it be okay if I go to Verona to check on him?"

The man never did anything for Nova, but not wanting to be a bastard, I nod. I take the phone from her. "Hi, I'm Nova's partner. Where's Mr. Allen now?"

"Oh hey," the deputy says, "I dropped him off at his place. I'm worried though. He seemed a little out of it, and he's never in town this time of year. He couldn't remember how to get home."

I glance at my wristwatch, then say, "We won't be able to get to Verona until six this afternoon. Can you do a welfare check during the day just to make sure he's okay?"

"Sure."

"Thanks."

I end the call, then dig my own phone out of my pocket. Dialing Sylvia's number, I wait for the call to connect.

"Hi, Easton," she answers.

"Hi. I need the private jet ready to go as soon as possible."

"Where are you going? You have to be on set in three days."

"It's a short trip to Verona. I'll also need a car. Nova's grandfather isn't doing too well, and we have to check in on him."

"Okay. Give me a few minutes to make the arrangements."

"Thank you."

Ending the call, I glance at Nova, who's giving me a questioning look as she says, "I can go on my own."

I shake my head. "No, I'm going with you. Call Charlotte and ask if she'll mind picking Lainey up from school and if it's okay if she can spend the night. Just tell her we have a family emergency to deal with."

"Are you sure?"

I nod and place her phone in her hand. "Call Charlotte, then text Lainey so she knows she's spending the night at Porsha's before you pack a bag for us. I'm going to tell Tyler so he can get the security team ready."

I dial Tyler's number, and when he answers, I say, "Sorry to do this to you on your day off, but we need to travel to Verona to check on Nova's grandfather."

"I'll let the others know," he replies.

I bring up Izak's number and listen with half an ear as Nova speaks to Charlotte. "Thank you so much. I'll pack a bag for Lainey and drop it off at your house on the way to the airport."

If my woman thinks I'm letting her go back to Verona alone, she's got another thing coming. She's not leaving my sight while we're there.

Nova

When we drive past the park in the middle of town, I glance at all the trees and flower boxes lining the sidewalks.

It feels like a lifetime has passed since I was last here.

I really hope we don't run into Trent. He's the last person I want to see, and I don't know how I'll handle it. With the therapy I've been receiving and Easton's support, I've been doing well, but I'm scared coming face-to-face with the bastard will stir up old demons.

Izak turns onto the road that leads to the mountain, and it takes another fifteen minutes before we pull up to my grandfather's house. It looks more like a weatherworn cabin between the trees than someone's home.

Taking a deep breath, I climb out of the vehicle and walk to the front door. Easton quickly catches up to me, and when I turn the knob and push open the door, the air is stuffy and smells of rotten food.

God, when last did he open a window?

Entering the living room, I see the man who never really cared about me sitting in the old armchair he's had all my life. Unable to help it, I still feel a flicker of sadness for him.

"Hi, Grandpa," I say to get his attention, the title feeling foreign on my lips.

His head snaps up, and I'm stunned by how much he's aged since I last saw him before winter. I ran into him in town when he came to get supplies, but all he did was grumble at me to get out of his way.

"What do you want?" he barks, a look of disgust making the wrinkles cut deeper into his leathery skin.

"Deputy Stone called me. He said you were wandering around town looking lost."

"Everyone should mind their own goddamn business!" He grumbles as he stands up from the worn armchair, and not even glancing at Easton, he snaps at me, "Leave before I get my shotgun."

I look at Easton and whisper, "Can you wait outside, just in case he grabs the shotgun?"

He looks at me as if I've lost my mind. "Hell no."

I glance around the house, and seeing the weapon on the kitchen table, I figure we'll have enough time to get out before my grandfather can get to it. There's a pile of dirty dishes and flies buzzing around the kitchen, which makes my stomach roll.

God. It looks bad.

Turning my attention back to my grandfather, I say, "You can't live like this."

"I'll live however I damn well please. Get out of my house! Get!" He shuffles in the direction of the kitchen, and it has me pushing Easton out of the house.

I'll be the most hated person in the world if I let him get shot today.

"There's no use trying to talk to him," I sigh as we walk to the car where Tyler, Ryan, and Noah are waiting. We left Eddie with Lainey.

I lift my hand and place it on my forehead as I glance back at the house. "I don't know what to do."

"Can I give some advice?" Easton asks. When I nod, he says, "He can't live here alone. He's clearly not getting enough to eat, and the place is filthy. I think we should put him in assisted living."

"He's going to lose his shit," I mutter.

"What else do we do, Nova? We can't just leave him like this. What if the deputy comes to check on him, and he decides to grab his shotgun?"

"I know." My teeth worry my bottom lip.

Just then, a sheriff's car comes up the dirt road, and we walk toward it.

Recognizing Deputy Stone, I wait for him to get out of his vehicle before I say, "Hi, Deputy. I'm so sorry about this."

His eyes lock on Easton, then shock ripples over his face, and he stares at him, completely awestruck. "Holy shit. Easton Rowe, as I live and breathe."

"Hi." Easton walks toward the deputy and shakes his hand. "I'm Nova's partner. We talked on the phone earlier."

"I had no idea. Hot damn." He shakes his head in disbelief. "I never thought we'd see you in these parts again." The deputy looks like he's a second away from asking for an autograph. "Everyone in town is so proud that you've made such a big name for yourself in Hollywood."

"Thank you," Easton replies.

I step forward to break up the 'fanboy' moment. "About my grandfather. He's threatening to use his shotgun, so we can't go inside."

"I should've taken the weapon when I dropped Bill off." Deputy Stone shakes his head. "He can't live like this, Nova. He's dangerous with that shotgun."

"I know." I look at Easton. "Maybe it will be best if we put him in assisted living."

"There's a nice place on Oak Drive," the deputy informs us. "But it's going to cost money Bill doesn't have."

"Don't worry about the money," Easton mutters.

I give the man I love a thankful look, then ask, "What do we do with him tonight?"

The deputy shrugs. "Leave him here until you've made arrangements for the folks from assisted living to come get him. I'll make sure I'm here so Bill doesn't shoot any of them."

"Yeah, I guess we have no choice. Thank you for all your help."

"Before you leave," Deputy Stone says as he takes a notepad and pen from his breast pocket. "I have to get an autograph for my son. If you don't mind?"

"Sure." Easton scribbles a short message on the paper before signing it.

"Thank you so much." Deputy Stone walks back to the driver's side of his patrol car, then pauses to say, "My condolences about Rachel. I read about her death in the newspaper."

Hearing her name makes my heart clench with sorrow. Easton just nods.

"You have a nice stay in Verona. I'll stop by tomorrow morning to check on Bill," the deputy says before climbing into the patrol car.

"Thank you." I look at the house again, and it's to see my grandfather peeking through the curtains with his shotgun in his hand.

Stubborn old man.

"Let's go," Easton says.

"We wasted time coming here today," I mutter as I head to the car. "I'm sorry. You should be at home resting and not out here dealing with my crap."

"Stop apologizing." Easton waits for me to climb into the back seat before he slides in beside me. He takes my hand and rests it on his thigh. "We're a family, Nova, which means we deal with shit together. Okay?"

I lean my head against his shoulder. "Thank you." I glance at the house as we're driven away and let out a sigh. "I've forgotten how far the house is from town. That was quite a walk for someone his age."

"And he survived it, so don't worry about him. He'll be fine on his own for one more night."

"I don't know why I worry," I mutter. "It's not like he ever cared about me."

Easton lifts his arm and wraps it around my shoulder. "Should we drive to Madison for the night?"

"We can go to Sugar River Inn? I know the owner. She's really nice." I give him an apologetic look. "It's close by, and we can get everything taken care of first thing tomorrow morning. I want to go home as soon as possible. I don't like leaving Lainey for longer than absolutely necessary."

"Sugar River Inn it is, then."

I give Tyler the directions, and when he pulls up to the inn, which has a charming feel to it, my stomach grumbles.

"What are we going to do about food?" Easton asks.

"I can run to the diner and grab us something to eat," I say. "But let's first check with Maggie whether she has a room for us."

"You're not running anywhere," Easton mutters. "Not without me."

I let out a chuckle. "I love how protective you are."

Tyler pulls our luggage from the trunk while we walk to the front door. Entering the home that's decorated with sunflowers and chickens, I call out, "Hello? Maggie? Anyone home?"

"Coming," Maggie replies, and a few seconds later, she walks into the foyer. "Nova. It's been a while since I last saw you in town. How are you, dear?"

"I'm good. Do you have a couple of rooms available?"

"Business has been as dead as a doornail. You can have your pick of the rooms," she replies, then her eyes lock on Easton, and her mouth drops open. "It's . . . it's . . . it's . . . Easton Rowe."

Honestly, I don't know how Easton does it. All the attention makes me super uncomfortable.

"Hi, Maggie," Easton says when she just keeps staring. "How about those rooms?"

"Oh, of course!" She hurries to the small desk and grabs keys from the keyholder.

"Four rooms, please," I add.

When we follow her up the stairs, Easton says, "I'd appreciate it if you don't tell anyone I'm staying here. I'll sign the wall in the foyer, which should be good for business."

"Of course. My lips are sealed. It's such an honor. Here are the keys. Have you all eaten? Should I make something for dinner?" She thinks for a moment, then her face falls. "Gosh, I don't think I have enough ingredients to feed you all. I didn't expect to be fully booked tonight."

"It's okay." I pat her arm. "I'll grab something from Reggie's Diner."

"Oh, good. Let me know if you need anything. You're welcome to make yourselves a cup of tea or coffee. There's also some lemonade in the fridge."

"Thank you."

Instead of leaving, she hesitates before saying, "I heard about Rachel. She was always such a sweet girl."

The whole town must know of her passing.

When Maggie walks away, she keeps glancing over her shoulder until she heads back down the stairs.

"I have no idea how you deal with all the attention," I mutter to Easton as I walk into the first room.

Tyler places our luggage near the double bed, then says, "Should I go to the diner to get food? That way, you can stay here."

Easton glances around the room. "Yeah. Thanks, Tyler."

"Just get us each a cheeseburger and fries. It's the best thing they have on the menu," I tell him.

When we're alone, Easton shakes his head. "Wow, this is one hell of a blast from the past."

"Yeah." I let out a chuckle.

We look at the double bed with sunflowers on the covers and pillowcases, then glance at each other.

"Maybe we can sit outside for a bit," Easton says. "I could do with some fresh air."

"Okay."

We leave the room and head back downstairs. Maggie's sitting in the living room with the TV on, and I almost burst out laughing when I see she's watching one of Easton's movies.

I take hold of his arm and push him to keep walking out the front door while teasing him, "Don't you dare offer to show her how to kiss."

He lets out a bark of laughter. "I only did that so I could finally kiss you."

We sit down by a small wrought iron table, and Easton shifts his chair so he's partially hidden behind a pillar.

"It's actually a nice night out," I say as I glance up and down the street. All the houses are on the older side, but the gardens are filled with pretty flowers.

Even though I wasn't happy in Verona, it's a charming little town.

We're quiet for a moment, then Easton shakes his head.

"What?" I ask.

He locks eyes with me, and just from the guilt on his face, I already know what he's going to say. "I should've let you stay with us after I became Rachel's guardian. That old bastard wouldn't have put up a fight. I don't think he would've even noticed you were gone."

"It's in the past," I murmur.

He shakes his head again while taking hold of my hand. "God only knows how you survived in that house."

"You and Rachel always gave me food," I remind him.

He raises an eyebrow at me. "And after we left?"

"I got odd jobs wherever I could."

"When did you move out?" he asks.

I glance at the other houses again. "A month after you left, I moved in with my first boyfriend."

When I didn't have any money to give him, he would beat the crap out of me. I ran from him, straight into Trent's arms.

A man comes walking up the road, and when he flicks his cigarette into the road, my eyes widen.

Oh no! Talk about the devil.

I sit dead still, praying Trent doesn't look our way.

"Nova?" Easton gives my hand a squeeze. "What's wrong?"

Trent glances in our direction, and my heart sets off at a crazy pace when his features grow dark. "The fuck? Where have you been, bitch?" He picks up speed, and turning up the path leading to the porch, he shouts, "You left me hanging high and dry. I got kicked out of the apartment because of you."

When Easton rises to his feet and moves out from behind the pillar, Trent's eyes snap to him, but then shock registers on his face, and he comes to a sudden halt.

I hear footsteps and notice Ryan and Noah coming out of the house. They keep a cautious eye on Trent, who seems to be rethinking things.

Not sure I can stand because my legs are a little numb, I remain seated as I say, "Leave, Trent."

Easton instantly growls, "So you're the bastard who likes to beat women?"

"Hey, now. I don't know what she's told you, but I never laid a finger on her," Trent says, holding up his hands in front of him.

"Leave this to me, guys," Easton tells the guards as he grips hold of the railing around the porch, jumping over it with ease. When he walks toward Trent, his tone is threatening as he asks, "Are you calling my girlfriend a liar?"

I dart to my feet and rush down the stairs, grabbing hold of Easton's arm. "He's not worth it."

Easton pulls free from me and gently pushes me a few steps back, then he swings around, and his fist connects with Trent's face.

My ex staggers backward before falling flat on his butt, blood gushing from his nose.

I gasp and dart forward, grabbing hold of Easton again. "Don't. Please!"

This is so, so very bad. What if it's leaked to the press? What if Trent opens an assault case against Easton?

God.

Easton

The fucker deserved it. I'll face whatever backlash I have to, but there was no way I was letting the opportunity pass me by.

"Trent Crawford," Maggie snaps from the front door. "Are you causing trouble again?"

"He hit me," Trent shouts as he climbs to his feet. "You broke my fucking nose. I'm going to sue you."

"All I saw was you causing trouble," Maggie says. "I called the sheriff."

Sylvia is going to lose her shit.

But it was worth it, and I'd do it again.

Not even a minute later, the patrol car stops in front of the house, and when Deputy Stone climbs out, I lean into Nova and say, "If I'm arrested, call Sylvia."

"Oh God," she whimpers.

"Crawford, I'm so goddamn tired of your shit," the deputy grumbles. "What did the troublemaker do, Maggie?"

"He just came up to Nova and Mr. Rowe and started yelling obscenities." Maggie comes closer, then she lies through her teeth as she adds, "I think he took drugs. He got himself beaten up somewhere, and now he's messing blood all over my cobblestones. I'm never going to get the stains out."

I think I love Maggie. Fuck, she's saving my ass right now.

"A night in the cell will do you good," Deputy Stone says while he puts handcuffs on Trent.

"I didn't do shit," Trent yells. "He hit me. You're arresting the wrong man!"

We all stand and watch as Trent is shoved into the back of the patrol car, then Deputy Stone says, "Sorry for the disturbance, folks. You all have a good night."

When he slides in behind the steering wheel and drives away, I turn to look at Maggie. "Thank you."

She shrugs. "That boy deserved the punch you gave him. He's never been anything but trouble."

Nova looks a little shell-shocked as she says, "Thank you, Maggie. God, I was so worried."

"Let's go inside and have some lemonade."

When we head into the house, I stop in the foyer and say, "Do you have a permanent marker, Maggie?"

"Yes." She hurries to the desk and digs in a drawer. "Somewhere in here. Where's that dang marker?" She packs everything out of the drawer before finally finding it. "Here it is."

I take the marker from her and check that it hasn't dried out before I walk in behind the desk and write on the wall.

Loved staying at Sugar River Inn. Easton Rowe.

I scribble my signature and add today's date before asking, "Do you want to take a photo, then you can add it to the wall?"

"Oh yes! That would be great."

She pulls out her phone, and letting go of my rule not to touch women, I place my arm around her shoulders and smile. She snaps a few photos, and I even press a kiss on her cheek before moving away from her.

"I'm framing them all," she says, tears shimmering in her eyes. "Gosh, who would've thought I'd get to meet you today? I'll never forget it."

I'll have Sylvia tell the press I stayed here so Maggie can get some publicity for her business.

Tyler comes walking into the foyer with bags in his arms. "Food's here."

"Come. You can sit in the dining room. I'll bring the lemonade," Maggie says, her face lit up with happiness.

It's times like this, when I get to make someone genuinely happy, that I love what I do.

I wait for Nova to sit down before I take a seat beside her. Tyler unpacks all the burgers and fries, and soon, we're all stuffing our faces.

Turns out that coming to Verona had a silver lining. I got to knock Trent on his ass. I would've loved to beat the shit out of him, but at least I got one very satisfying punch.

I place my hand on Nova's leg and give her thigh a squeeze. "You okay?"

She nods but then scowls at me. "Never do something like that again. I was worried out of my mind."

"Everything sorted itself out," I say before popping a greasy fry into my mouth.

"Lucky for you," she mutters, then she places her hand on top of mine, and a smile tugs at her mouth. "I don't condone violence, but it felt good watching you punch him."

When we're done eating, we head up to our room, and while Nova closes the door, I fall back onto the bed and let out a sigh. "I'm tired."

"Let's get changed, then you can lie on your stomach, and I'll give you a massage until you fall asleep."

My head pops up. "Now that sounds like heaven."

She slaps my boot. "Come on. Boots off the bed and get changed into your sweatpants."

Chapter 32

Nova

I look at my reflection in the mirror and brush my palms over the silky fabric of the dress I'm wearing. It's the blue one with flowers that I got with Lainey two weeks ago.

The past week has been quiet since we returned from Verona. Luckily, we were able to get my grandfather admitted to the assisted living facility on Oak Drive. Easton paid for everything, and we were back in LA by late afternoon.

That's twenty-four hours I never want to experience again.

I drink in the sight of the long dress and high heels I'm wearing, and I have to admit I feel beautiful. Lifting my chin, I say, "You're going to make Easton proud today."

Nodding, I turn around and leave my bedroom. Just as I step into the hallway, Easton's door opens, and he freezes when he sees me. His jaw goes slack, and with a look of pure awe, he says, "Christ, Nova. You look breathtaking."

I walk to him and adjust the lapels of his leather jacket. "And you look way too hot."

"Yeah?" He grins at me. "Hot enough that you'll move your things into my bedroom?"

My heart beats a little faster as my eyebrows lift. "Really?"

"I don't like us being in separate rooms." He wraps his arms around my waist. "I want you in my bed every night."

I press a soft kiss to his mouth, then wipe the gloss off his lips with the pad of my thumb. "I'd love to move into your bedroom."

"Good. When we get back later, we can carry your clothes over to my closet." Looking happy, he pats my butt. "Let's hit the road."

We head down to the living room, where Lainey's sitting on the couch, wearing a pretty pink dress.

"Are you ready, my sweet girl?" I ask.

Her head snaps up, and when she sees what I'm wearing, she smiles widely. "Gosh, you look so beautiful. I love that one most."

"Thank you. I have the best personal shopper in the world."

We all leave the house, and I wait for Lainey to get into the back seat of the SUV before I shut her door. Easton holds mine open for me, and as I climb into the passenger seat, my eyes devour him.

He seriously looks way too hot today.

The corner of his mouth lifts because my desire for him is probably written all over my face.

When he slides in behind the steering wheel, I glance over my shoulder to make sure Lainey has her seat belt on. Satisfied, I click my own into place before I place my hand on Easton's thigh.

"Are you nervous?" I ask as he follows the other SUV with the guards to the gates.

"No." He glances at me. "Are you?"

I shrug. "It's not like I'm the one who's being interviewed."

"Still. After today, everyone will know we're in a relationship. The press will watch your every move."

"Don't worry," Lainey says from the back. "I'll teach Nova how to deal with them."

Easton let out a chuckle. "Yes, because you're an expert already."

"Yep."

She's just like Rachel was at her age.

My heart squeezes at the thought, and memories of Rachel fill my mind during the drive.

As we get close to our destination, nerves spin in my stomach, and by the time we park in a secluded area, my heart is beating a mile a minute.

After we climb out of the car, we all gather for a moment, and Easton says, "Just stay behind or next to me. When we meet up with Sylvia, you'll stay with her while I'm busy with the convention."

I nod while reaching for Lainey's hand.

Easton places his hand on the side of my neck and looks deep into my eyes for a moment before pressing a kiss to my forehead. "You're going to be great. Don't forget to breathe."

I smile nervously. "Break a leg."

He gives Lainey a kiss on the top of her head before he starts to walk.

We enter the building, and I notice there are only security personnel. Once we've walked down a hallway, we stop by a door, and Tyler takes hold of the knob. "Ready?" he asks Easton.

My heart sets off at a crazy pace, and I curve my lips up into the smile I practiced in the mirror after watching video after video of red-carpet events.

"Let's do this," Easton replies.

The door opens, and Lainey's grip on my hand tightens. I glance down, giving her a loving smile before I look up again as we move forward.

"Easton's here!" someone calls out, and a second later, cameras start flashing. Luckily, it all seems organized as Easton keeps walking.

"Easton, can you look here?" a reporter calls out, and Easton pauses for a moment so the man can take a photo.

This keeps happening all the way to an area that's been converted into some kind of lounge slash dressing room. Milla Hamilton is already here talking with another actress, Angela Reeves, who plays Milla's mother in the movie.

From what Easton has told me, Angela dies early in the movie, and that's when his character makes a vow to protect Milla's character.

Angela notices Easton and smiles. "Hey, look who's here. I haven't seen you since New Zealand." She walks closer. "I'm so sorry to hear about your sister."

"Thanks, Angela."

Lainey lets go of my hand, and she makes a beeline for Milla.

Sean Russell comes into the room hollering, "Let's get this show on the road, people. The main star has arrived."

He's met with barks of laughter before they all talk about the convention.

I glance around, and spotting a couch that's about to become my best friend, I walk to it and take a seat. The high heels might be the end of me today. It's going to take me a while to get used to wearing them.

I watch as Easton interacts with his costars, wondering if I'll ever get used to all his fame.

Maybe I will, maybe I won't. It doesn't really matter, does it? And honestly, I think I've handled it pretty okay so far.

Sylvia comes into the room with Robert, the producer, and they talk with the actors for a short while before everyone begins to move toward the door.

When Easton glances around and sees me sitting on the couch, he comes toward me, holding out his hand.

I get up quickly, and placing my palm in his, I ask, "What's happening next?"

"You and Lainey can wait with Sylvia while I answer a few questions. Once we're done promoting the movie, you'll join me onstage, and I'll make the announcement."

My stomach feels like it's going for the gold medal in gymnastics as it dips and spins. "Okay."

We leave the lounge, and Lainey comes to take my other hand. As we near the auditorium, where a long table has been set up on a stage, I can hear what sounds like hundreds of voices.

Dear Lord.

Sylvia joins me and Lainey, and smiling, she says, "You look gorgeous, Nova."

"Thank you."

Lainey and I hang back with her while the actors and producer walk out onstage.

A roar erupts, then Sylvia takes hold of my arm and says, "If you stand here, you'll have a clear view of Easton. When he indicates for you to come, just walk straight to him, and don't forget to smile."

Oh, sweet baby Jesus in a manger.

Sylvia doesn't notice my nerves spiraling and continues to give instructions. "You'll alternate between smiling at the reporters and looking at Easton as if you're madly in love."

"I am," I blurt out the words.

A wide smile spreads over her face. "I know, but right now, it looks like you're going to puke." She digs something out of her handbag. "Take one of these. They're travel sickness pills. They'll help."

I wave my hand quickly. "Oh no, I'm not nauseated at all. Just nervous."

"Okay. Remember," she ticks off what I have to do on her fingers, "smile at the reporters, and look madly in love with Easton. If you're asked a question and you feel you can answer it confidently, then go for it." She spots someone and says, "Excuse me."

While she hurries off, I glance down at Lainey. "How are you holding up?"

She pulls her hand from mine. "I'm bored. Can I go sit in the lounge and play on my phone?"

I glance at her bodyguard while I nod. "Just take Eddie with you."

Once she walks safely into the lounge area, I turn my attention to Easton and watch as he laughs at something Sean is saying.

I get lost in looking at my man, being all charming and playful while answering questions.

God, I'm the luckiest woman in the world.

An hour passes before all the actors stand up, and the producer is the first out the door, saying, "Good luck, little lady."

"Thank you."

Easton hangs back, listening to a reporter asking, "What's next for you?"

"Another action movie, of course," Easton answers with a chuckle.

"Will you ever consider acting in a romance?" someone shouts.

"Romance movies aren't my thing," he holds up a hand, "but I do have something romantic to share with you all." He looks at me and holds his hand out.

Here goes nothing.

I walk toward him, and my nervous gaze sweeps over hundreds of people.

Oh. My. God.

Instead of taking my hand, Easton wraps his arm around my shoulder, giving me a sideways hug, and I quickly return it while making sure I'm smiling.

"I'd like to introduce you all to my girlfriend, Nova Allen," he announces.

"So the rumors were true?" a man shouts. "How long have you been dating?"

"A month," Easton answers. "But I've known Nova since we were kids."

"Was she your sister's friend?" a woman asks.

"Yes. Rachel and Nova were best friends since their first day of elementary school." Easton holds me tighter to his side. "Nova came to help us through Rachel's last weeks. We wouldn't have made it without her."

I place my hand over his heart and look up at him.

When he glances down at me, someone shouts, "Kiss her!"

He doesn't miss a beat, and leaning down, he presses his mouth to mine for a few seconds before smiling at the crowd again.

When everyone cheers, I let out a chuckle and grin at the flashing cameras.

That's right. This amazing man belongs to me.

"You make a beautiful couple," a woman in the front comments. "Nova, when did you realize you love Easton?"

"When I discovered I had hormones at fourteen," I answer honestly. "But Easton was focused on raising Rachel and starting his career, which I fully supported. I mean, any girl would wait fourteen years if it meant she would get a chance with the love of her life."

"Oh, definitely," she replies with a chuckle. "I love your dress. Where did you get it?"

"Actually, I don't remember. Lainey picked it for me."

"Will you and Easton coparent Lainey?"

I nod. "Yes."

"Do you find it difficult becoming a mother figure for her?"

I shake my head. "Lainey is an amazing little girl. Sometimes, it feels like she's the parent in the house."

Laughter erupts, then a man asks me, "So you're living with Easton?"

Easton takes over, answering, "Yes."

"Can we expect wedding bells in the near future?" the man asks.

Easton glances at me, and the corner of his mouth lifts. "If it were up to me, I'd marry her right now. You'll have to ask Nova that question."

Crap.

I look from Easton to the reporters and let out a chuckle before saying, "I guess he'll have to propose and find out."

They love my reply, and I slowly let out a breath of relief.

I don't read too much into what Easton said and continue to answer questions before posing for what feels like a thousand photos.

When we're finally done, Easton leads me off the stage and presses a kiss to the back of my hand. "Welcome to my world. There's no escaping the madness now."

I let out a burst of laughter. "It wasn't as bad as I thought it would be."

"They loved you," he comments. "You were amazing."

I lean into his side as we walk and rub my hand over his chest. "Not half as amazing as you were."

Chapter 33

Nova

"I'm so glad you could make it," Charlotte says as I walk into the foyer of her glamorous home.

I glance around at the soft-pink-and-white décor, which gives a warm feel to the atmosphere.

"Thank you for the invite. Gosh, your house is beautiful."

When Charlotte invited me to join their fundraiser committee, I didn't hesitate to accept. In honor of Rachel, I want to continue her legacy by pursuing everything she was passionate about. Until now, my life has revolved around Easton and Lainey, and I feel the need to do something else that's also worthwhile. Besides that, I have to make a good impression with the press, and what better way to do that than to be involved in a fundraiser?

"The other moms are already here. Let me introduce you," Charlotte says. I follow her to a formal lounge where three women are seated on sofas. "This is Jamie Bridges. Her daughter, Casey,, is a year younger than Porsha and Lainey," Charlotte says as she points out a woman who's wearing sweatpants and a T-shirt that says 'Bite Me.'

"Hi. I love your style," I tell her.

Although Jamie smiles, it doesn't reach her eyes, instead she looks at me with something akin to contempt.

Chin up, Nova. Not everyone's going to like you, and you'll just have to deal with it.

"This is Jane Carlson. Her son, Josh, will be a sophomore next year."

I give the woman a friendly smile, which she returns, making me feel better after Jamie's haughty look.

"Nice to meet you," I murmur.

"And last but not least is Tori Douglas. Her twins, Shiloh and Tyrel, are in Porsha and Lainey's class."

Ooooh, the mother of the boy who gave Lainey and other girls chocolate.

A grin tugs at my lips. "Hi."

"This is Nova Allen, and she'll be our fifth supermom."

"I don't know about supermom," I mutter with a playful tone. "But I'll give it my best try."

Charlotte and I sit down, and she gestures at the coffee table that's loaded with finger foods, juices, and flavored waters. "Help yourself."

Jamie lets out an audible sigh, and when I look at her, I can swear she just rolled her eyes at me.

Choosing to ignore the woman, I smile at the other moms.

"We're so sorry about Rachel," Jane says, compassion softening her features. "She was such a beautiful soul."

I'm getting used to my heart clenching whenever Rachel is mentioned. It's comforting in a way because I never want to forget her.

"Thank you," I murmur.

"Okay, school is almost over," Charlotte says, drawing the attention away from me. "I think we need to get the raffle set up so we can gather funds for the kids who would like to go to summer camp but can't afford to."

We spend the next hour coming up with ideas of things to raffle, then Jamie says, "You know what would bring in a lot of money?"

She gives me a mocking smirk, and I just know I'm not going to like what she has to say.

"What?" Charlotte asks.

"A chance to win a date with Easton."

Oh, hell no.

Instead of losing my temper because the whole world knows I'm dating Easton, I suck in a calming breath, force a polite smile to my face, and say, "There's no way Easton would agree to something like that. The best I can do is to get an autographed photo of him and some merchandise from his latest movie."

Jamie rolls her eyes again, but luckily, Charlotte jumps in. "That would be great, Nova. I can ask my husband for memorabilia that was used on one of his sets." When she sees the surprised look on my face, she explains, "My husband is a producer, so I know all about the pressures of the film industry."

"Oh wow." The corner of my mouth lifts. "I didn't know that."

"We need to discuss the cost of the raffle tickets," Tori mentions, turning our attention to her.

Jamie remains quiet while Tori and Jane do most of the talking, and I begin to get my hopes up that Jamie won't say anything else in an attempt to upset me.

When we're finally done and we're enjoying the finger foods, Jamie raises her eyebrow at me, and I groan internally.

"How does it feel to be Easton Rowe's girlfriend?" she asks, her tone dripping with contempt as if she finds it hard to believe that Easton would be interested in someone like me.

Before coming to LA, her behavior would've made me feel insignificant, but after living with Easton for two months, my self-confidence has skyrocketed.

"Hush, Jamie," Charlotte mutters with a frown on her forehead. "I'd like for Nova to come back after today."

"What? It's a question every woman wants to hear the answer to," she defends herself. "Easton never dated, no matter how hard every single mother at the school tried to get his attention."

"It's okay, Charlotte," I say. With a polite smile, I reply, "Obviously, it's a dream come true. Easton is an amazing man. He really has a way of making me feel loved and protected."

Jamie looks like she's sucked on a lemon while the other women practically swoon, and I take it as a sign that I've won this round.

Jane leans a little forward, hanging onto my every word. "And?"

"That's it. I'm not sharing anything else," I reply while chuckling. "We'd like to keep our personal lives as private as possible."

Charlotte steers the conversation to what's happening in the kids' lives, and I let out a relieved sigh.

Yep, I'm getting the hang of being a Beverly Hills mom and representing Easton in social settings.

Rachel would be so proud of me.

Easton

When we walk into the restaurant, Nova asks, "Why are there no other people?"

"I booked the entire place for us so we wouldn't be interrupted every five seconds," I mutter.

The manager of the restaurant smiles at us, then she says, "Mr. Rowe, it's such a pleasure to have you here. Please have a seat. Your server will be with you shortly."

"Thank you," I murmur as I lead Nova to our table.

My woman's wearing a stunning cream pantsuit, so I'm happy there aren't many men around because her cleavage is next-level sexy.

Slowly, her style has been changing, and she's becoming more confident with her sexuality.

It's one hell of a turn-on to watch Nova evolve into a sexy siren, but I still get her to blush in bed, and I hope that never changes.

When we reach our table, I'm satisfied to see it's decorated with red roses and candles. I pull out a chair for the love of my life, and once she's seated, I move my chair a little closer to hers before I sit down.

My eyes drift over her beautiful face, then I admit, "I'm the luckiest man on this planet." I reach for her hand and hold it in mine. "You look absolutely breathtaking tonight."

Her lips curve up. "You must really like this outfit because it's the fourth time you've complimented me."

I lean into her and brush my knuckles over her cleavage. "Can you blame me?"

"A server is coming," she warns me, and I reluctantly pull back.

We're given our menus, and after glancing over the selection of dishes, Nova asks, "What are you in the mood for?"

"You, but seeing as that's not on the menu, I'll settle for wagyu tacos and sushi." I look at her. "What are you having?"

"Hmm . . . I'll have the wagyu tacos as well and the spinach and cream cheese dim sum."

I gesture for the server to come closer and give our orders to her and also ask for a bottle of wine.

When we're alone again, I turn my attention back to Nova and say, "Filming will end soon, then we'll have to attend a premiere and a few conventions."

She takes a sip of her water. "Will you have some time off afterward?"

I shake my head. "Right after the premiere of *The Eradicator*, I'll begin to work on the next movie."

"What's it called?" she asks.

"*Man of Wrath*."

The server brings our wine and pours some into the glasses before giving us privacy again.

Nova's eyebrows draw together with a worried expression. "When will you get time off again?"

"Over December and January, but I have something important planned for those months."

Something I've been planning for the past couple of weeks.

Her shoulders sag. "Damn, will you at least get to spend Christmas week with us?"

I let out a chuckle. "Of course."

When our orders arrive, we discuss Lainey's upcoming summer camp while we enjoy the delicious food.

After our plates are cleared from the table, I say, "There's somewhere else I want to take you."

Nova nods and takes a last sip of her water before getting up.

I thank the server and manager on our way out, and luckily, I've already discussed our plans with Izak, so I don't have to tell him where to go.

We get into the back seat of the SUV, and Nova gives me a questioning look. "Where are we going?"

"You'll see."

It's a twenty-minute drive before Izak steers the SUV through the gates of the studio.

To keep Nova in the dark a little longer, I say, "I just need to get something from my trailer."

"No problem."

Izak stops near the studio where we're currently filming, and after we get out of the SUV, he drives off because we're spending the night in my trailer.

"Where's Izak going?" Nova asks.

"He'll be back," I answer vaguely, pulling her toward the alleyway between the two buildings where Jason is waiting for us.

"Hey," I greet him. "Thanks for doing this."

"Sure, man. Let's get you geared up."

"Geared up?" Nova asks, a world of confusion on her face.

I nod and point at her high heels. "Take those off."

Even though she has no idea what I'm up to, she does as she's told.

The second Jason holds a harness out to us, her eyes widen. "I'm not jumping off the building."

"Yes, you are," I reply while chuckling. "With me."

Looking very unsure, she lets me help her into the harness, and while I put on my own, she stares up at the rooftop. "I'm not so sure about this, Easton."

"It's safe," I assure her.

Jason double-checks that our harnesses are secure before walking to the control panel. "Give me a thumbs-up when you're ready, Easton."

I wrap my arm around Nova's waist and tug her tightly to my body. "Will you be my leading lady tonight?"

She lets out a burst of laughter. "Yes."

I give Jason the signal, and the next second, we're hoisted into the air.

"Oh God." Nova chuckles nervously while wrapping her arms around my neck.

Once we reach the top, I help her onto the roof and say, "Stay right here. I'm going to run toward you. Don't duck out of the way."

"I'll try not to," she says, her features tense. When she glances down, I grip hold of her chin and shake my head. "Eyes on me."

She does as she's told while I walk to the starting point. "Ready?" I call out.

"No, but what the hell. Let's do this."

"That's my girl." I break out into a run, and when I reach her, I grab hold of her as I dive off the roof.

Nova lets out a shriek, her arms quickly wrapping around my neck to the point that she might strangle me.

I turn our bodies midair right before my back slams into the safety net. As we bounce on the net, I roll her over and kiss the living hell out of her.

Minutes later, I lift my head and stare deep into her sparkling eyes. "Will you be my leading lady for the rest of my life?"

She nods, and it's clear she doesn't realize what I'm asking.

"Will you be the mother of my children?"

Her smile turns affectionate, and she nods again.

I frame her face. "Nova, will you marry me?"

Finally, it sinks in, and her eyes go wide with surprise while her lips part, then her features go slack with disbelief. "Easton."

I tilt my head, and my tone is much more intimate when I repeat the question, "Will you do me the honor of becoming my wife?"

She begins to nod, then emotions flash over her face, and I can feel the wave of happy energy bursting from her. "Yes. Yesyesyes!"

I seal my mouth to hers and savor her answer for a long while before I break the kiss so we can climb off the safety net. It takes me minutes too long to get us out of the harnesses, then I pick my woman up bridal-style and carry her to my trailer.

When I set Nova down on her feet and open the door, I'm glad to see Sylvia managed to put up all the fairy lights. There's a podium in the living room with red silk flowing over it and a box perched in the middle.

I walk to the podium, and picking up the box, I turn to face Nova as I go down on one knee.

Nova

My heart can't contain everything I'm feeling, and as Easton goes down on his knee, a sob bursts from me.

I cover my mouth with a trembling hand, my gaze glued to him as he says, "Nova Allen, I choose you. I'll keep choosing you every single day of our lives because no one compares to you. Your smile lights up my world, your selflessness keeps me humble, and your love gives me strength. Please let me love you for the rest of our lives because, until you, all I did was act. But with you, I get to be the real me."

I nod like a crazy person and struggle to rein in my chaotic emotions so I can reply. "I chose you fourteen years ago, and I'll continue to choose you forever. I'll be a safe space for you where you can be vulnerable, and I'll always do my best to keep you grounded and make you feel loved." When I walk closer to him, he climbs to his feet. I look into his eyes as I whisper, "I will never love another the way I love you."

He opens the box, revealing a diamond ring that leaves me speechless. I can only blink like an idiot at the massive glittering stone.

Easton removes the ring and takes hold of my left hand. When he pushes the diamond onto my finger, another sob bursts from me.

"Dreams do come true," I whisper while lifting my head to look at the man I've loved all of my life. "You're mine."

"Forever," he murmurs as he wraps his arm around my lower back, "and always." I'm tugged against his chest, and right before his mouth claims mine, he says with a hoarse tone, "Every single beautiful inch of you belongs to me."

Epilogue

Nova

I'm sitting by the island and sipping on my first cup of coffee for the day when I hear the front door open.

"Yes, I'll be back on set tomorrow afternoon," I hear Easton say. "Okay. Talk to you later."

I quickly place the mug down, and darting to my feet, I run toward the foyer. When Easton comes into view, I let out a happy shriek before throwing myself at him.

Chuckling, he lifts me off my feet, giving me a tight hug.

"God, I missed you," I say before I start kissing him with all the longing I've felt. The past two weeks he's been in New Mexico for filming have been way too long.

Between kisses, he murmurs, "I've missed you too." Keeping me pinned to his body with one arm, he walks deeper into the house. "Lainey?"

"Sleeping," I mumble, eager to devour my husband's mouth.

We got married on New Year's Day and spent a wonderful week in Bali for our honeymoon. Since then, Easton has been working on his new movie, spending most of his time away from home.

It wasn't easy at first, but he makes an effort to fly back every two weeks so we don't have to go months without seeing him.

I'm carried into the guest restroom because we won't make it to the bedroom. After kicking the door shut, Easton pins me against the nearest wall.

When I begin to shove my leggings down, he pulls down the zipper of his pants. We desperately reach for each other, and he lifts me off my feet again. I quickly wrap my legs around him, and when he enters me with one hard thrust, I moan into his mouth.

Yes. God, yes.

Easton takes me hard and fast, and when my orgasm hits, he muffles the sounds escaping me by kissing the ever-loving crap out of me. His body jerks against mine, and I savor the groan rumbling from his chest.

He thrusts twice more inside me before stilling, and with our foreheads pressed together, we lock eyes.

"Fuck, that felt good," he says breathlessly. "Lucky for me, I get to spend tonight at home, so we can continue this later."

"I look forward to it." When he pulls out of me, my body shudders, and it makes him grin. After being together for close to a year, he still loves how sensitive I am for him.

We take a few seconds to clean up and get dressed before we leave the restroom.

"I was busy having coffee. Can I make you a smoothie?" I ask.

He shakes his head. "I'll have coffee as well."

While I prepare the beverage, he asks, "How is Lainey doing?"

"She's okay." I place his coffee in front of him before sitting down on a stool. It's been exactly a year since Rachel was taken from us, and Lainey's understandably sad.

We're all sad, but we've decided to celebrate Rachel today. That's why Easton came home.

"At least it looks like it will be a nice day for a barbeque," he mentions.

"God, I've been craving your grilled steaks."

"I hope it's not all you've been craving," he teases me with a smirk.

"I just jumped you the second you walked into the house, so that craving has been satisfied for the time being."

He lets out a chuckle. "You can welcome me home like that any time."

"Uncle Easton," Lainey shouts as she comes flying down the stairs. "You're home!"

"Of course. I told you I'd be back in time." He climbs to his feet to hug her before pushing her back so he can look at her. "How have you managed to grow so much since I last saw you?"

"The growing pains suck," she mutters. "Nova rubbed my legs the other night because the pain kept me awake."

"I'm sorry, sweetheart." He gives her another hug. "Hopefully, the growing pains pass quickly."

She glances between us, then asks, "Can we watch the video now? I can't wait until later."

"Of course," I reply. "I already brought the memory drive down. It's on the coffee table."

While Lainey goes to switch on the TV and plug in the memory drive, Easton and I take a seat on one of the couches. He wraps his arm around me and pulls me into his side.

Lainey grabs the remote and plops down beside me before bringing up the video on the TV screen.

She presses play, then grips the remote to her chest.

We all look at Rachel's smiling face as she says, "Wow, has it already been a year?"

"Yes," Lainey whispers, her face crumbling.

I rub my hand up and down her back while my own eyes mist with tears.

"I hope you've all been living your best lives." Rachel's face is filled with love. "Lainey, I know you miss me, my beautiful girl, but I hope you've spent the past year laughing more than you've been crying."

Lainey nods, her chin quivering.

"Because every time you smile, the sun shines brighter, and the world deserves all the light you can give it." Rachel takes a deep breath. "I want you to remember that wherever I am, nothing can stop me from loving you."

"I love you, too, Mommy."

I blink faster, but it doesn't help, and my tears begin to fall.

Rachel's expression grows mischievous as she says, "Easton and Nova, I really hope you finally got together and that you're happy. Rachel is a really good name if you decide to have children. Just saying. If you still haven't told each other how you feel, sorry, cat's out of the bag."

I let out a burst of laughter.

"Please don't spend the whole day mourning me. Go have fun, or relax. Get something greasy, and stuff your faces. If it's a nice day, have a barbeque and swim. Just live your lives and be happy because I'm happy knowing you're all together."

Lainey nods, her attention glued to the screen.

"I love you. Always and forever." Rachel gives us a moment to look at her while she smiles.

"I love you, Mommy," Lainey whispers through her tears.

I clear my throat before I say, "Love you, Rach."

"I love you, Rachel," Easton murmurs, and as if Rachel knew precisely how long it would take for us all to say the words back to her, she blows us a kiss before getting up to stop the recording.

Don't worry, Rach, we're living our best lives. I'm happily married to Easton, and Lainey is turning more and more into a mini you.

If you or someone you know is experiencing domestic violence, help is available at https://nomoredirectory.org/.

Acknowledgments

Thank you to my son, Sheldon, and my daughter-in-law and bestie, Tayla, for putting up with my crazy deadlines. You are the loves of my life, and I'd be lost without you.

Thank you to my parents, who have been my biggest cheerleaders. I know the past six months have been hard, but your determination to power through difficult times has taught me always to stand strong, no matter what happens.

Thank you to my agent, Mark Gottlieb, who noticed me in a sea of authors and decided to take a chance on me. You chose the plot for *Things That Break Us*, and I hope I've made you proud.

Thank you to Maria Gomez and the team at Montlake for making my biggest dream come true by publishing *Things That Break Us*.

Thank you to the best PA, Leeann Van Rensburg. You put up with all my crazy voicemails and texts at all hours of the day and night. You're my partner in crime, and I'm so thankful for you.

Thank you to Sherrie Simpson Clark, who's the strongest person I know. You inspire me so much with your positive outlook on life, and I hope to become half the woman you are.

Thank you to Brittney Bailey and Sara Van Acker for always being ready to beta read for me. I value the time you give to me.

Thank you to Sheena Taylor, who polishes every book I write. You always push me to do better, and God only knows where you get the patience to put up with my bad habit of waiting for a deadline to start writing.

Thank you to every reader and blogger who's loved and promoted the words I write. Every book is for you, and I'm so thankful you choose to read them.

Connect with Me

Thank you for reading *Things That Break Us*.

If you want to hear all the news first, you're welcome to join my Facebook group, Michelle Heard's Readers Group.

You can also sign up for my newsletter.

Website

https://michelleheardauthor.com/

Newsletter

https://landing.mailerlite.com/webforms/landing/p6m4o4

Facebook Author Page

https://www.facebook.com/MHeardAuthor

Facebook Michelle Heard's Readers Group

https://m.facebook.com/groups/118971435201074/

Instagram Author Page

https://www.instagram.com/authormichelleheard/

TikTok

https://www.tiktok.com/@author_michelleheard

Amazon

https://amazon.com/author/michellehorst

BookBub

https://www.bookbub.com/authors/michelle-horst

Goodreads

https://www.goodreads.com/author/show/18108320.Michelle_Heard

About the Author

Michelle Heard is the *USA Today*, *Wall Street Journal*, and Amazon bestselling author of over sixty romance novels—and counting. She specializes in love stories as heartwarming as they are heart-wrenching, about characters who would burn down the world for each other.

Before she began writing, Michelle had a career in banking. Now she lives happily in South Africa with her son—her right-hand man when it comes to all things publishing—and her daughter-in-law, who is also her best friend.